AN OCEAN OF MINUTES

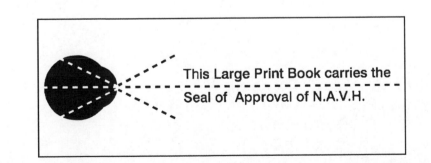
This Large Print Book carries the
Seal of Approval of N.A.V.H.

AN OCEAN OF MINUTES

THEA LIM

THORNDIKE PRESS
A part of Gale, a Cengage Company

Farmington Hills, Mich • San Francisco • New York • Waterville, Maine
Meriden, Conn • Mason, Ohio • Chicago

LIBRARY OF CONGRESS CIP DATA ON FILE.
CATALOGUING IN PUBLICATION FOR THIS BOOK
IS AVAILABLE FROM THE LIBRARY OF CONGRESS

ISBN-13: 978-1-4328-6766-9 (hardcover alk. paper)

Published in 2019 by arrangement with Gallery Books, an imprint of Simon & Schuster, Inc.

Printed in Mexico
1 2 3 4 5 6 7 23 22 21 20 19

For Ryan, who sees the seabirds home

SEPTEMBER 1981

People wishing to time travel go to Houston Intercontinental Airport. At the orientation, the staff tell them that time travel is just like air travel, you even go to the same facility. People used to be apprehensive about airline travel too. But when you arrive at the airport, it is not the same at all. Before you can get within a mile of the terminals, you reach a bus stop moored at the edge of a vast concrete flat, where you must leave your vehicle and ascend a snaking trolley, like the ones they have at the zoo.

A quarantine taxi makes its way to that lone bus stop, the airport appearing through a million chain-link diamonds. The driver is encased in an oval of hermetically sealed Plexiglas. In the backseat, Frank is wearing a yellow hazmat suit. The color marks him as infected.

Now is the time for last words, but Polly's got nothing. Frank keeps nodding off and then snapping awake, stiff-spined with terror, until he can locate her beside him. "We can still go back!" He has been saying this for days. Even in his sleep he carries on this argument, and when he opens his eyes, he moves seamlessly from a dream fight to a waking one. Already his voice is far-off, sealed away inside his suit.

She pulls his forehead to her cheek, but his mask stops her short. They can only get within three inches of each other. The suit rubs against the vinyl car seat and makes a funny, crude noise, but they don't laugh. Polly would like to breathe in the smell of Frank's skin one last time, a smell like salt cut with something sweet, like when it rains in the city. But all she gets is the dry smell of plastic.

The news outlets went down weeks ago, but that didn't stop the blitz of ads for the Rebuild America Time Travel Initiative: billboards painted on buildings, posters wheat-pasted over empty storefronts, unused mailboxes stuffed with mailers. *There is no flu in 2002* and *Travel to the future and rebuild America* and *No skills necessary! Training provided!*

At first, the ads were like a joke, gallows humor for people who were stranded once the credit companies went down and the state borders were closed to stop the flu's spread, people like Polly and Frank, who got trapped in Texas by accident. Later the ads made Frank angry. He would tear the pamphlets from the mailboxes and throw them on the ground, muttering about opportunism. "You know they don't market this to the rich," he'd say, and then an hour later he'd say it again.

They stayed indoors except for the one day a week when they traveled to the grocery store, which had been commandeered by five army reservists who doled out freeze-dried goods to ragged shoppers. The reservists had taken it upon themselves to impose equal access to the food supply, partly out of goodness and partly out of the universal desperation for something to do. One day the glass doors were locked. A handwritten sign said to go around the back. The soldiers were having a party. With their rifles still strapped on, they were handing out canned cocktail wieners, one per person, on candy-striped paper dessert plates that looked forlorn in their huge hands. Ted, the youngest, a boy from Kansas who had already lost his hair, was leaving for a job in the future. He was going to be an independent energy contractor. There was another sign, bigger and in the same writing, on the back wall: *2000 here we come!* It was a rare, happy thing, the soldiers and the shoppers in misfit clothes, standing around and smiling at each other and nibbling on withered cocktail sausages. But just that morning the phone had worked for five minutes and they got a call through to Frank's brothers, only to be told it had been weeks since the landlord changed the locks to Frank's apartment, back in Buffalo. The landlord was sympathetic to Frank's predicament, but he could no longer endure the absence of rent. "But what about my stereo?" Frank had said. "What about my records? What about Grandpa's butcher knife?" His voice was small, then smaller, as he listed off everything that was now gone.

Frank was usually the life of the party, but that afternoon behind the grocery store he picked on a pinch-faced woman, muttering at her, "Why don't they stop the pandemic, then? If they can time travel, why don't they travel back in time to Patient Zero and stop him from coughing on Patient One?"

"They tried." The woman spoke with her mouth full. "The earliest attainable destination date is June of '81. Seven months too late."

"What? Why? How can that be?" This clumsy show of anger was new. Frank was normally charming. He was the one who did the talking. Later, his sudden social frailty would seem like a warning of the sickness that arrived next. It unsettled Polly, and she was slow to react.

But the woman didn't need someone to intervene. "That's the limit of the technology. It took until the end of '93 to perfect the machine, and twelve years is the farthest it can jump. Or, to be precise, four thousand, one hundred, and ninety-eight days is the farthest it can jump. Do you live under a rock?"

The tips of Frank's ears pinked and Polly should have made a joke, offered comfort. But she was distracted. In that second it stopped being a fiction. Time travel existed, and the plates of her reality were shifting. She felt a greasy dread in the center of her chest. She wanted to drop her food and take Frank's hand and anchor him in the crook of her arm, as if he were in danger of being blown away.

Now they are pulling up to the lone bus stop, and they can see the new time travel facility, across the lot bisected by trolleys. The facility is a monolith, the widest, tallest building either of them has ever seen, and something primal in Polly quails. The only thing remaining of familiar airport protocol

11

is the logistical thoughtlessness of the curb: once you reach it, the line of unfeeling motorists waiting behind you means only seconds to say good-bye.

"You don't have to go," Frank says.

"Say something else. Say something different." Polly is smiling and shaking her head, an echo of some long-ago courting coyness that once existed between them. It has landed here, in the wrong place entirely, but she can't get control of her face.

"You don't have to go," he says again in his faraway voice, unable to stop.

Polly can only muster short words. "It's okay. We'll be together soon. Don't worry."

The sole way Polly was able to convince Frank to let her go was through Ted, the reservist from Kansas. He and his buddies had a plan to meet in 2000. They had chosen a place and everything. "We can do the same," she said to Frank. "I'll ask for the shortest visa; I'll ask for a five-year visa." It was a setback when she got to the Time-Raiser office and they offered minimum twelve-year visas. But still he would meet her, on September 4, 1993, at Houston Intercontinental Airport. "What if you're rerouted?" he asked. He had heard about this from another patient, who had heard about it from a cousin, who knew someone

12

who worked at the facility, who said they could change your year of destination, while you were in mid-flight. Polly said reroutements were a rumor, a myth. Why would they send you to a time totally other than the one you signed up for? That would be like buying a ticket to Hawaii and winding up in Alaska. But to calm him, she came up with a backup plan. If something went wrong and either of them couldn't make it, then the first Saturday in September, they'd go to the Flagship Hotel in Galveston, until they find one another. "Not just the first," he said. "Every Saturday, every September." This was overkill, a lack of good faith, but he was distraught, so she gave in. And if the Flagship Hotel is gone, they'd meet on the beach by its footprint. Even if, between now and '93, aliens invade and the cities are crumbled and remade, the land will still end where the sea begins at the bottom of Twenty-Fifth Street.

Still he is not satisfied. He puts his head back. His skin is so gray and drawn that it looks about to flake off, and it's as if the brown is fading from his hair. When Polly speaks again, it sounds like when she is drunk and trying to conceal it, enunciating each of her words, a single phrase requiring maximal concentration: "If I don't go, you will die."

"You'll be gone twelve years. When you come back, I'll be forty."

A set of comforts she repeats to herself have become like the chorus to a song. Men age well. I'll still be young. We can still have a baby. But now her face, her throat, and her lungs flush with hot, hideous panic, like water rising over her head. She grabs the inside of his upper arm so hard that she can feel his flesh give way, even through all the sealed layers.

"You meet me on the other side. We'll see each other there."

He yelps and tries to pull away, but she won't let go.

"We can still do the things we talked about."

They will get back to Buffalo. They will eat meatballs at Polly's favorite restaurant on Seneca Street. They will push their bed under the window and every night after dinner they will lie there and chat, with their feet pressed against the cool wall. They will have a baby with curly hair, a warm, happy weight in his arms, kicking her chunky legs. But Polly can't say this out loud and expose it to a jinx. She wills him to know what she means through only the pressure on his arm, as if transmission requires just touch.

His face swims in the fog of his suit. He smiles. He's got her pictures in his mind.

One car behind them honks. Then others join in. The voice of their driver, made tinny by the intercom, says, "You gotta go." They squeeze each other's hands so hard, the skin of his suit bites the web between her fingers and there is no way they can touch skin to skin, and the seat of her heart falls away and so does her resolve. She says over and over, "Don't forget about me," and she tries to memorize his shape. But there is no more time. All the cars honk like the end of days. As soon as the car door opens she is taken to Decontamination, and they do not get to wave good-bye.

Since no one carries much luggage, there are no bags to block pathways or take up seats, and a trolley bench can fit three. Polly has the middle seat between a man and a woman. The trolley passengers sit with their few belongings on their knees, in paper bags or in a battered briefcase, like the one the woman next to Polly holds. They must bring their papers and then they may bring anything else they can fit in a small bag, excluding weapons or flammables. They can bring photographs, but they've been told there is no point: photo paper can't survive the journey.

It is a stifling end-of-summer day, and heavy colorless clouds sink towards the tarmac. Plenty of them are traveling in groups — brothers and sisters, friends and couples — but no one on the trolley speaks. Once they're out of the bay, the trolley makes a wide loop, and the travelers get a clear view of what they're leaving behind. The woman on Polly's left twists her neck sharply, like someone looking away when a nurse gives a needle.

They travel through a parcel of trees, musty and dappled, the electric motor whirring, like on a children's field trip. Polly inflates with a bright, absurd calm, an anesthetic for this excision. She thinks: This is all right. Now we just have to get on the boat. She must remember to tell Frank that time travel is much more efficient than air travel; these trolleys mean no more getting lost on the way to Departures, no more taking the wrong ramp, going up when we should be going down.

The man has his travel handbook open to the Frequently Asked Questions list, but his eyes are on the back of the seat in front of him. Polly read hers the same way, with rapt attention cleaved by stretches of averted gaze. The first part is easy — *Those with special skills may be eligible for an O-1 visa for aliens of extraordinary ability* — because she has one of these limited visas. Another part offers material for grim jokes: *You must not have any living descendants — i.e., children — or they must travel with you. Ensuring travelers have no descendants remaining is to diminish confusion or genetically incorrect alliances in the future.* But then the text declines into reality: *TimeRaiser can convey the whole cost of your travel expenses and you will be bonded to TimeRaiser for an agreed-upon period.* Only the small print spells out in blunt letters the atrocity of what she's about to do: *Attempts to mitigate the pandemic or generally shift outcomes of events through chronomigration lead to poor outcomes, hence international and federal law permits only correspondence with the past that is solely of administrative significance and of a non-personal, non-historical, non-legislative, and non-narrative nature. Human cargo may only pass to the future and never back.* She had read this passage to the end only once, and even then the hatches of her mind sealed shut before understanding could reach the inside.

The woman next to Polly is crying, at first

with restraint, but now holding her fist to her teeth, her knuckles turning shiny with spit. When she begins to make noises, Polly wonders if she should pat the woman on the leg or tell her not to worry.

The trolley stops in the mouth of a hangar. Travelers peel away in strips. Some head deeper into the hangar, into a vaulted hall lit by fluorescents. Others take up position inside the red lines chalked on the floor that show where to wait for the mandated extra health screenings and bactericidal showers in advance of boarding the special planes with quarantine cabins, flying to TimeRaiser facilities elsewhere: Shanghai, Frankfurt, Harare, Caracas, or Sydney.

In the midst of this clamor, the crying woman moves in slow motion. She gets to her feet once, but the weight of her bones and her sadness topples her, and she sits down again so heavily, the flimsy bench shudders. The staff, dressed like hospital orderlies, try to move her forcibly, but the woman says, "Wait, just wait. I'll do it." She is short and wearing sandals with multistory heels, the fabric straps crusted with sparkling purple stones. All the other travelers wear cheap shoes with zero decorative function. Polly suggests that the woman take off her sandals to make it easier to get down.

The woman doesn't acknowledge Polly, but she removes her shoes. Her feet are dirty and the skin of her heels is cracked and fissured, and the shoes look even more out of place.

Polly and the woman are among the last to reach the inner door of the hangar, where travelers break into shorter lines, waiting for an agent to take their passport and their ticket and their fingerprints. Polly's ticket says *GALVESTON SEPTEMBER 4 1993*. It's twelve years. It's a quarter of a blink of an eye in the life of the universe. Polly shuffles her documents around to find the order that will best please the agent. She makes sure the *O-1* embossed on her visa card is prominently displayed. Her passport is fresh and the pages still have that scent like money.

It was only last Thursday that they went to the makeshift clinic, where whole hallways were tented off, transit areas for the lucky sick, the ones awaiting transfer to the treatment centers. There, a nurse in a trim turquoise hazmat suit told her Frank was positive for the flu. She laid out the test strips like a card dealer, so Polly could see she had already run the test three times, with the same result for each pass. The medication he needed was thousands of dollars. They could give him the free treatments dispensed by the public health service, but their efficacy was not so good. Though there was time travel, she said. Polly had not understood her. Was she saying that Frank should travel? Oh God, no, the nurse said, they didn't let carriers go, but Polly could go, so long as she passed the medical evaluation. TimeRaiser offered family health benefits. Once Polly signed on as an employee, even though they weren't yet married, Frank could go straight to treatment; she just had to write his name on the line.

Polly tries to focus on the floor tiles, the grouting and the shiny chips in eggshell white. But her mind keeps retracting to an evening last week when Frank took her up to the roof of their apartment to watch the sun set, that last day before his symptoms appeared.

Months earlier, they'd chosen the complex because it had been emptied of life. Then the emptiness turned oppressive. But the roof was specked with soda cans and butts from hand-rolled cigarettes, clues of others in this world who also came to snack and watch the sky.

They sat on a waxy banana box, back-to-back, and Frank produced a treat from his jacket pocket: a warped, fun-size box of raisins. They ate the raisins slowly so they would last until the sun went down, chewing each juiceless bead until only threads remained between their teeth. A wind-beaten pigeon approached, hopeful. "Don't fold," Frank said. "Don't waste anything on that sky rat; I saved those for you." Polly said, "But he's hungry," and held a raisin to its jerking beak. A second pigeon soon joined the first. "And another mouth to feed," Frank said, watching wistfully as she gave away the last raisin.

The sun setting over his shoulder, the noise of the wind, the churr of the gravel, his brown hair curling into the folds of his ear. What she would give to forget that moment, to unremember that last chance to trace those inimitable ears and fit her face into his neck.

An agent processes her papers, disinterested in his primary role in the drama circling him. Everyone is given regulation clothing and slippers, all of it blue, and the travelers, now divided into women and men, remove their clothes in communal changing rooms, each person with eyes fixed firmly on the wall. When Polly pulls the limp blue material over her head, it tears under her armpit and the edge of her dingy bra is visible. She keeps her hand tucked into her armpit until she sees other women contending with far worse rips across the seats of their pants. There is no one to give them replacement sets of clothing, and when they arrive in the future, it will look as if the '80s were even more destitute than they were. Polly throws away her home clothes in one of the many black bins down the middle of the room.

Something's torn in her bra, and the underwire has broken through, rubbing the soft of her skin raw. She is preoccupied with trying to tame it discreetly through the hole in her armpit as she walks, when she hears shrieking and she sees women stopping just before the exit instead of going through. Polly sees the crying woman from the trolley, kneeling, the contents of her case spread around her, as if she has lost something dear. She is making thick, strangled sobs.

It is an unacceptable noise. It triggers an avalanche of dread that comes plunging over Polly, and her ears and airways fill with it, and for a second she is too heavy to move. The only way she can get out from under it is to narrow all her emotions into a fine point of rage. She wants to scream at the woman, Do you think you are the only one suffering here?

In another immense room with naked bulbs,

the politeness has dissolved with the quiet. There are no signs saying what to do. Passengers make mobs in the corners of the room, along a row of desks, by a line of white bins filled with plastic-coated radiation-proof jackets. There are not enough jackets in the necessary sizes, and people are shouting and sniping at each other. Polly takes an extra-large because they are easy to reach. The bins with the smaller sizes are almost empty. Polly looks around with queasy confusion. She sees what did not register before. She is among the tallest in the room, and the palest. Almost everyone is small and black-haired. They are mostly women. They are not the same race as her. She doesn't know what race they are. Maybe they are from Mexico. She suffers layers of clammy embarrassment. It's impolite that she noticed their difference; it's backwards, like something Frank's mother would do. But now she's somehow in the wrong place for her kind, like she's wandered into the men's room. Did she miss the sign that said this was the area for foreign nationals? Are they being streamed by language?

When she puts on her jacket, it gapes around the arm holes and at the middle no matter how much she cinches the straps, and she is afraid of what the radiation might do to her exposed areas. Passengers have oozed out of the lines so chaotically that the agents have left the desks, now patrolling the room like herders.

One grabs her papers and shouts, "Can't you read? You're O-1 not H-1. Get out of here. Over there!" The agent points. It's an imprecise gesture that takes in the whole back end of the hall. Alarms are blaring. Polly goes back into the changing room. It is the only other exit aside from the distant gangway to the next phase. She'll wait in the changing room until it seems safe to go out and find a kinder agent. She leans against one of the black bins of unpeopled clothes, filled with cotton and rayon and striped polyester, little pearly buttons, a tattered blouse that maybe once was a favorite. She looks away. She notices a small door she didn't see before, one ignored by everyone else, marked *O-1.*

It opens into the first compact space Polly has seen, with wooden folding chairs and low chipboard walls and no ceiling. There is a potted plant in the corner and a reproduction of Van Gogh's *Café Terrace at Night* hanging on one wall. There's a clothes rack of plastic jackets, many in each size. The shouting from over the wall is muffled.

The only other person waiting in the room is a woman who looks like she could be anywhere between twenty-five and forty. The paper suit provides no cues. She has fine blond hair and a tiny tight mouth, and keen, angular posture that strains the seams of her shirt. She is staring straight ahead, cracking her knuckles one unlovely pop at a time.

The chafing from Polly's bra has gotten worse. She twists to shift the protrusion creating a dint in her flesh, but whatever it is, it has snagged itself on her skin. Her neighbor has moved on from popping all her knuckles to drumming on her seat like the ticking of a watch, and the relief Polly felt when she entered the room is gone. The sense of foreboding crests. Though Polly is for private space and against mindless chatter, she thinks she has to speak. Then the woman looks at her, as if noticing her for the first time, and says, "What's your special skill?"

"Pardon?"

"Your special skill? How did you get an O-1 visa?"

"I'm an upholsterer and a refinisher. I repair and restore old furniture."

The woman laughs uproariously. Polly preferred the drumming.

"That is absolutely fascinating."

"It is?"

"It's fascinating that that's what they're after."

"What do you do?"

She laughs again. "Acupuncturist. Isn't that absurd?"

"What do you mean?"

The woman leans in, whispering. "Did you read the list of O-1 qualifying jobs in the guide? The first one: engineer. Fair enough. Makes sense. You need engineers to rebuild a country. And we've got architect, surveyor, that's fine. Then there's movie star and Grammy-winning musician. So that's dumb but still, understandable for morale. But who else is on the list? Natural-medicine doctors, chiropractors, massage therapists, beekeepers. And now upholsterers? Do you have any idea what they mean to do with these people?"

"No."

"Why don't they want the kinds of skills people want today? Like scientists, doctors, scholars. Lawyers."

"They already have those people. They need people to fill the jobs no one wants."

"No," she sneers. "The jobs no one wants are what the H-1 visas are for. Canning beans. Building bridges. But we're O-1.

Extraordinary-ability visa. But abilities for what? They don't want lawyers. I'm a lawyer. I had to lie on my application. I had to say I knew acupuncture. I don't know acupuncture. I don't know massage. I've never massaged anyone in my life. Except erotically." She laughs again, a high whine. "Aren't you afraid this whole thing is a sex thing?"

"Excuse me?"

"Sex trafficking." Her tiny mouth works furiously to get the words out. "Are we going to be sold as prostitutes?"

Polly fixes her eyes on the Van Gogh painting. The first time she ever laid eyes on it, in a guidance counselor's office, she thought it was magic: the way the painting was like a window, as if you could walk right into the scene. Just by looking at it, you were somewhere else.

"You and I are more sexually appealing than those people out there," the blonde says.

Polly's seen the painting too many times. She can't get the light in the painting to do what it used to.

"I worked my whole life. Sixty-hour weeks." The woman dispenses with the whispering. "Sunk all my funds into a luxury condo, and then the pandemic struck." She slaps her hand down on the folding chair next to her, and two things happen. The chair snaps shut and then it falls forward, its legs catching on the underside of the planter as it goes. The planter hits the floor and smashes, a loud, irreversible noise.

The woman stares at the pieces, appalled.

"Quick! Help me get it back the way it was."

She jerks the chair out of the way and it scuttles across the floor and knocks into the coat rack. The woman starts kicking dirt madly into the corner, under the furniture, and after a second Polly helps her. Polly is in a state now too, without knowing what retribution they are trying to escape. They are trying to be inconspicuous, but the woman can't stop herself from emitting little yells of panic. On her hands and knees, she blunders into more chairs, and the chairs kick the walls, making knocking sounds, like someone looking for a hollow spot in a sealed room.

Security guards arrive, slow moving and unworried. The woman rushes at them. She's shouting, "I still want to travel! I still want to travel!" but all they see is her charging. In a smear of motion, they half trip her and twist her around, then bind her wrists together.

"All right, all right," they say to her.

"Can I still travel? But can I still travel?"

The guards don't answer. They take her away. The inside door is opened by an official with a clipboard, in a sharply pleated military dress, cursing and grappling with the radio clipped to her front. When she hails someone on the other side, she says, "Female passenger, last name Bauer, O-1 status, has been transferred to Discharge. Eighty-six Bauer, please." She addresses Polly. "Nader? This way." She waves her through the door, into an even smaller room. This one does have a ceiling, with perforations for soundproofing. Obviously, Polly assures herself, this is a consideration for the travelers' sake, for their privacy — not for concealing company crimes.

"I'm Colonel Simpson. I'm an army psychologist. I'm going to inspect your case and perform a physical and mental evaluation to ensure you're travel ready. Should you decide not to travel, now's the time to say so. If so, you'll have to return any TimeRaiser payments made to you — advance pay or health benefits to friends or family members — plus a thirteen percent processing fee on these advance payments or health benefits. Are you ready?" She says

29

this all so rapidly it's difficult to catch each word. She pushes a box of Kleenex at Polly and nods at her dirty hands.

"I'll be honest with you," the psychologist says. "We're having a bad day. That was the second meltdown in ten minutes, and an O-1 at that. At this rate we're going to be sending only half our entrants through."

The psychologist uses a blood pressure cuff, then a stethoscope. Polly's heart is still speeding from the broken plant, and how easily the guards subdued that woman, like they were folding a piece of paper.

"If I fail the evaluation," Polly says, "do I still have to pay the processing fee?"

"Yes. So don't fail the evaluation." She flips a page. "Full name, age, and birth date?"

"Polly Nader, twenty-three, June 12, 1958."

"And you're traveling to Galveston at September 4, 1993. Your ethnicity? Nader — what is that? Jewish?"

"I'm Caucasian."

The psychologist peers at her. "What kind of Caucasian?" She puts her cheek on her fist and stares until Polly says, "My father was Arab." She only left this out from habit. It's complicated to explain, extraneous information that usually no one has time for. But now it must seem she's hiding something.

"And your mother?"

"Caucasian."

Polly's windpipe clenches, but then the woman only says, "So you look white. Okay . . . let's just keep things simple. I'll put 'Caucasian.' Height and weight?"

"Five foot five, one hundred and twenty-five pounds."

"Hair color and eye color: brown and brown."

The psychologist opens Polly's briefcase and uses a white spatula with blue felt on its tip to sift her papers. She's cautious, like a person handling evidence, then Polly realizes she is just that. She finds Polly's baseball cards.

"What's this?" Rollie Fingers looks preposterously out of place.

"I thought they might be worth money in the future."

There are two versions to this story. The truer version is that the cards are traveling with her because they belong to Frank; they have the synecdochical magic of a beloved's beloveds. But she thinks the psychologist will be more likely to comprehend the official, pragmatic version.

This backfires.

"Then technically I should confiscate them."

What Polly would like to do best is put her head between her knees. But that would be a sign of weakness, and it's clear that here things go poorly for the soft.

"Aren't there special considerations for me because I have an O-1 visa?"

Simpson regards her with drawn-together brows. Then she laughs.

"You know what? You keep the baseball cards. What does it matter, really? I don't know where you're going, you don't know where you're going. Makes the rules seem arbitrary, you know?" Simpson scribbles on a form, copying down the information on Polly's visa. "I like your style. You're a negotiator. My God, you should see the basket cases we've had today. Just now a woman had to be forcibly removed because she was refusing to leave her shoes behind. Her shoes! And there were all these old biddies around her saying, 'Don't worry, sweetheart, those shoes won't even be in fashion in the future.' It was comical, in a morbid way. And the shoes only had sentimental value. A gift from her mother. Touching, but we can't invest in people who can't even get through customs. I see you even travel light," she says happily. "No photos."

"They said photo paper would be damaged in travel."

"Sure, but that doesn't stop most travelers. Unless Rollie Fingers is your boyfriend."

Polly shakes her head no, answering her question seriously, just in case.

Now that the woman is inclined towards her, Polly asks in a high, watchful voice, "Do a lot of people travel to get medical treatment for a friend or family member with the flu?"

"Isn't that the draw? That or basic survival."

"I was wondering if you knew what strategies are most successful? For meetups?"

"What's a meetup?"

"When people try to find each other again? Once they arrive?"

"Oh, a meetup. I see. You know, I have no idea. No meetups have ever happened."

"No one has ever been successfully reunited with someone they left behind?"

"Literally speaking. Chronologically. It's never happened before. The first travelers aren't scheduled to arrive for another twelve years. But I can give you a contact form. Would you like a contact form?"

"Yes. What's a contact form?"

Simpson removes a sheet from the back of

her clipboard.

"Write down the name and number of anyone you'd like to keep abreast of your changing travel plans. It's in case of reroutements. In case your services are deemed more useful in a different time."

"Reroutements? I thought that was just a rumor."

Just like that, with the slightest lift of her voice, Polly lets slip her weak spot. Wariness slides into the psychologist's expression. They can't afford another basket case.

"Don't you worry about that," Simpson says. "I shouldn't have mentioned it. You won't be rerouted. It would say, if you were going to be. Somewhere in here, it would say." She makes a show of riffling through Polly's file. "Can you sign the statement now?"

"I don't have a phone number for him yet. He's on his way to the hospital now."

"Which hospital?"

"St. Luke's."

"Great. Good." The psychologist takes back the contact form and writes *St. Luke's.* "Can you sign this statement now? It just says you agree to the terms. There's others to get to." The psychologist touches her bare wrist as if she is wearing a watch.

Polly finds herself pinching the pads of

her fingers, one by one. Their Saturdays-in-September idea is suddenly sickening. It is like a plan a mother would make to keep from losing her children on a subway. It's a plan able to withstand early closing doors and a snarl of stairways, not the ocean of minutes that twelve years holds. But uselessly her mind has gone blank. Strange, random thoughts wander into the empty space. Is it dinnertime? She is entering a world where the notion of something as normal as dinnertime does not exist.

"Should you wish to break your contract now, I can set you up with a repayment plan for the associated costs plus the thirteen percent that you'll owe us. Otherwise, I need you to sign this final statement saying you are prepared for travel."

It was then that Polly began to experience a feeling of dislocation that did not leave her for many months. The pen in her hand and the paper on the table appeared far away, like she was watching them on a movie screen. I'll see him in just a few hours, my time. This time tomorrow, he'll be waiting for me. We can still have a baby. The happy weight in my arms.

She heard the psychologist say, "Time-Raiser is a good company. We'll protect you. Today, or rather tomorrow, is the first day of the rest of your life. It's a gift."

On that movie screen, the hand drew ballpoint loops on the line: her own signature. That was almost the last thing she remembered of the whole trip. When she met other travelers in the future, she could not remember the sort of details they wanted to trade, because they were details that came after the paper was signed. Which gate did she leave from? Which class was the boat? Was she put in a lie-down seat or a sit-up one? Did she wear a radiation-protection apron or blanket? Shoptalk was a way to divvy up what they'd endured without actually talking about it.

She could not remember the recording, played right as she pitched into a many-year sleep. A tender voice told of Polly being past the point of return and hence authorized to hear the story of the future that was waiting, how the tiny but intrepid TimeRaiser — Texas born and bred! — had endeavored to prevent the pandemic by inventing time travel, and when that didn't work, they did not relent, but tamed the flu by snatching carriers from right under its nose.

The last thing she remembered was this: when she was left alone in the last holding area, she finally located the snag in her bra. It was not the underwire. It was a photograph Frank had tucked into the padding pouch. It was of the two of them at New Year's, confetti strands in their hair. Her aunt Donna had set the zoom too close and each of them had an ear missing. On the back, Frank had written, *Something to remember us by.*

She couldn't explain what she did next. Polly flipped the photo over and folded it in half. And she tore it up. Then she pressed the shards between the pages of her travel handbook and put it all in a garbage can in the corner.

Afterwards she tried to console herself by imagining that horror had distilled her down to her most animal self, who had no use for photos; she had been out of her mind. But the truth was that she had done it because Frank believed they needed props, aids to remember each other. He believed in the possibility of a future time-line in which she could forget him. This was intolerable.

She would regret this always. It would sit like a bubble in her lungs. Even if the travel had wiped it blank, she would still wish she owned the piece of paper that had housed the outline of his face, with the ruts his writing made in the back, where he had written his message without signing his name.

■ ■ ■ ■

When the pod unsealed and they climbed out of the time machine, the light struck them like a blunt force. Their skin was burning, their nostrils about to rupture, their eyeballs ready to burst. People were screaming and weeping and Polly heard her own voice, severed from her body, crying about her eyes. She was on a gurney. They tied a plastic bag around her neck so she would stop getting sick down her front and they put a strap around her chest just to measure her heartbeat, although it felt as if they were tying her down. A serene voice was speaking to no one in particular, and Polly caught the words "side effects" and "normal" and "subside," but the voice soothed nobody. She kept trying to sit up to reassure herself she wasn't restrained, until they cuffed her wrist to the bed. They forced her to drink a sweet gelatinous liquid and she threw up again. She was crying and apologizing and someone was holding her head.

"Frank?" she asked. Everything in the terminal had been rebuilt on a petrifying scale, curved windows like tsunamis of glass, and she had to shut her eyes or she'd upset herself again.

"Is Frank one of the nurses?" someone said.

"I'm supposed to be at the airport. I have to get to the airport."

"You're at the airport."

"Which airport?"

"Houston Intercontinental Airport."

"Okay." She relaxed against the restraints.

A second later she grasped that this wasn't everything she needed to know.

"Hello? Hello?" she shouted.

Nobody came.

"What year is it? Is it nineteen ninety-three?" Polly couldn't move her head; her skull was pinned down; she could only see the ceiling. It was not like her to be so visibly needy, all her insides on the outside. Even her own self was foreign.

Someone in another bed, who was even more confused than she, said, "Nineteen eighty-one."

Polly tried again for someone in charge. "What year is it? Please?"

Finally, an official replied, "It's nineteen ninety —" then the last number was garbled.

"It's nineteen ninety-three?"

"I said nineteen ninety —"

"It's nineteen ninety-three?" she mewed.

The world started to revolve and she cried out until she realized someone was turning her gurney.

"See for yourself," the voice said.

Now she was facing the exit. A digital clock in the ceiling said *5:17 p.m.*

"What is it?" she heard herself say.

"It'll show the date. You have to wait till it clicks over."

And then it clicked. Like a red neon portent, the clock pulsed *September* and *4* and the numbers *1 9 9 8.*

SEPTEMBER 1978

Polly lives in Buffalo and works as a secretary at a bookkeeping firm, on a side street off City Hall, in a neighborhood that used to be grand but has lost its identity. Around the corner, Frank works at a bar where the city grease on the windows acts like tinting and the carpet will smell forever. The crowd is an unusual mix of men with huge, craggy faces, and jolly fifty-something women who laugh together like ducks honking, and passersby in dinner jackets or construction wear or snug rock-band T-shirts who come once and never return. Polly likes to come here after work every day and drink a screwdriver, because there's not one thread of commonality to make anyone feel left out.

Two months ago Polly's boyfriend moved out of their shared apartment, taking with him all of Polly's furniture. This was more absurd and humiliating than if Chad had committed a generic betrayal, like sleeping with a friend. Polly had to move back in with her aunt Donna, who she'd lived with from age thirteen to eighteen, after her mother died in a car accident. Donna is a thirty-something travel agent who looks like a pipe cleaner: gangly, with a long face and close-cropped, dyed-black, bristly hair. All Donna has to say about Chad is that no one treats you bad unless you let them. "It's only stuff," Polly tells Donna. "This is a good thing." "Now when faced with trouble, I can remember I survived this." Eventually, Donna tells her that if she has nothing bad to say about Chad, she is not allowed to say anything at all.

Polly has already gotten up twice to use the pay phone in the corner to call Chad's last-known number. She keeps her finger on the edge of the switch hook so she can hang up right before the call goes to his answering machine. She doesn't want to waste a quarter on nothing. Summer has turned into fall and she will never track him down, and she is calling only for the pleasure of annoying him. It is an empty pleasure.

Polly sits down. Frank has taken away her drink, but she wasn't finished, and she can't afford a new one. He is before her, with a dish towel over his shoulder like an old-fashioned barkeep.

"Another?"

She shakes her head without looking up. A fat, disgusting tear is making its way down her nose. She hears his cords swish as he reaches for something. He holds out a napkin. She takes it, her chin still down, and before she can thank him, he is off to get someone else a bottle of Black Label.

She waits before wiping her eyes. She does not want to be caught tending to her tears. She pretends to study the scalloping at the napkin's edges. How much does it cost to put scalloped edges on every napkin? Such an act of beauty that goes mainly unseen.

Donna likes to remind Polly that she has to earn her keep by entertaining Donna. "You're such a drag," Donna says. "Go do something daring so I can live vicariously."

Polly prefers to stay home and drink home-brew wine and watch TV with Donna's two massive cats, Chicken and Noodles.

"What happened today?" Donna yells as a way of greeting when Polly comes home. "Gossip! If you don't give me some gossip, you're getting kicked to the curb!"

"We did some training on the new in-house phone system. Everyone got new extensions. You're gonna love hearing about this."

Later, Polly makes the mistake of telling Donna about Frank. "There's a dishy bartender who works around the corner."

"And . . . ?"

There isn't really anything else to say. She edits the story. "Today I sneezed and he gave me a napkin."

"He. Likes. You. Quick, go back now. Where's your coat?"

"You're not serious. I'm in my Ziggy pajamas."

It is also only the second commercial break during the *Laverne & Shirley* season premiere, which they've been awaiting for weeks.

"You should go. You've been wanting to meet someone."

"I could go tomorrow."

"Maybe tomorrow he'll meet the love of his life and you'll have missed your chance. As soon as the credits go, take my car."

"If it's meant to be, it's meant to be, whether I go out there or not."

"You have the worst attitude. No one has ever had a worse attitude than you."

At ten p.m. the bar is a backwards, smoky facsimile of its daytime self, even if it is a Wednesday night. The tables are littered with the gunk of drink, and the stools are crammed with bodies searching for a bewitching stranger to hold between their knees. Frank is leaning against the bar with his face resting on his hand, talking to a woman in green everything. Polly opens the door to exit, but this makes the bell overhead tinkle, and Frank sees her.

He waves to her and produces a screwdriver and places it on the bar. And then he winks. There's a cherry in the drink, which must be a night thing. She had a book on her, but Donna confiscated it so that she wouldn't look like a schoolmarm. She has nothing to do with her eyes. Around her, the bar screams with mirth.

Polly likes to think of herself in a certain way — self-assured, nonchalant. But the glare of this nighttime world exposes her shyness, her inexperience. Her high school friends are already engaged to their high school boyfriends. Polly stares miserably at the cherry.

He is just her size, the height she'd be if she were a man. He has strong shoulders and a sweet face, a sinking combination.

Polly thinks, Stay or go, but quit feeling sorry for yourself. Her goal is to make herself immune to her surroundings, so she does not see how Frank looks around, pretending to scan the room but lighting too long on Polly, how Frank looks into the mirror over the bar, in order to see her face. This is how it begins, and she misses it. And so, when he places a matchbook in front of her, she looks at it confused, almost angry it seems, judging from her expression in that mirror over the bar. She puts the matches in her pocket and her money on the counter and she leaves. A few days later, she puts her hand in her jacket pocket, where she has forgotten the matchbook, maybe intentionally, and she is stupefied when she opens it and sees Frank's name and number scribbled across the flap.

Frank suggests they go for a walk in Delaware Park. It is an endearing, old-fashioned suggestion, and Polly has to tell herself not to get her hopes up. When she arrives, he goes to hug her, and she is taken aback. Their bodies mismatch, one of his arms jammed awkwardly around her neck, while a six-pack of beer in a black plastic bag swings in his other hand, perilously near her ear. Why did he bring beer?

"Heh," he says. "Almost clocked you in the head." They step through the archway and her stomach gives a nasty twist. Sometime after, when it is too late to mention,

46

she thinks about how he said "clocked" — a funny word she can't remember ever hearing him say again. She remembers too his hand was so busy with his shirt, which rode up his pale belly when he hugged her, and she realizes he must have been nervous. She didn't know him well enough to read the signs.

The beer and the crude noise it makes when he opens it has her reconsidering the whole date. It is not at all that she is against drinking; she is just against drinking inelegantly, in the park. But they walk and get to talking, and when they return to where they began, they take the loop again. He tells her he is an out-of-work historian. He's working at the bar to help a family friend and he's going to get his high school teaching credentials this fall. She admits that what she really wants to do is learn upholstery, as unexpected as it sounds, and she even tells him why. She has never told anyone before, but Frank asks. She wants to learn so that she can fix her mother's love seat, moldering inside the discount locker where it's lingered for years.

They talk and talk, and she asks him how old he is, and it takes him a second to remember: he's twenty-five. The more years I have, he says, the less I remember them,

47

and isn't that terrible? She thinks it's such a nice thing to say. When it begins to rain, first they huddle under her puny umbrella, and then eventually he puts his arm around her, and the contact makes her voice crack. Gusts of rain heap up marshy piles of leaves, and the cars going by kick them down in streams of taillight red.

Frank asks if she wants to come to his place to get out of the storm. It is across the street and around the corner. "It's just up ahead," he says after they have walked five blocks. "Just around this corner," he says after another ten minutes. By the time he says, "It's just the next street over," the rain has stopped. The dark sky has cleared and it's daytime again.

"Do you still want to come in?" Frank asks, which makes Polly consider that the rain wasn't just a cover to get her into his house, which means that now that the rain has stopped, he doesn't want her to come in anymore, which means that she should decline.

"I guess I'm okay," she says, and his face falls. It's embarrassing how clearly his feelings show, and they both know it, and he kicks his foot at a congregation of squirrels and pigeons pecking at something on the ground.

The pigeons go up and the squirrels go out. But one hysterical squirrel makes the bad choice to go straight into the road. There is the gruesome thump of a Buick going by, fatally close to the curb, and Polly screams.

The animal is making spooky moves, blinking its one milky eye and trying to get off the road, not grasping that its haunches have been flattened. In an awful turn, Frank laughs.

"What should we do?" he says. He bends down to take a look and instantly steps back.

"We have to put it out of its misery."

"We should call animal control."

"That will take too long. It's suffering."

"Maybe another car will finish the job."

"Another car will just run over its feet again. Its head is too close to the curb."

"What do you want me to do?" He has sidled off, away from the gore, to almost out of earshot.

"Stamp on its head."

Frank cringes, his entire face crinkling to a point at its center.

"Do you have a quarter?" Polly asks.

"Why?"

"To buy a newspaper. There's a box over there."

"Are you going to read him to death?"

Polly drags a newspaper out of the box and opens it with a single, trim motion. She removes the first three pages and leaves the rest on top of the newspaper box. She takes the front pages and lays them over the animal delicately, like a sheet over the dead, mindful not to look in its heartsick eye.

"Are you ready to do it?" she asks him.

This is a defining moment. But Frank doesn't say anything.

"Fine. It's only a squirrel," she says.

"Wait. This is his final hour. Should we say something?"

Polly brings her heel down hard and fast, too fast for either her or the animal to ponder it.

At first they keep walking, both a little stunned.

"How were you able to do it?" Frank says after a while.

"Don't think about it. You think too much."

She doesn't actually believe this. She doesn't know why she says it. And then it just seems like the best thing to do is leave. There is a bus coming. She has no idea where it goes.

"It's getting late. I should catch this bus."

"Of course." He jams his hands in his pockets and blows out his cheeks. "That's not how I imagined I'd act in that situation."

"What did you imagine you'd do?"

"I'd be you."

The bus comes and the bus goes.

"You changed your mind?" he says.

"When it got close, I saw it was the wrong one," she lies.

She thinks that he will say, *Well, come on up to my place then,* but instead he says, "If you have to go, let me drive you home."

He leads her to his car, pointing out his window near the top of a small apartment building on Colvin Avenue. She longs to go up there, but he's unlocking the car. What could she say to change their direction that would also leave her pride intact?

He puts Carly Simon on the stereo. They cross Delaware and they cross Elmwood, they cross under the train tracks as a freight train in multicolored rust rolls overhead. They are almost into Riverside now, and still she can't think of anything to say. She thinks about saying she forgot something in the park, but then she can't think up what to say she left behind. She can't say her wallet, because then she'll sound reckless. She can't say sunglasses; it's a cloudy day. She can't say umbrella, because it's sitting at her feet. Maybe he wants her to say something. Maybe he is relying on her to husband their time together, as if, for some reason unbeknown to her, she is the only one who can. His eyes flick around, but that could just be safe driving; she could be misreading this too. Today's record is poor.

Then they are near her street and it's too late. The hems of her sleeves and the knees of her tights are wet from the rain, and the cold sets in. Snot trickles down the inside of her nose and she tries to sniff genteelly.

"I wish I still had that napkin you gave me," she says.

"What napkin?"

"Never mind."

They are at a stop sign. He reaches into the backseat and brings out a plastic sleeve of those cocktail napkins with their scalloped edges. It's the length of his arm. He drops it in her lap.

"Stick with me and you'll never run out of napkins again."

He reaches over the armrests and touches her on the leg. It's just a small thing, a quick squeeze on the round of her knee, and then his hand goes back to the wheel. Something in the gesture is genuine, familial, like they have known each other a long time. She wishes that were true.

He takes the corners with one hand on

the wheel and the sun comes dusty through the windshield and the singer warbles as Frank squints to make out the street signs. He looks like a photograph. Polly wishes that time could just stop right here, and stay in this very moment, for good.

Polly traveled an hour from Houston on the back bench of an old panel van. She couldn't keep her eyes open, as much as she wanted to resist the nakedness of sleep. The bus driver had the heat on and the only window didn't open. Her shirt was steeped in sweat.

At the terminal, once she passed a whole hour without vomiting, they'd said that despite the lingering effects of travel, she had withstood the journey well and was cleared to go. She had not wanted to leave. "Someone is expecting to meet me here," she said. She asked to be taken to the passenger pickup area, and she made a fool of herself, babbling details they had no use for, about how he'd expected her in 1993 but maybe he came every year? But there was no passenger pickup area. That was not the way the system worked: no one was allowed to remove Journeymen except Time-

Raiser personnel, and only after they'd been photographed and printed. They did not explain this to her. They just kept saying, "Yes, all right," as they guided her through cloth tunnels with flapping walls like the insides of a cocoon. She kept checking every head for Frank's face, even after they loaded her onto the van: the blurred features of the men at the final guardhouse, the single maintenance worker in a dim pool of lamplight by a fence. The tendons in her hands were aching like she was clinging to a lifebuoy, and she couldn't unball her fists. Their first plan had failed, by five years.

But as soon as she got to her lodging, she would call Donna. Donna would know where to find Frank. Polly would call the police if she had to. It would all be sorted out by the end of the week. Her mind bleared the particulars of her situation, laboring to protect itself from itself.

Now they were driving over water, and Polly turned to look out the window in the back door. She saw everything backwards, only after the van had passed it by. On the left, a cluster of five or six bonfires swam in the sky. On the right, a lightless hotel loomed over water like a mangrove. Its balconies gave the look of a tremendous honeycomb, but stark white against the total night. The hotel had no neighbor but brush as tall as houses for miles. They were at a checkpoint and she heard her name, distorted, as though the voices were speaking through a tin-can phone. Every time she tried to inch forward, nausea pinned her. A row of uniform junipers lined the road like the highway was wearing blinkers. She glimpsed guards at a checkpoint, reading maps by flashlight. For the first time she thought to be concerned that there was no light. No streetlights, no headlights from other cars, no table lamps on sills.

When she opened her eyes this time, a garden of golden huts was rolling past. Then came an empty concrete plain a mile wide, then came objects that Polly could not compute. They passed ten or fifteen of these somethings: a familiar shape, like a house or a church or a corner store, but the outline was wrong, baggy and shaggy like a beast. Then she understood. Strip malls, warehouses, and offices were canopied in shrubs and grasses that seized their first stories. Anything higher was bound by jumbo-leafed ivy that smothered doors and windows with wiggling tendrils, bricks and mortar transmuted into jiggling, unearthly life-forms.

It was like seeing the face of a loved one where a moustache is missing, or an eye.

Her fear was present but vague, like an emotion she had once felt a long time ago.

She woke again, banging her elbow against a rivet. She finally remembered the most important thing: the day of the week. What if it was Sunday and she'd already missed the first Saturday?

She dragged herself, seat by seat, up the aisle, pausing only when the nausea became dire. She writhed into the bench behind the driver as the van plunged into light.

"You all right there, miss?" He had a pockmarked face, like an old dish sponge.

"What day is it?" The tires hit gravel, rattling Polly's teeth, and she looked for a sick bag.

"Friday."

Her relief was so intense, it was painful, like blood coursing into a sleeping limb. With all these guardhouses, Frank hadn't been able to make it to the time travel facility in Houston, but he'd be in Galveston.

But was she in Galveston? This was not Galveston. She'd been once, and it didn't look like this.

"Where are we?"

"Galveston."

"That's where we're going?" she asked.

"That's where we are."

"We're in Galveston?"

57

"Yes. Is something wrong?"

"We're not in the outskirts?"

"We're in Galveston."

"Why does it look" — she struggled to think of a nice word and could not — "abandoned?"

"Pandemic took ninety-three percent of us, through sickness or flight, but each remaining has the strength to do the work of twenty." Then he scowled, his bottom lip pinning his top lip to his nose. "I'm giving you information out of order. We're not supposed to say that first." He popped a finger up against the windshield. "Look! It's not abandoned at all."

A boulevard was unfurling out of the desolation. Thick, hooded figures rose out of the median. Now Polly's fear swamped in from that long-ago place, swift and searing. But the figures were just bushes, hedges, painstakingly carved into animate shapes.

"Tyrannosaurus rex," said the driver, pointing out the topiary shapes as they passed. "Mickey Mouse. Spiral. Cups and saucers?"

There were explanations, things that could help create sense. She just had to corral the right questions from the wilds of her mind.

"Ninety-three percent of what?" Polly asked.

"What?"

"The pandemic killed ninety-three percent of Americans?"

"Not necessarily killed, also chased away. This is Harborside Drive." The driver continued the tour. "It's the first thing the vacationers see when they come off the ferry."

"Where do vacationers come from?" But she thought of a more pressing question. "Where are the other travelers? The ones I arrived with?"

"I'm not positive. They probably went to the holiday resorts at Rockport, Padre Island, Lake Charles."

"Why am I here?"

"To work in a holiday resort. Right?" With one hand on the wheel, he used the other to flick through a stack of bound papers on the seat beside him. "Polly Nader?"

She wanted to ask him to watch the road. "Yes." Then again, they hadn't met a single car.

"You're here to work for Henry Baird, head decorator at the Hotel Galvez."

They turned right, into darkness.

"We've only completed development around the perimeter of the island." The driver drew a circle in the air with his finger. "Like a roller rink. You and me are going a

59

smidge inland. It's more rustic."

The headlights found a lone, gawky high-rise, age-spotted and brown, crisscrossed on one side with fire escapes but gaping open on the other, this height-wise hole covered by a flap of plastic that slapped in the wind, like a giant's skirt. They pulled up in front of a set of double doors. There were no lights on behind the frosted glass.

"Here we are! Best digs in town: Moody Plaza. For O-1s only."

It looked nearly condemned, but she took comfort in hearing O-1 was still a coveted status.

"Don't worry" — the driver pointed to the stories-high plastic flap — "they're fixing that."

When he unlocked the passenger door, instead of the sweet breeze she longed for, a wall of heat socked her in the face. Her tongue swelled. She wiped the sweat from her eyes and the driver said, "You never been to Texas before?" Her body had reverted to its default: though she understood she was in Texas, she had expected the air of Buffalo.

He had to unlock a box to get at the light switch for the lobby. "Energy conservation program," he explained. "You're on the fourth floor. What a break. You could've been on eleven."

The stairwell landing was the width of a broom closet. Up close, the driver looked drained. He started when she tapped his arm to get his attention.

"Will there be time for me to go to the Flagship Hotel tomorrow?"

"You'll have orientation; first things first." His voice was muffled as they ascended in single file, her eyes on the back of his dust-colored vest. He was a big man and walking behind him was like facing a wall. "There could be some time for sightseeing later in the day."

"So I'll be able to go tomorrow? And tomorrow is Saturday?"

She saw his face as they drew abreast at the turn of the stairs. He was gazing at the risers, thoughtfully or vacantly; she couldn't tell. But he said, "Yes," and that was all she wanted.

"What street are we on?"

"Twenty-First."

They could not be far from the Flagship. She was so lucky.

"Can I make a phone call?" she asked.

"A phone call? Who do you know here to call?"

"I want to call my aunt." She was sur-

61

prised by his rudeness, but she tried to keep civil.

"Where's your aunt?"

"In Buffalo."

"How do you know?"

Polly didn't know what to say. His questions were so odd. "She's my aunt."

He paused on the third-floor landing to look at her.

"So you have a phone number for her?"

"Yes."

"Is it a current phone number?"

"Yes!"

"You're sure it's a phone number for right . . . now . . . ?" He said this courteously, as if his line of questioning could cause insult.

"Of course." And then a nightmarish cold gripped her. "Oh no," she said. "It's 1998."

"That's what I'm trying to tell you."

She put her hand out and felt the reassurance of the wall. She said, "Oh boy, oh no," because she couldn't tender what was truly in her mind — What have I done? What have I done? — to an awkward stranger.

"It's okay," he said. "I see this all the time. People's minds have trouble catching up with their bodies. They should list it as a symptom of the motion sickness."

"Can we call now anyway? To see if she's there?" She hated the weedy tone in her voice.

"I have to go home. I live on the Bolivar Peninsula. If I don't go now, I'll miss the boat."

"Oh." She didn't know what he was talking about. "Is there someone I can speak to? Maybe it's you, or a superior, about my situation? I was supposed to go to 1993."

"I'm not positive who you can speak to. But listen, your aunt has waited years for you. Trust me, she can wait one more night." He smiled and so she smiled back, a reflex. "I'll put you in touch with anyone you want to talk to tomorrow."

A headache, a pounding, grinding, screeching thing, had joined the nausea. He led her to her door on the fourth floor and dropped the key in her hand. He pointed out the bathroom down the hall. He pulled a jar of beans from his vest pocket. "To fortify you." A dank, salty wind blew up and down the hallway through the gash in the south wall.

She could not remember what the travel handbook had promised in terms of accommodations. She had not asked too many questions; the official accommodations hadn't mattered, because she was going to

63

have her own, at Frank's, there was no doubt.

She could unlock the door, but she could not get it open more than halfway. She reached her arm inside and fumbled for a light switch. But there wasn't one, at least not anywhere light switches are commonly mounted, scaled to basic human dimensions: within a foot of the door, within five feet of the floor. It was a small but eerie discrepancy. She turned to the driver for help, but he'd gone. She hadn't heard him say good-bye.

Her gut crowded with sudden childhood fright, her capacity for the strange exceeded. She had to make a phone call and find out where Donna was, where Frank was now, no matter what. But as she turned towards the stairwell to find the driver, the light within it clicked off. The darkness throbbed. She took one step down the stairs, and her mouth filled with sick. She flailed her way back to her room and clung to the wall. She inched forward, toe by toe, until she found the switch, four feet from the doorway, at waist height. Slapdash electricals for a once-grand room that had been divided and subdivided into sorry slices. Brown light shone from a bulb in a plastic seashell cover. She had not been able to get the door open because it was blocked by the bed. There was no sink. She spat into a tiny garbage can.

There was a phone hanging next to the bed, a fleshy plastic lump on a cord. She grabbed the receiver. But the phone had no buttons, not on the front or the back, the receiver or the cradle. It was like a face without features. Her need to vomit spiked all the way up. Her groin contracted and sweat spackled her nose.

She turned off the light and lay down. She pressed the back of her neck against the bed and clasped her hands and jammed her thumbs against her ribs to steady her heart. Of course she would see him tomorrow. Of course he would be waiting on the first floor of the Flagship, sitting in those bulbous burgundy armchairs, where he had a view of the door. Of course she would get there hours before he even formed the thought that she might not make it. And by tomorrow evening, this acid fear that she would never again see his face would have lasted less than a day.

Polly did not remember falling asleep, but she was woken by a baying like a car horn. The phone was ringing, and her heart zippered into her throat. She lifted the receiver, hearing Frank's voice before the other end spoke.

"GOOD MORNING!" a voice screamed so loud, Polly screamed back. It carried on, unperturbed. "IT IS 0700 HOURS AND TODAY IS SATURDAY, SEPTEMBER 5, 1998! THE TEMPERATURE IS 92 AND RISING, SO GET OUT YOUR SUN HATS AND SANDALS! THE ASSIGNMENT FOR POLLY NADER TODAY IS: ORIENTATION. YOUR SCHEDULE IS: AT 0730 HOURS, PROCEED TO THE LOBBY FOR PICKUP." The voice was female and violently cheerful. It paused before every personalized value, and then a low, gloomy voice interjected with Polly's name and assignment.

Polly had slept in the clothes she had traveled in, the shabby hand-me-downs of a stranger, given to her at the airport to replace her torn blue suit. A towel and navy coveralls hung by the door. She put on the coveralls. She didn't have any toothpaste. She kept sucking her teeth, embarrassed by her breath.

There was no sign of the driver from last night. A different man in the lobby waved her onto an old school bus and yanked it into drive before she could find a seat. There were three other passengers, all asleep. Polly's nausea was gone, replaced by the

66

sensation that her insides had been suctioned out. The highway and the ferry terminal were new. Everything else was junk. Kudzu spread like gangrene across the boarded-up buildings, its leaves the size of dinner plates.

A headless palm tree stood alone in a field of wan grasses. Shipping containers lined up end to end on cinder blocks made a winding, rusty snake. There were too many containers to count. They had holes cut in the sides for entry and exit; the containers were makeshift homes. The bus stopped where a crowd had formed along the narrow road shoulder. The people were dusty and creased, with grit in their hair and big, scarred hands, and skin darkened by the sun. They didn't look like new arrivals going to get oriented. They boarded, coming and coming, the driver counting each body with a clicker. Polly got wedged against the metal siding, three to each bench made for two.

This bus was not going to an orientation. This must be a mistake. She didn't fit in with these people. Why hadn't the driver noticed his error?

Or maybe they were going to drop her off somewhere else. This was some kind of public bus. She relaxed. She'd taken a million public buses. Like random shapes that turn out to be words, she understood this context all at once. Her seatmates had the scent of body and onion, but it was just the smell of a regular ride.

A paper bag was passed. Each passenger removed something, then sent the bag on back, not looking at what their hands were doing. Polly took the bag stiffly, holding it with as few fingers as she could, in case it was dirty or wet. Beneath the bag's rolled rim lay a heap of gleaming tomatoes. She extracted one hesitantly. Was she meant to eat it like an apple? The woman beside Polly tore into hers, red juice running down her chin. A strip of skin with a chunk of flesh still attached swung from the gouge she'd made. Polly's stomach turned and she dropped the tomato into her pocket. Her face was hot, her mouth tight.

On came the checkpoint and the juniper blinkers and the floating bonfires. But now she saw that the fires were attached to oil refinery towers. From afar, the refinery looked like someone had punctured the coast with a hundred different needles — sewing needles, knitting needles, spindles, syringes. A cyclone fence circled the towers, so tall she could see it from across the water, nearly half the height of the highest tower, garlanded with bales of razor wire.

Now they passed flowering shrubs with cirrus strands dancing in the bus's wake, and more topiary. Then a high wall of shrubbery, so you could see only the pastel shingles of the vacation homes arrayed on the other side. Then they reached the bowels of the resort: drab utility buildings and the putrid smell of garbage. Here they stopped, by a shipping container.

Polly stayed in her seat until the bus driver honked his horn and shouted, "Gulf Pearl. Come on, everybody off." Maybe he made everyone get off at each stop for an administrative reason. After, he'd let her back on. But as soon as her foot cleared the step, the driver shut the door.

"Wait!"

She knocked on the door, but he started the engine. She shouted and banged on whatever part of the bus she could hit as it slid past her. She ran, shuffling pathetically in the too-big shoes given to her in the airport yesterday. With a screaming and a crunch, the bus stopped.

"Are you loco? ¿Estúpido?" the driver yelled.

"You're supposed to take me somewhere else. I'm going to orientation." She had to shout through the door.

He opened the door.

"That's not what this says." He jabbed his finger at a clipboard, making it skitter across the dashboard. "Eighty pax to this cycle center. I'm just the transporter. I go where the manifest says." He had a scraggly little moustache like a teenager, though he was older.

"Is this orientation?"

"It's a cycle center."

The others had vanished down a lane the width of a body beside the shipping container.

"What's a cycle center?"

"Journeymen come here to ride bikes."

"For exercise?"

A guffaw urped out of him. "No. It's the job."

"I'm not supposed to ride a bike. I was brought here as an upholsterer."

"A what?"

"I restore furniture."

"You were brought to the cycle center to fix furniture?"

"No, to here. To this year."

"I don't got time for games! I gotta be in Baytown! All you have to do is go in there" — he pointed out the window to the containers — "and ride an exercise bike."

"No, you've made a mistake." She

70

wouldn't be dismissed like the night before. "I'm not supposed to be here." But where was here? It was the first Saturday in September, the sun had already begun its climb up the sky, and she didn't even know where she was. "Where are we?"

"I can't make small talk with you! Let go my door!" He pulled the lever to shut the door.

She threw everything in the door's gliding track: foot, elbow, palm. The rubber edge crunched down. "I have to get out of here. I have to be somewhere else!" She was shouting. Anyone who knew her would be shocked; she'd been pushed past the point, they'd better heed. But this driver didn't care. She had to think of something else.

"I'm O-1," she claimed. "I have special, important skills. I don't belong here." Both yesterday and many years ago, in the great hall with the radiation jackets, she had not been like the others, and everyone accepted that she belonged somewhere else. Why couldn't he see it? "Look at me. I'm not like them!" She began to cry, out of shame that she had said such a thing, and out of fear that she had to.

"What do you mean, you're O-1? How can you be O-1? Bullshit."

"But I am," she said, though she didn't

have any papers to back it up. What had last night's driver told her? "You picked me up from O-1 lodging."

"No I didn't," he said.

But now he was flicking through his clipboard, folding and unfolding a map.

"Oh, crud. I went to the wrong goddamn building. Oh, fuck." His face crumpled. "I can't lose this job. I'm supposed to deliver eighty. If you don't ride that bike, I'll only have seventy-nine. I'll be out on my ass. We just had a baby and we'll be kicked out of housing. Oh, fuck."

"I can't. I have to get somewhere. If I'm not there in time —"

He started the bus. But she wouldn't let go of the door and he was beginning to drag her. He leaned out of his seat and raised his fist, and she tried to duck, but she was trapped in the door. Then he stopped. He put the bus in park and put his head on the steering wheel.

"Where do you need to go? If you let go, I promise I'll come back and take you later."

"The Flagship Hotel, on Twenty-Fifth Street, in Galveston."

"It's 0815 now. I've got the Baytown run, but I'll come back for you at 1300 hours. I promise."

"I can't wait," Polly said. "You have to

72

take me back now."

"Please." He put his hand in his pocket. "I carry her little sock." He laid a small white thing in his palm and held it out for Polly to see. It was grayed and grubby from use, making it even more forlorn and sweet. Abruptly, even after he had taken her miles away, even after he had tried to strike her, her adversary became like her: parted from. Her perspective toppled, and so did her unyielding. Maybe one p.m. wouldn't be too late.

"What did you say the people are doing here?"

"Pedal power." He flung out a hand, gesturing to the whole resort compound. "The air-conditioning runs on clean energy from pedal power, powered by people like you. You get exercise and healthy living, the vacationers get lights and A/C." Polly understood all the words he said, but they didn't make sense together. "You're new, right? Long story short, we sold the oil fields. Now we get our energy elsehow." He looked at his watch. "Go to container one-five-four-six, one-five-four-five, or one-five-four-three and take the empty bike — there'll only be one. Just work fast, so when I pick you up, it looks like you worked the whole day. Be back at 1300 hours. I promise."

There were at least twenty shipping containers, lined up so precisely that at first she saw only one. They were numbered with spray paint, the fourth labeled *1546*. Inside, exercise bikes were planted three across and ten deep. Everyone was already hard at work. It smelled like an intestine. No one looked Polly's way. The floor was intricately webbed with cables that ran from the bikes and up the wall, where they connected to a rack of car batteries the length of the container. Some of the bikes were sleek and new; some were regular street bikes jammed into the network of cabling. The only vacant one, at the back, was an amalgam of salvaged parts glued together. When she climbed on, the bike rocked in its moorings. There were three army-regulation tin bottles slung from the right handlebar and a box cobwebbed to the left. When she pedaled, green numbers appeared on the box's face.

There were long, clawed slits in the ceiling, presumably for air, but too narrow for sun. No one talked. Two fans wheezed, far at the front. The man ahead of her was wearing orange sweatpants, pilled and printed with white loops of sweat salt.

Panic came in waves, like cramps. Why had she agreed to this? That driver was never coming back. How would she find a way back to the Flagship?

But around her the others cycled in that grim-faced, customary workplace silence. If they had been wailing or protesting, it would have been different. But they weren't, and so they made this normal. You did not have to cycle fast to make the green numbers change. She didn't know what they were counting, but the whirring and the pumping began to lull her. The driver would surely return, he couldn't have made up his baby, people didn't lie about things like that. The cycle farm seemed inhumane only because she was being forced to take part; otherwise she might think it quite clever. By evening she would be with Frank.

When Polly took a drink from one of the bottles, she expected the flat taste of water, but the liquid inside was warm and tinny, like blood. She told herself not to be such a princess and gulped it down. By the time the counter reached 200 — minutes, miles, or amperes, she didn't know — she needed a bathroom. But she was afraid to leave in case her ride returned. There were no clocks, and no one appeared to be wearing a wristwatch. Her best guess was that it was noon. Only an hour to go. She'd go to the bathroom when the driver came back.

She tried every trick she could to keep herself distracted — counting the rotations of her pedals, singing the alphabet backwards under her breath, replaying *The Black Stallion* in her head — but eventually she could no longer endure the heaviness in her bladder. She leaned as far forward as she could and whispered, "Excuse me," to the man in orange pants, but he couldn't hear over the whizz of the bikes. She tried again. A woman in the next aisle frowned at her. Polly was lancing the silence that kept them afloat.

"Please," she said to the woman. "Sorry, but do you know the time?"

The woman pointed over her shoulder. At first Polly thought she was signaling to Polly to keep her eyes to herself, but then she turned and saw a clock right above her head.

1330. The driver wasn't coming. She'd been so brainless. She'd have to find a way to the Flagship herself. The bike wobbled as it released her weight.

When she opened the back door, she stepped straight into shrubbery. The heat rose, viscous and deadly. Her coveralls were stifling, but at last she felt the release of taking action. First she had to find a bathroom. She could hear the sound of children laughing and the shriek of a swing set. Wind chimes tinkled. But as she walked, she found only container after container. She reached the final one before a wall of hedge. A plaque said, *70% of the air-conditioning in Gulf Pearl Vacation Homes comes from pedal power, provided by the independent energy contractors in centers like these! Our eco-mmitment in action!*

The children's laughter got louder. The playground must be on the other side of the hedge; there'd be a bathroom close by. Polly tugged at the hedge. Her fingers hit plastic, a black box. A speaker playing a recording of children's laughter, swings, and wind chimes.

She could think of no healthy reason for the recording. She wanted to leave and never come back, but her bladder was ready to burst. Pale purple stepping-stones led to an enormous gazebo, but no toilet. Instead, a set of ten deck chairs sat in a circle, each occupied by a naked man or woman wearing a bell jar on their head. The glass distorted their features. They swiveled their Martian heads to gaze at her. Their bodies glistened with oil, like Christmas hams.

Polly staggered away. In traveling, she'd expected what she was used to, or its opposite. Once, she'd seen a history textbook drawing of what ancient explorers predicted they'd see in uncharted lands: people with eyes in their feet, people who walked on their hands. But this was not an upside-down 1981. It was a totally alien sign system, with no cipher for translation.

She would just pee in the bushes. But she had to take off her coveralls completely. She tried to cover her body with her arms and, so distracted, she peed on her socks.

She followed the blacktop until she reached the main road. She fell back, to the side, whenever anyone passed, in golf carts, in trishaws, or dragging wagons of equipment on foot. She could make no peace with any of her choices. Every step, she felt sure she'd made the wrong decision. It was too far; she'd never make it in time. But she could not turn around and go back to that indifference. The horizon was flat and endless, brown like teeth. A trishaw passed, carrying an old man in a straw hat who was scanning the horizon as if on safari.

It was long past four when she reached the checkpoint. She'd done nothing wrong, but when a patrolman looked her way, she hid in the roadside growth. Exhaustion, thick and gluey, overcame her. Insects made a constant, high-pitched whine, like an incessant request never granted. She patted her pockets for the tomato from the morning bus ride. Maybe vitamins would help. But it was gone; she'd lost it at some point without knowing. She rooted around in her pockets, but her fingers only captured bits of thread. The tomato had been an act of kindness that she'd returned with disdain. She blinked and exhaled and blinked, trying to disperse her remorse.

But there was nothing to stop her from going on through the brushland and emerging way down the road, where the patrolmen couldn't see. Hope that she might yet make it before the end of Saturday shimmered. She still had a couple of hours.

She wriggled forward, watching for bent grasses like tripwires. Then the ground gave way, turning into a puddle. She could smell rotting food. Her feet sunk into a muck of plant and animal liquefied by the Texas sun. She could not get her feet free. They were pinned under by roots or monsters. Terror struck. She was not going to make it by nightfall. She might not even make it back to her lodging. There was nothing to hang on to, to yank herself free, but leaves that tore like tissue. She sat down so her seat was in the wet too, but this was the only way to get enough leverage to finally pull herself clear. Gulping and sobbing, she crashed back to the road, almost getting run over by a trishaw.

Someone said her name. The dream of finding Frank in less than one day became actual. He was calling her from the trishaw, holding out his hand.

But it wasn't Frank. It was the old man in the straw hat.

"Polly Nader? Are you Polly Nader? You must come with me."

The old man was tall and skinny, with tufty silver hair like moss. He had a pile of papers in his lap, including a photo of her.

"Thank God! I thought they'd botched it and sent you to 2010 or something and I was going to have to start all over again. I'm Henry Baird. I'm your boss."

She was slow to respond, and his smile dissolved.

"I thought I specified English-speaking." He frowned. "English? ¿Inglés?"

But when she answered nervously, his smile repaired itself.

"I thought we were going to have a communication problem. My God, I've been calling around all day and then I finally got in touch with your superintendent. Two buses arrived at the same time and you must have got on the wrong one. I went all the way to that, whatever-it-is place, calling your name in all those cycle rooms, giving you

81

up for a runaway, and then you're here, in the bushes. Did you get lost?"

"Yes." She was overcome by her disappointment that he was not Frank, and unable to say more.

"Well, don't get lost again or I'll have to dock your hours. You've already missed all of today. What happened? Why are you all wet?"

Mist by mist, her dream dissolved. She would not see Frank today. She put her hand on her waist and squeezed her side to hold herself together. There were many more Saturdays to go.

"When I realized I was in the wrong place," she said to the old man, "I thought I'd walk back, to see if I could still catch the orientation. I misjudged the distance."

"Well, I'll take you back to your lodging. Don't want you getting lost again."

Polly had never traveled by trishaw. It looked safe enough, everything welded together, but it was a grisly thing to be traveling by human. Baird appeared unbothered, because he had an expansive, lordly way of speaking that obscured how tense he was, until he stopped talking. Then he vibrated with nerves, the vibrations moving him through the world a half second faster than everyone else. He convinced the trishaw driver not to charge for waiting time; he insisted no energy was expended while the driver was waiting, in fact he'd received the chance to recharge, as if Baird had supplied him with an extra can of oil. Baird had the might of someone who couldn't manage not getting his way. Like so many before, the heat-scoured driver gave in, because it was easier.

After this was accomplished, Polly said, "Excuse me, sir. What sort of work am I doing for you?"

"Furniture restoration! Correct? Don't tell me . . ." He started to mutter.

"Correct, furniture restoration," she said, and he relaxed.

It was the first positive proof she'd received, one thing going according to plan, and she took it as a sign that eventually everything else would too. The numbness of battle left her body, and sensation returned: shoelaces cinched around her ankles, wind rustle, an earth that held her.

"I've been waiting months. Lucky you volunteered for travel, or it would have been me teaching someone the trade from scratch. What a headache that would be. But the process of requisitioning you — a nightmare! First, all the paperwork, then they have to send it to the relay point —"

"Relay point?"

"The machine can only go a max of twelve years in one jump. You don't recall your layover? Ha. Really a very stupid system, so vulnerable to error, because they have to send it back twelve years and then the people there send it the rest of the way and some numbskull at the relay was spaced out when my order came through, and the request changed from September 1998 to September 1993. Can you imagine?"

"What?" she said, but softly, really to herself, and he kept going.

"You can picture my face when I saw the figures, the dates, shimmer and change in the catalogue — that eight turning into a three. I had a fit! I bitched and I moaned and they fixed it, with something like only seconds to spare, in the buffer time. What if I hadn't been there? I said, 'No, it has to be 1998.' "

Bile shot up her throat like someone had stepped on her stomach. She launched herself to the edge of the bench and evacuated her insides over the side. Sick splattered on the wheel.

"Dear, oh, dear, oh, dear!" Baird banged on the coupling between the bicycle and the carriage, but the driver turned only long enough to say, "Sorry, can't stop." Baird squeezed himself into the farthest corner of the bench, and once there, tossed a handkerchief at her.

She wiped her face. "I was expecting to land in 1993, I was meant to meet someone."

"The hard truth is that whomever you made arrangements with is probably dead." He crossed his arms. "Sorry."

He went silent, but not for long. They reached a string of construction sites, and he burst out, "I bet you don't even know what we're doing here," as if they were in the middle of a discussion. "We're creating a vacation belt. The buckle is here, in Galveston. We're already attracting hundreds of vacationers from Japan, Norway, the United States."

"But I heard last night the pandemic wiped out ninety-three percent of America."

"So?"

"How are there vacationers from the United States?"

"They're from the United States. We're in America."

She started to think he was a bit crazy.

"Their economy is thriving. How could we get some for us? We have the time machine, a stream of cheap and willing workers spewing forth. We sell rebuilding services to any country that needs it — Germany, Venezuela. But also: Galveston as the new Acapulco. We have workers to build resorts, and workers to work in them. Things have restabilized in the countries able to maintain quarantine. They're stabilizing elsewhere too, in places that are now rebirthing. If everyone is back to work, then everyone needs a place to vacation."

"Which countries kept quarantine?"

"I hate that question. It makes me think of where I should have been." He sighed. "England, Iceland, Singapore, Sri Lanka, Hawaii. Islands. Our friends in the North."

Did he mean Canada? "How long did the pandemic last?" Where was Frank in all of this?

"Forever."

"Where do the building materials come from? For the resorts."

"The workers manufacture them."

Polly stored all these details for review at some later date, when she'd have time to make sense of this vicious world.

"Health tourism," Baird was saying. "All-natural everything. Very big. Therapeutics are the biggest fad since the pandemic."

"Where are you from?" she asked.

"Connecticut."

"No, I mean, when are you from? When

did you leave from?"

"When?" He laughed. "I'm not a Journeyman. My word. Why? Do I look like a Journeyman?" His face puckered with offense.

"Oh. I don't know."

"I'm an American. I'm not a Journeyman. I don't look like a Journeyman."

"You don't. I'm sorry."

"Well." He tugged at the bib of his overalls like it was a waistcoat. Silence crackled between them. She had exposed her ignorance. She vowed to never again speak before screening her words first, until she cracked the etiquette of this place. She was so flustered she didn't think to wonder why Americans and Journeymen were opposites, instead of counterparts.

"You traveled to benefit someone, didn't you?" he said. "That's who you were supposed to meet in '93?"

She nodded.

"Who'd you travel for?"

"My cousin." She was going to be careful, until she knew what was safe to reveal and what wasn't.

"I thought about making that choice, but in the end I couldn't." He gazed at his thumbs, sly and uncomfortable. "It was for my boyfriend."

87

Pain enveloped them and she couldn't tell if it was his or hers.

"They wouldn't allow you? Because you are . . . ?" She struggled. She didn't know what word was polite. Did they still say "gay"?

"Homos? Something like that."

What must they have suffered? This was the key to everything about this man: the rudeness, the jitters, the blundering. No wonder he was thoughtless: all his thoughts must be expended on trying to forget.

But they had arrived now, back at Twenty-First Street. There was still summer light in the sky. She was only four blocks away from Twenty-Fifth Street. Even if she was on the wrong end of the island, it could not be more than an hour's walk to the Flagship. Possibility and ache rebounded.

The driver from yesterday was waiting for her at Moody Plaza, in a room off the lobby that smelled of newspaper and mushrooms. Tidy, tightly spaced shelves were stacked with wooden toothbrushes, cakes of soap in paper, pajama sets, and jars of food. Under the window was a picnic table littered with packs of cards and old books. Two men were playing a game of twenty-one. The driver shooed them away. "It's twenty minutes to closing time," they protested.

"Item twelve," he replied, pointing to a list of policies pasted to the door: *#12 Time-Raiser reserves the right to revoke this space for confidential purposes at any time.*

"You got on the wrong bus," the driver told Polly. "You got on a bus that arrived at 0715 instead of 0730. If you're not careful, next time there'll be serious deductions off your LifeFund."

"Life fund?" she asked.

"Uh-oh. Did you miss your orientation today?"

He tried to figure out if she could attend another orientation. But the next one wasn't till the twelfth, and such a wait was against policy. He'd have to do it manually, now.

"There's a protocol for how to lay things out. To avoid undue distress. I'm no match for the video you'd view at the real orientation, with images and music. All I have is a basic script."

"I was hoping to go for a walk this evening. To get my bearings." She spoke so slowly, it sounded like she was making up a lie, but it was only because she was trying quite hard not to cry. She was so close. If she left right now, she could make it before this Saturday slipped away.

"Oh no, it's not safe for you to go walking

about. Anyway, the shuttle will take you everywhere. You don't need to worry about your bearings."

"Can I make a phone call?"

"I'm Norberto. I didn't introduce myself."

"Can I make a phone call now?"

"It will cost you."

"How much?"

He directed her to sit in front of a grubby old desk that was leaning in a corner, labeled *Concierge.* The top of the desk was immaculate — pens sat perky in a cup, a coffee cup rested on a coaster — a puzzling thing, considering the scored surface of the desk, blotched here and there by the gum of long-gone Scotch tape. There was a long-distance rate chart on the wall.

"Where do you want to call?"

"Buffalo."

Norberto studied the chart. "Connection fee is . . . fifteen dollars. And then it's two fifty a minute. Dang! You still want to call? You know most likely the folks you're calling won't be there anymore?"

"Yes."

"Okay. It charges to your LifeFund. What's the number?" He dialed Donna for her. "Yup. Disconnected."

"Can I listen?" She put the receiver to her ear. She heard nothing.

90

"Nothing means it's disconnected," he explained.

"Can you dial again?"

"It's going to add up."

"I understand."

She heard the song of the number as he dialed, watching to make sure he did it right. There was a ring and she shouted, "There!" Then the sound cut out before the first bell finished. The phone transmuted from a portal into only plastic. She tapped her other ear to make sure she hadn't gone deaf. She asked if it was properly connected and he showed her the translucent line running into the wall and told her about cables being laid two years ago by Journeymen.

"Can I call someone else?"

Norberto dialed the bar where Frank had worked. The same thing happened: the first blurt of the ring and then the bottomless silence.

"Do you want to make another call?"

She tried Frank's parents. The phone rang. Then it rang again. Polly screamed.

"Hello?" A scratchy voice spoke.

"Mrs. Marino! It's Polly!"

"Wrong number," scratched the voice, and hung up.

"That's sixty dollars plus ten dollars," Norberto said.

She nodded without hearing him; her brain was clicking too fast. It confirmed nothing except that the lines were out of service. They'd experienced a national disaster. A global disaster. It was silly to think she'd get them on the phone. It didn't mean Frank and Donna were dead. There would be other ways.

Norberto opened a binder filled with sheaves of paper in plastic holders, and it hit the desk with a fat slap. He moved like an old man, but he could not have been over forty.

"Ready?" he said.

She nodded.

"What year did you come from?"

"1981."

"Let me see . . . 1981." Colored tabs dotted the fore edge. Polly tried to count how many. "There's some preamble. Greetings and introductions. I'll skip to the meat." He started to read: " 'Welcome to 1997' — I mean 1998; sorry. It says 1997, but it's 1998 now. 'We are so happy to have you join us. You're a participant in a pivotal point in human history: not only can we time travel, we've perfected a method for carrying it out humanely, with as little disruption to history as possible. Today is the first day of the rest of your life, and you have a chance to begin again.' "

The text itself had the artificial intimacy of a motivational speaker, but Norberto read the words in a stuttery monotone. He ran his finger along the page so he didn't lose his spot, and his effort made the words genuine.

" 'You will find many changes have elapsed in the time you were in transit. We will let you uncover these in your own time, save for one. The borders of our land have been redrawn. No longer within our borders: Colorado, Connecticut, Delaware, Idaho, Illinois, Iowa, Kansas, Kentucky, Maryland, Nebraska, New Jersey, New York —' "

Her aching legs felt far away, as if she were sitting in one room and her body in another.

"Excuse me."

"Yes?"

"Are you listing states in alphabetical order?"

"Yes, ma'am."

"I'm having trouble following. Maybe if I look at a map?"

They had to get up and go back to the entryway to see the map that hung there with the heading *America, c. 1997.* The poster showed a squashed shape, not the one she knew. The top half of the country

93

was black: Washington, Oregon, Idaho, Montana, Wyoming, Colorado, and anything north of the Mason-Dixon Line. The states that remained were in neon: Nevada, Arizona, the South. California was called New California.

Norberto had brought along the binder with the script, holding it out like a missal. He continued the list: " 'Ohio, Oregon . . .' "

Polly became very aware of the sounds of her own body, of her epiglottis closing in her throat, of the rush of air in her ears.

"Sorry," she said. "Can you just tell me what happened?"

"You don't want to hear the script? I have a pamphlet you can have." She shook her head no. He tucked the binder under his arm. He smoothed a curling corner of the map, rubbing it with his thumb like a stain.

"You know why they invented time travel?"

Polly didn't know what to say. "So we could time travel?"

"To go back and stop the pandemic from ever happening. But that wasn't possible — you heard why? Because they could only reach as far as June of '81? So instead they sent the vaccine that scientists had working by the late '80s to '81."

"They did? When?"

"When was your origin point? September? It went in November. It was a good idea. I don't know what went wrong. I don't know disease science, why the vaccine worked in '93 but not in '81. The flu didn't go away. It mutated, got nastier. But only in the South. TimeRaiser distributed the vaccine to Texas first, thinking it would be a leg up. By summer of '82, we had problems with water, sanitation. Disease spread like a house fire.

"So the North cut us loose. They set up roadblocks and a regional border from coast to coast, and they sealed that border. There was pushback, but they had the United States military, so that only lasted three or four days. The border was supposed to be temporary, only for the worst spikes of the disease, but by the end of that year the government dissolved, and people living in the North decided to keep defending their border."

She could not control the cinching of her ribs and the closing of her throat.

"How about now? Can people cross that border now?"

He grimaced. "They cross it now to get the oil. By the early '90s the South was desperate to get the oil back online, to get leverage once more. Errors were made. After the ninety-three percent, there wasn't the necessary expertise. Around '92 the North agreed to come down and fix the wells and refineries, but only on the condition they get nine-tenths of access to the oil. Greedy bastards. What was the question?"

"Can I cross the border now?"

"Borders reopened in '93, when eradication was declared in the Americas. But we're different countries. We're America. They call themselves the United States. United, my butt." Redness flared around his hairline. He rubbed the back of his neck, like he was trying to rotate it. "I'm speaking out of turn. I'm sorry if I'm causing undue distress."

Like most people, it was impossible for Polly to have an immediate emotional response to the behemothic movements of global powers. Instead, she could make sense of this only in narrow slices, at the place where politics intersected with the needs of her own small life.

She said, "If you were sick, say, in 1981, and you were treated in Houston even after the countries separated, you'd just stay wherever you were treated, wouldn't you?"

"It's hard to say, really. It would depend on a lot of things. Some people roved. Other people stayed put. People had all sorts of strategies for getting through the hard years."

"When were the hard years?"

"That's a personal question. We can't get personal with tenants." Again Polly had that sour feeling of violating a rule of engagement invisible to her, and inborn in everyone else.

He returned to his desk and pulled a stuffed envelope from his desk drawer. She sat and spilled its contents into her lap. There was an ID card and manual and a stiff red book — a passport — embossed with *America — Conditional.*

"Do you need to buy anything?" Norberto asked.

It took her ages to say, "Can I buy a toothbrush?"

He took out an index card. "Let me have your ID for a second." He printed her name and the nine-digit number on her ID. Then he wrote down the date and made a list below it.

Long-distance phone call $17.50
Long-distance phone call $17.50
Long-distance phone call $17.50
Long-distance phone call $17.50

"What's this?" Polly asked.

"Oh, right. This is your LifeFund. To streamline your financial experience, all your pay is deposited into your LifeFund, and any living expenses — lodging, food, medical, purchases at any TimeRaiser PX like this one — are deducted out of it."

"What if I need to shop at a regular store? Or buy . . ." She trailed off.

"You can get everything you need at the PX. TimeRaiser will pay for your transportation to and from your workplace. It's completely free. There are no regular stores."

He put some beans in a pot on a hot plate behind the counter, pouring them into two yellow children's bowls when they were done, because he hadn't had dinner yet either. The beans tasted like paper pulp and her guts clutched painfully.

"Any questions?"

Her brain was not able to sustain the information he'd given. It held it for a pause, then rejected it, like a coin slot dropping a bad dime. Instead, a query from this strange day floated to the boggy surface of her mind.

"What is that place I went to today? The

vacation homes and the cycle center."

"Where did you wind up again?"

"I think it was called Gulf Pearl."

"It's a resort."

"It's not like other resorts."

"In what way?"

"I don't know." She was too modest to ask him about the naked people. "I thought that there were children. But it turned out to be a recording of children laughing. There was a speaker hidden in the bushes."

"Sounds nice." He was rinsing their bowls in a tiny sink, and she thought he might have misheard.

"What?"

"Having a recording of children laughing. Nicest sound in the world."

"There were naked people," she blurted, "with jars on their heads." Saying it out loud, she wondered if she had hallucinated it.

"Jars?" His face furrowed. "Or do you mean something like diving helmets?"

"Maybe. Yes."

"Hyperbaric oxygen therapy. The helmets deliver one hundred percent oxygen, for beautifying and to promote longevity. Don't know why they'd be naked."

"Why does everyone speak Spanish to me?"

99

It was this question, not the ones about fake children and jarred heads, that ruffled him. He stopped his work and turned from the sink. "Texas used to be Mexico, you know." Then she saw he wasn't startled by the question; he was annoyed by it.

"I know," she said, though she didn't really know Texas history. "But why does everyone speak Spanish, to me?"

The phone rang. He said, "That's my nightly check-in. Look around awhile."

There were corkboards papered in ads for swaps: *Exchange boots for water filter? Exchange towels for dictionary?* Norberto was holding the phone to his ear, but he didn't speak. He listened, and from time to time he pressed the keys.

When he hung up the receiver, she asked, "Can you tell me which way the seawall is?"

"You can't go for a walk right now. I'll be locking the doors for the night soon. You won't be able to get back in."

"I was just curious."

"The sea is two ways. As the crow flies, if you go out our door and look right, that's north, and that's Galveston Channel, and if you look left, that's south, and that's the Gulf."

"May I ask you something?" Her own politeness was a comfort, willing that the kind of manners she knew were applicable still. "I don't know if you know I was rerouted? I thought I was going to arrive in 1993." She couldn't read Norberto's face. "They said if I was rerouted, they would get in touch with anyone expecting me and tell them where to meet me." He led the way out of the store. "I filled out a form, an emergency contact sheet. How do I tell if they got the information to the person who was expecting me? How do I know if he knows I came late?"

"Oh. I'm not positive. That's not my area." He opened the door to the stairwell for her.

"Do you know who I can ask?"

"I'll look into it."

She didn't move.

"I'll look into it," he said again, and though she stayed there, he went away.

Polly sat on the bed with her back to the window. Behind her, on the other side of swampland and age-corroded strip malls and fallen-in churches, and chalets with marble sinks and migrants sleeping in cans, Frank must be trudging up the beach and walking away. This was an idea that did not make sense.

There was no socket for a radio, no books.

Her room was the size of a large sandbox. There was a cupboard, a hot plate, and a fridge no bigger than a shopping bag. The fridge was dark and warm. It had a coin box; she would have to feed it tokens to keep it cold. There were instructions next to the light switch: if the light was on more than two hours per day, she'd pay overage fees. There were five jars of food in the cupboard, with handwritten labels: black beans, kidney beans, potatoes. There was a polished-steel mirror, but she kept away from it, not wanting to see a stranger's face. The rest of the space was bed: a single mattress on a frame lifted high off the ground, so there was storage underneath, although did anyone who lived in these rooms have much to store? She had seen the container houses. She should be grateful for this room.

She would unpack. She opened the cupboard and laid her case on the floor. She had hardly anything in it — only toiletries, some papers, and Frank's baseball cards.

What Polly had liked most about baseball was not the game but all the red-faced, cheery people, the foolish happiness of doing the wave, the ordinariness of headlights in the parking lot afterward, on their way home. The cards were so fastidiously sealed, and it was that, most of all, that distressed her, the pains he had taken to keep them pristine, how sincerely she had ferried them over. She heard the sound of waves crashing, but really it was that plastic sheet, gusting in and out at the hallway's end, like the south side of the building had gills.

Pain came in like an ambulance siren, far away and then everywhere inside her head. She had missed Frank twice. Buffalo was in another country. She had lost five years. So she did what anyone would do in the face of such malicious silence: she closed her eyes and went to sleep.

Laughter woke her up. It was past midnight, and the lampless dark was full. She heard breathing, as if someone else was in the room.

She fumbled her way to the weird light switch. But she was still alone. It wasn't Frank.

The breathing was outside; it was just loud. There was more laughter. Then a moan. It was coming from next door, or right above. Polly tried to slam the window shut, but the swollen frame denied her. The breathing found its rhythm.

She pulled the pillows and the blanket and the sheet and then the mattress over her head because the sound of other people's sex was everywhere, and it was unbearable.

The march of goosebumps across his shoulders, his hand in her hair, his toes lacing her ankle, his arm on her waist like a roller coaster bar, her body unlocking, the catch of her heart.

February 1979

Frank is on his hands and knees in the bushes, a slurry of snow and mud and likely dog piss seeping through his jeans, his forehead almost touching the frost-flecked basement window of Chad's apartment. Chad is drinking can after can of Schmidt's in front of the TV, watching *The Love Boat.* As soon as Chad got home, he hit the head, then the fridge, then the couch. There are no lights but the harsh spray from the bulb in the bathroom. He hasn't even bothered to take off his coat. He is paunchy, already beginning to bald. Frank almost feels bad for him. But Frank can see Polly's mother's things at the edge of the frame. Chad put the dining table on its back, then nestled credenza, nightstands, and ottomans in its underbelly, then piled chairs on top, legs-up so the interlocking seats made a kind of lid, and used cords to keep this tidy little mountain together. There is great spiteful-

105

ness here: for a slob who doesn't even bother to take off his snow boots in the toilet to employ such precision. Frank is waiting for Chad to drain beer number three before he makes his move. Get the guy all relaxed, warm, good buzz going, then pounce. Or maybe he should wait for beer number four.

It's just that there is a station wagon in the driveway and only one doorbell. Which means this is likely some kind of family home. So Frank should come back in the daytime, when he won't be waking anyone. But Frank knows it's now or never. Already this mission has required almost too much premeditation to complete. He had to snoop through Polly's address book when she wasn't looking (in vain), he had to bring Chad up casually to find out where he worked so he could follow him home — and it was near impossible to talk about her ex-boyfriend casually — and he had to borrow his brother Johnny's pickup, sitting only a few feet away at the curb, so tantalizingly near. It would be so simple to get in the cab, blast the heat, and drive away. No one would be the wiser. Polly wouldn't be disappointed. What she didn't know couldn't hurt.

But it was the worst kind of story, the type

that made you want to cover your ears, like hearing about a dog being beaten, or that someone had shamed your mother. Polly told him, in the corner of a Chinese restaurant, how Chad had taken the furniture. Frank already knew this: she'd told him early on, laughing, it was such a silly story. He imagined cheap stuff, ugly stuff, shoe box quality. But that day she let go the detail she'd held back: the furniture had been her mother's. The only matter left of her mother. All Polly had now was a patio table and a love seat. "I'm not crying because I'm upset," she kept saying. When he tried to take her hand, she put it in her pocket. Chad had forced Polly to admit his badness, life's badness. He made her give up her belief that things would be all right in the end, that quality in her Frank found most touching, because more than others she had a right not to believe it. Chad made Polly defenseless. Frank couldn't sleep thinking about it. His Polly, his sweetheart.

Frank rings the doorbell, and then right away wishes he hadn't. He could get shot. He makes for the truck, but it's too late: a light bings on, the door is opening. It's not a shotgun or a sleepy grandpa: it's Chad. Chad in real life, not the one through the half window, who Frank just now realizes

107

seemed as real as the characters on his TV. This one is bitter breathed, almost beast-like — though small, Frank reminds himself.

Might as well get to the point. "Give me Polly's furniture," Frank says.

"Get stuffed," says Chad, and slams the door.

But here is Frank's plan: to be unrelent-ing. His foot is already in the doorway, and it doesn't hurt too much when Chad whacks him in the boot with the door. Chad does this several times, each time expecting a different result but getting the same: Frank still in the way.

Chad's hands are revolting: hooked and edged in shit-toned yellow from too many cigarettes. Those hands tangoed in the waves of Polly's hair, traced that dip at the bottom of her spine where perfect bone gives way to pretty rump. What'd she see in this troll? Maybe, he has some type of Travis Bickle, boring bad-boy thing, maybe, if you like that kind of thing. But while Frank is thinking, Chad stretches one of those hor-rible hands to its fullest extension and, with fast, full speed, slaps Frank in the ear.

The pain is searing, white, magnificent. Frank doesn't give up his spot, but he doubles over, his nose now dangerously close to Chad's knee. But then it occurs to him he's in a great position for tackling. He bursts forward, slamming his skull into Chad's belly. He hears the guy gasp, but shortly Chad has him in a headlock. Now they are bucking in the foyer, Frank trying to get free, Chad trying to choke him out. Frank has the advantage of reach; he manages to get Chad's hair. He grabs and grabs and hears Chad's far-off voice calling him a fuckin' girl. Frank gives up on the pulling and switches to whacking, getting great enjoyment from trying to sock Chad right where his hair is thinning. "I'll kill you!" Chad shouts. One of his bedroom slippers goes flying and something delicate crashes.

But now there is another voice. "Bastards!" it cries, and then they both feel the cold and the wet. They separate, stumble back. A woman stands at the top of the stairs, brandishing an empty water glass. In the other arm she carries a toddler with vertical hair and a glazed look. The lady looks to be Chad's sister.

"I'm calling the police. This is the last straw. Tomorrow morning you're out of here."

"No, Melissa. We were just horsing around."

Melissa glowers. The baby sucks its fist. Chad gives a sickly smile.

"I oughta put a lock on that basement door."

"We'll go downstairs. Night-night. Night-night, Thomas." The baby half grins. Chad whacks Frank on the shoulder. "Come on, buddy," he says. They amble down together, but at the foot of the stairs Chad says, "I'm gonna fucking murder you."

"I'm not leaving without that furniture, man."

"Then get comfy, dillhole, because I'm not giving it to you."

Frank has been in very few physical conflicts in his life. He is also a champion of breaking up bar fights. Neither of these facts are due to physical prowess. Instead, it's because, one, he has a preternatural ability to comprehend when another man would rather die than lose face, and, two, he never has the need to save face himself. He says he can't take credit for this. "I was just born this way," he tells Polly. "Hmph," she says. "Or it's the result of a well-loved life."

"Listen, pal —"

"Not your pal."

"I work at a bar. You give me the furniture, every time you come in, I'll give you a Schmidt's on the house."

Chad sets his mouth. But he is in a parka, with one denuded foot.

"This stuff isn't even useful," Frank says. "In fact, it's downright inconvenient."

Frank may have gone too far with that one. He holds his breath.

"And a whiskey," Chad says.

"Huh?"

"Gimme a beer and a whiskey."

"If you'll help me get this on my truck."

"Old Crow. *Reserve,*" Chad specifies.

Together, they are strangely efficient. In fifteen minutes it is all on the truck.

"You want your cords back?" Frank asks.

"Nah."

Frank gives Chad a matchbook with the bar's address. He will only come twice, and then Frank will never see him again. Frank will not tell Polly what he's done. Instead he will festoon his apartment with her mother's furniture. Ottomans under the coffee table. Kitchen table over the coffee table. Rocking chair wedged in the gap between the couch and the window. Then he'll invite her over. He will wonder how long it will take her to notice, but she will understand almost before he has the front door all the way open. In fact, she will not come in. She will stand on the threshold. He will not rush her. She will gaze around the room, counting the pieces silently, making sure every one has come home. Finally she will enter.

She will laugh. She will go to the rocking chair and rub the knobs at the ends of the arms, shiny from her mother's palms. Her hair will smell of cold, and she will say it for the first time of millions: "I love you." It will be one of the best moments of his whole life. To other girls, Frank is a Chad. But Polly will do for him what love can do: it will be as if she has said, Look how strong you are. A hero.

He gets a few blocks from Chad's before it hits him: he pulled it off. He turns on the radio, cranks it, looking for a manful anthem. Instead he gets Dionne Warwick, singing "I'll Never Love This Way Again."

But when the piano booms like a drum and her voice storms the chorus, Dionne is epic, warlike. "Yes!" Frank shouts. He winds down the window. He shouts at the night like a loon: "I'm going to marry this girl."

"GOOD MORNING! IT IS 0645 HOURS AND TODAY IS MONDAY, SEPTEMBER 7, 1998! THE TEMPERATURE IS 86 AND RISING, SO GET OUT YOUR SUN HATS AND SANDALS! THE ASSIGNMENT FOR POLLY NADER TODAY IS: REPORT TO HENRY BAIRD AT HOTEL GALVEZ. YOUR SCHEDULE IS: AT 0730 HOURS, PROCEED TO THE LOBBY FOR PICKUP."

On Sunday she'd been unable to leave her room, for opening the door would have been to admit this was really happening. She'd pulled her bed away from the window so she could sit on the edge of the mattress and look out. She'd tried to examine what she saw with detachment — blocks of houses with trees growing out of their roofs, roads mutating into woods — as if she was only a visitor to this place, because she was. In no time at all, she would be out of here.

At the day's end, she discovered that, if

she lay in bed with her head at the foot, she could watch the sun go down. She wrestled the window open, and she could hear music playing somewhere down the line of rooms. One song played all day, an electric guitar descending the saddest scales as Bobby Womack and a chorus of soul singers chanted its title again and again: "If You Think You're Lonely Now." She had let all the imaginings she'd kept out come in: the earflaps of a woolly hat, buttoned under the chin; Springsteen whistled out of tune; the only way to slice a lemon; arms wide for a hug as he walked towards her, crossing the street.

By the time the sky was dark, she'd cried enough to give herself a headache. She felt ashamed, though she was her only witness.

In the morning she decided she wouldn't indulge this nonsense anymore. She took a grim look in the mirror, a small square that contained only her face and a slice of shoulder. Everything was as it had always been: moon face, crooked teeth, snub nose. Exhaustion had turned her lips bright pink. In another life she had dyed her hair mahogany, but now it was long and ragged, back to no-color brown. She had brought some makeup with her, but wearing it with coveralls would look bizarre. For a moment the room darkened. Without the physical trappings of her identity — her own clothes, her scent, her blusher — how could she look like herself?

She couldn't think like this. She was in the grip of the peculiar but popular idea that if she lacked hope, the cosmic powers would shun her. Believing this was more pleasant than realizing that the cosmos has no preference.

She waited until 0720 to go downstairs, to be sure she wouldn't mix up the buses. Vacant minutes before, the lobby was now so full of Journeymen that bodies were backed into the stairwell. Norberto was shepherding people through, pointing the way with a miniature dustpan. When he saw Polly, he strode through the crowd.

"How are you settling in?"

"Did you find out anything about the contact form?" She'd wanted to be cooler, more safely indifferent, but the question sloshed out.

His face didn't change. The skin was cratered along his jawbone, the scars of adolescence.

"I asked you if the person expecting me in 1993 received my emergency contact form?"

"I can place a call to a friend."

"Really?"

"Check in with me later."

Of course, he might have been just saying what she wanted to hear, but she felt so cheerful anyway that she smiled at everyone on the bus. This time she paid attention to the route. She wanted to be able to find her way to the Flagship Hotel without asking anyone. But the road had few distinguishing marks. That juniper hedge closed off street after street, and without exits they were no longer streets but nameless earth. They turned left, passed a sign that said *Service Road — Authorized Vehicles Only,* and they drove past the container homes. Here there were no junipers, the ruins on display. Empty plots had a bald, startled look, still bearing the footprints of a house: a moat of grass around a singed rectangle where somebody once made lunch and watched TV. At the corner of Avenue K, two men on either end of a tree saw were in a back-and-forth dance with a stump. Polly looked to see if one of them might be Frank, the silly clench of her heart. But they were old men with scarlet faces streaked with dirt.

"All manual." The girl in front of Polly had twisted around. Her perfectly styled red bob curled around her jaw. How had she managed to get it that way? "No motor-operated machinery. No fumes. It's better for everyone."

Past a row of houses, clobbered into one single lump, was a line of laundry and a ladder.

"Do people live here?" Polly asked.

"God. No one could live there."

Then the road humped up, as if the land were taking a deep breath. Over the ridge came the sea, every wave crested by a tiny sun. Polly was jolted by the delight of recognition. The sea was still the same.

The driver called out, "Hotel Galvez!" A quarter of the building was new. So white, it hurt to look. As for the other three-quarters, stories had collapsed on the ones below, cathedral windows and balconettes like faces with their bones removed.

An official in a guardhouse took Polly's ID and matched her name against a list the width of his desk.

"To the back and through," he commanded. Polly looked but did not see an entrance. "Go on. ¡Anda!" He carried on shouting at her from across the courtyard. "¡Más! ¡Más! To the back!"

A staircase, hidden by a small stacked mountain of black tiles, led to a third-floor chamber. The hall was unfinished, all the beams in the ceiling bared like one hundred ribs, urine-hued insulation wadded between each plank. Queen Anne banquet chairs tied together formed an unnerving pile of carved feet. Fan chairs were trussed back-to-back like hostages.

"Over here!" Baird was at a drafting table, placed randomly in the middle. He shoved a coffee-table book her way. "This room will look like this one day." A glossy photo showed a lushly carpeted ballroom with a blue, glowing ceiling. "The Starlight Roof at the Waldorf Astoria. You've been?"

"Not sure," Polly said. She had never been to the Waldorf.

"It's going to be the cornerstone of Galveston. I won the bidding war for redesign, because I had the best idea. We're not just restoring the Hotel Galvez but all the lost hotels. Each suite in the vein of one of the greats. The Plaza, the Savoy, the Mauna Kea, the Shangri-La.

"I was decorator at the Waldorf. Used to party with the Beatles and Lauren Bacall. Then we went to visit my mother in Palm Beach and got stuck below the border. And now I'm here, in overalls. Dressed like a Journeyman, right?" He waggled his eyebrows.

Something was off about him. He was different from before. His face was red and his eyes were wet and beady. Maybe it was just a good mood.

"Start with the brocade cushions from the MGM Grand. Count them and process them for cleaning and repairs. There are targets to hit to stay in business, so work smart. This way."

She followed him behind a plastic curtain, and she passed through a wormhole, back into the world she knew. There was the lathe and the band saw and the sanding station, in whose languages she was fluent. There were the coils of reed spline, fiber rush, and seagrass, as identical to the lay as homophones to a foreigner. There was the shelf of half-pint cans of wood stain, their names like the names of old friends. Polly could cry. She weighed a mallet in her hand. Stamped on its handle was *TimeRaiser.* She put it back, name-side down, but the brand was on both sides. The wormhole spat her out.

"Those wicker thrones are from the Flamingo. The gentlemen's valets are from the Golden Nugget. We scavenged Vegas. None of this is really from the Great Hotels. Vacationers won't know the difference. The real reason they picked me? I can repurpose junk. I'm cheap."

"Who scavenges it?"

"TimeRaiser workers. Like monkeys.

Shinnying up the rubble. Dangerous, though. These are my pride and joy." He showed her a set of Sheraton-style mahogany side chairs, oval backed with ribbon-form splats and green leather seats. "These four are from the actual Starlight Roof."

"How did you get them from New York?" Was it easy to cross the border? If Frank had wound up back in Buffalo, could he get to Galveston for Saturday? But he never would have left Texas without her.

But he didn't answer her question. He pointed to a pine box the size of a small room, saying, "And that's the blood closet." She awaited further explanation, but one of the brass studs on a Starlight Roof chair had come loose, and he bent to examine it.

"Is it . . . a wood-staining room?" There was no need for a special room for stain.

"Blood storage. Guests deposit their blood, the closet keeps it cold, the blood doesn't age, five or ten years later they reinject it, and they feel brand-new again. Young blood." He snorted at his own joke. "I've been given every assurance the closet will be moved in time for the launch of the Starlight Roof."

The pine box had a porthole window. Soda fridges were manacled by bulging machinery, its hum vibrating the floor.

Liquid dangled in frosty bags, blood brown and milky green.

"Some of the blood has turned white," Polly said.

"That's cat milk."

She waited for Baird to grin and show he was teasing, but he didn't.

The worksite swarmed with Journeymen working elbow to elbow, laying brick, sanding floors, shingling roofs. But Polly and Baird were alone in an expanse of space and silence. She found a dropcloth and started on the pillows. This work was a blessing, a distraction from the bog of fear and hope inside that spumed with every thought of Saturday. Baird set himself down on a couch. There were over thirty silk cushions, patterned with audacious birds of paradise in fuchsia and gold, and they all stank of motor oil and cat piss. She tried to think nothing of it when Baird undid his upper buttons and rubbed his chest. She tagged each cushion, indicating the necessary repairs — *hole: thread bridging; grease stain: kerosene; filthy: soak* — the days of its life to be deleted. The imminent satisfaction of erasure calmed her.

Baird was insensible to her technique. He was lying down. Polly kept her eyes averted, imagining he was just working out a problem and at any moment he would get up and hotfoot it over to his desk. But an hour passed and he started to snore, loudly. She rustled the cushions, she dropped a rasp, but the snores persisted. She went over and stared at him. He had a big, old man's face. At rest, his mouth sagged and his eyes were sunk with deep lines of sadness.

His eyelids quivered.

"Leonard?" he said.

She shuffled back, almost tripping over a caddy of hand tools. Then he burped and turned. A bad, sweet-sour smell permeated the air, and finally it dawned that he was drunk.

She went back to work. The most logical thing was to work as soundlessly as possible so he wouldn't wake until he'd slept it off, and the problem took care of itself. There could be a reason for his odd behavior. Maybe today was an anniversary, something distressing.

If she were him, she'd turn to drink too. His lover had stopped while Baird carried on, and now forever they were sealed on opposite sides of that irrevocable moment. How much better off she was. With every cushion, I get closer to Frank, she said to herself. This was her first proclamation of hundreds: with every cushion, every stitch, every pen stroke.

Baird slept until the PA system announced the last shuttle for the day. Polly stood as far back as she could and prodded his shoulder with a finger until he opened his eyes.

"It's time to go, sir," she said.

He emitted a loud, shocking noise between a low and a yawn: a bare, vulgar sound. When he was finally upright on the edge of the couch, he looked like an ancient, blinking baby.

"When I feel sad, I look at all this."

She thought he was rambling. Then she followed his gaze out the window, to the seafront, where the land was in an acute state of deconstruction. Three blocks away, like a seam joining the squares of a quilt, the scene changed at the lip of a finished resort. The completed resort looked like a fairy village: candy-colored houses, kiddie trains ferrying guests from massages to dinner, a Ferris wheel by the sea.

"Open the window. Do you know what we're doing?"

They could hear the evening-shift workers shouting over a jackhammer's pounding.

"We're getting the past back, but better. It will be the way we like to remember it instead of the way it was. People will pay anything for that."

She watched him fill out the progress log for the day. *Progress on the throw cushions well underway. Night stands for the Ritz suite ready for delivery midweek* — though the tables he appeared to be referring to were still under tarps, untransformed.

The shuttle was full of Journeymen who had worked on the middle wing all day, their clothes and faces stiff with ashy gunk. At the containers, the traffic slowed altogether, one lane blocked by other buses dropping off workers. Women were lined up in the sun, waiting for their turn to enter a poky open-air enclosure made from corrugated tin. It was a shower pit. From the bus, you could see right inside. Towel-clad women dunked buckets into a blue water drum in the center and then they poured the water out, little by little, over their heads.

"I wish they would build a privacy roof," the red bob said, her hair still perfect. "For everyone's sake."

At Moody Plaza, Norberto was sitting in his office, writing price cards.

"Did you call your friend today?"

"My friend?"

"About the contact form?"

"Right. No, I didn't. Let me call him tomorrow."

"Sorry to keep asking you, but it's really very important. It's urgent."

"I'll do what I can." He went back to his cards.

On Tuesday evening a woman with bright eyes and dirty-blond hair, who'd got off the same evening shuttle, held the stairwell door for Polly and smiled. She was slow to unlock her door — because her key was stuck, or to give Polly a chance to strike up conversation? But Polly lost her nerve and scurried inside. She was bad at meeting strangers. Still, the longing for information seized her like a bottleache. Had any other Journeymen found the people they had left behind? Had anyone been to the United States? Did they know how to find Donna?

On Thursday, Polly spied the woman as she got on the shuttle. Even more serendipitous, beside her was an empty seat. Then the woman waved. Polly jostled past a passenger hoisting a bucket and dived into the empty seat.

"This seat is for my sister," the woman said.

The passenger with the bucket was looking down at Polly in surprise.

Polly stood to flee, but the crowd kept her in place. Then the sister with the bucket

125

kept insisting Polly share the seat. She wouldn't quit and finally Polly sat, clinging to the back of the seat in front, to keep from slipping into the aisle.

The sister's name was Misty and she was only just twenty, and her older sister's name was Sandy. They shared the room on the fourth floor and they were both massage therapists at the resorts. Misty was very enthusiastic about 1998; they had come from 1984, which was so awful you couldn't even imagine. Sandy didn't feel the same. That evening they showed Polly everything: the laundry facilities, the library (a single bookshelf in the lobby), and the game room (the picnic table in Norberto's store), where there were nightly poker games.

"How do they bet?" Polly asked.

"You a card shark?" Misty said.

"No, I ask because . . . I didn't bring any money with me."

Always, Polly was patting her right breast pocket, feeling for the reassuring plastic rectangle of her ID. She wished she had just a few dollars. Donna had always taught her to keep some money in a can. "For your independence," Donna had said.

"Doesn't matter. It's not legal tender. Pre-1982 currency is invalid. That country doesn't exist anymore," Sandy said.

"There's nowhere to spend *money* money anyways," Misty said.

"Of course there is," Sandy said. "You could use it to leave. We could do business with each other."

"Not legally," Misty said.

"That's the point," said Sandy.

"She's a conspiracy theorist. You can buy chips." Misty pointed out a parts cabinet, mounted on the wall behind Norberto's desk, with stacks of olive and beige casino chips in its drawers.

"One Journeyman tripled his bond that way," Sandy said.

"That's not true, don't be so negative."

"It is true."

"Not triple. Maybe double. Maybe. How many months on your bond?" Misty asked Polly.

Even in the worst-case scenario, where Sandy was correct about everything, once Frank came, Polly would be immune. She would still be under bond, but her life would be hers again.

"Thirty-two," said Polly. "You?"

"Fifteen, at the end of this month."

Sandy didn't volunteer her bond length.

"She tripped," Misty said. "She was carrying too many sacks of towels and she broke her wrist. So she has a few extra

127

months to work off."

"So do you," Sandy interrupted.

"Nothing to be embarrassed about."

"Spent too much in the PX on God knows what," Sandy said.

"The bond is not so bad. Just think of it like a college degree," Misty said.

Polly smiled at her. This was a good idea.

"Now, that's unintelligent," Sandy said.

Sandy and Misty knew what kind of canned vegetables to expect this week, based on the time of year. They knew that Moody Plaza was the only housing for O-1 visa holders in Galveston, and by the time it was full, it would have layers and layers of decorators, tennis coaches, and osteopaths. They knew how wild the vacationers were for anything branded "healthy living" — anything to ward off the memory of sickness and death at the border of their towns, their houses, their skin. They knew the food-growing centers were in Tyler, Texas, and they were pleased about how close they were to Tyler, when the food had been so much worse in 1984 Tucson. They gave Polly tips on how to make the most of the pathetic cakes of soap Norberto sold, where to pick flowers. Misty told her about the Christmas beauty pageant and who would win this year. Sandy told her about the one newspaper, the *Texas Chronicle,* how it came out once a week and hardly had any news. Polly used her little funds to buy a copy anyway, and saw she was right. It contained mostly development reports from across the South. There was an international section with reports on Zimbabwe and Australia. But the photos looked just like Texas, although the captions said otherwise; she checked them twice.

Because she could see that giving this tour gave them pleasure, Polly didn't interrupt to ask how to find someone in the United States until they ran out of tips. Sandy suggested mailing a letter. But it was as expensive as anything, and what if Donna had moved? Was there a phone book?

"Of course!" Misty said, and Polly's heart fired into her mouth. "There's the Demographics Center. They'll run a search for you."

But Sandy interjected. "It'll cost you. I wouldn't bother. The results always come back the same."

"Hush," Misty hissed.

"What?" Sandy said. "She should be properly informed. Usually the reports are disappointing."

"What do you mean?"

"She's just talking about what happened

to her," Misty said. "You go to the Demographics Center if you want to."

"What happened to you?" Polly asked Sandy.

"Well. I came to save my husband, but his state was too advanced for them to cure. Of course, they didn't say so before they got me on the boat. He didn't make it. Now I'm stuck."

Misty put her arm around her sister. Her shoulders straightened at the touch. "But Shirley on the sixth floor found her brother. He's in Florida and they'll see each other once her bond is done."

"Good for her," Sandy said. "What about me? TimeRaiser created a mess and then made a mint fixing it. How do we know they really sent the '93 vaccine to '81? How do we know it wasn't actually an even more virulent version of the flu masquerading as a vaccine? How do —"

"Who are you looking for?" Misty cut her sister off.

Polly was livid to feel herself turning red.

"If it can only travel twelve years back," Sandy continued, undeterred, "then why didn't they travel to June of 1981 and rebuild a new machine there and keep on going?"

"Because the machine can't ever get

beyond June of '81."

"Why not?"

"Because it's a product of its time. You can't rebuild it without its limits."

"That's pure propaganda. They can but they won't!"

"Is it a boyfriend?" Misty said.

"What?" said Polly.

"Who are you looking for?" Misty repeated.

"It's my aunt," Polly said, but she knew she sounded like a liar. "And my boyfriend," she admitted.

Sandy sighed, the specific exhalation of someone about to tell it like it is. Polly knew what was going to happen before it happened, the ill about to come from Sandy's mouth, like an incantation, a thing that becomes actual when words hit air. But she couldn't prevent it, short of covering her ears.

"Don't get hung up on the one, dear," she said. "When did you say you were from?"

"1981."

"You're too smart to be that faithful."

"Sandy!" Misty issued another impotent warning.

"Have you considered that it's been seventeen years?"

"You're so embarrassing!"

131

"You girls! You dragged yourself out of a worldwide pandemic only to waste away over a man?"

It wasn't that Polly never considered that she could have been forgotten. It was that she was always thinking she'd been forgotten, and every minute was a dogfight to unthink it. She retreated from what Sandy was saying until her mind seized an opposite thought: if Frank was in Galveston, wouldn't they know him? Could he even be living in Moody Plaza? Why had she not thought of this before? It was such a simple solution that it had the absolute sensation of truth.

"Do you know Frank Marino?" Polly said.

"Who's that?" said Misty. "A singer?"

"I have to go," Polly said.

"My sister upset you. Ignore her," Misty said.

"I have to check the swaps board. I think I saw something I need."

But she had to get through only one more day that wasn't Saturday, and then she would climb the Flagship's shallow steps, with their paint blistered by the heat, and enter the lobby and find him there and know for sure that she could never be forgotten.

But she had to work on Saturday.

"Every day but Sunday," Misty said as they boarded the shuttle. "We could be like those poor H-1 people, only every third Sunday off or something."

It was all right. The Hotel Galvez was much closer to the Flagship than to Moody Plaza. It was on the same street, just a few blocks down the coast; she could walk there after work. Frank wouldn't come all this way and not wait till sundown. This dreary work of heartening herself was still less painful than the reminders of Frank and Donna that any minute could call up. Eventually this white noise of optimism would completely fuzz over her memories of their minutiae: their laughter, musk, tics, gripes, singing, skin.

Baird was too engrossed by a half-stripped wingback chair to say hello. All week he'd either been asleep or aggressively busy. She forgot him, her focus lasered on the last of her injured cushions, and it was mid-afternoon when she noticed him gone.

He was sitting on a three-legged stool at the far end of the hall, in front of a chair from the original Starlight Roof. She watched as he rubbed his thumb over the grooves of the splat. He traced the stains in the upholstery and followed the curve of the top rail with his palm. For at least five minutes he ran his hands from seat to splat to top, like in a trance, until with the careful precision of a drunk he put the chair back.

Nostalgia drove their work; without sentimental value they'd be out of a job. But you could not get too involved with the nostalgic impulse yourself. It would not do to think about what parties the chair had seen, what faces the mirror had held, whose hands had palmed the table, and what had become of them. If you got too involved, it would be like doing surgery on your wife. It was only a chair.

"It must be emotional to work on those chairs," she said.

"What?" he snapped.

Why had she said anything?

"Don't be silly," he said. But his breath slowed, his mouth parted, his head tipped to roll the tears back to their ducts. He was remembering: the night the Starlight Roof reopened, that feeling that at last he'd returned to a home he'd never seen; their Park Avenue rental, so high up that no one could peep him as he mooned at the skyline from the tub while Leonard soaped his back; Leonard bringing home one of the chairs from the Starlight Roof as a surprise. It became Baird's favorite seat during parties; it was the best place to watch Leonard dance.

"Okay." He patted his chest. "Okay."

She could see what was happening to him. It chilled her, as if he were showing symptoms of a disease she carried. To feel sad about the past is to recognize the past as passed. She would get to the hotel and find the lobby empty. She would get to Twenty-Fifth Street and the Flagship wouldn't be there; in its place would be only the coast swept clean. All week, doubt had festered underneath. She hadn't asked anyone if the Flagship was still standing; she didn't want to know.

This uncertainty continued to dog her as she walked away from the crowd of workers ringing the shuttle stop like a cloud of dust. Soon there was nothing but a hedged-in resort to her right and the road and the water to her left, and it felt like crossing a colossal stage, the Gulf a vast arena, every wave a seat. She could not remember exactly how the Flagship looked. Was it red or tan? There was an embossed nautical design the height of the shorefacing wall, but was it a mermaid, or a dolphin? The hotel was evaporating before her eyes.

Polly wanted to think of something nice. She started singing to herself, the first song

135

that came to mind. She sang "Love Will Keep Us Together" and entered the dangerous realm of memory. Neil Sedaka was on the radio, the silverware was lined up on a cheesecloth laid on the kitchen table, and Donna was wriggling around in her chair because she needed to pee but she wanted to get through the teaspoons at least before she broke her rhythm. Polly stopped singing.

She could hear the sounds of a swimming pool. She came across a rectangular stone: a footstool for seeing over the hedge. She braced herself for sinister sights. What sort of things might they get up to in this desperate little town at the whim of pleasure? A game of polo with humans in place of horses? A barbecue with live cows? An orgy while children looked on?

But the swimming pool was real, bearing so many marks of authenticity. An end-of-summer emptiness tinged the scene. A little boy hovered at the pool's edge, visualizing himself entering the blue. His father called encouragement from a deck chair, as pasty a father in the ordinary world. An older girl, late to return to college, wore a dual-toned bikini, one cup purple and one cup white, just like the one Polly had tried on in a department store the last time there was a normal summer. The only unusual mark was a sign that explained the pool's use of *all-natural salt-water-derived chlorine.*

The girl in her bikini was almost more unsettling than the foreign horrors Polly had envisioned, because her alikeness insisted that Polly's own decent world was on the same spectrum as this one. This alien world could infect her own, until it would have to be acknowledged that strangeness and evil were everywhere, even at home.

What was she doing? Polly got down as the little boy jumped. She got to walking as fast as she could. Now there was a small construction site, abandoned when the money ran out, bent rebar poking out of the ground like grass. She had been walking twenty minutes. She should have passed the hotel already. The road behind and in front looked exactly the same. Keep going or turn back? Keep going. But when should she stop?

Out on the water, a switch was flicked and floodlights boomed. It was a boat. No, it was a pier, but she could not see if there was a hotel, because a hill of garbage blocked what was once the next intersection. The hill hadn't gathered organically. It was built of tables and chairs, window frames, a tub. And it was not so much a hill as a wall, circling whatever sat in the middle. She'd have to go around it to reach the open road on the other side. Anything could be inside the wall. A harmless bus stop. Gang HQ. A nest of rats.

She should turn back. She must have passed the Flagship site ages ago. That wasn't true. It was a big hotel; it would have left some remains, an urn for a peace lily stuck in the sand. But there was no one else, no man to go ahead and check the hill was safe to pass. You don't need that, she told her quaking self. Before Frank, you managed just fine.

When she was halfway round the hill, she saw that the pier was part of a harbor. Small boats departed to meet a ship anchored a half mile out. She saw something familiar wedged in the wall, out of context, upside down, slit by animals and pounded by rain. It was a burgundy armchair from the Flagship Hotel. She had to touch it to be sure. She went to it as a man in uniform came out of the wall.

They saw each other at the same time. They spoke simultaneously. Polly said, "Excuse me," but he screamed, "CBP! Hands on your head! CBP!" as he drew his weapon.

Other men streamed out of the trailer

guarded by the garbage wall, maybe twelve or fifteen of them.

"I was just going for a walk!" Polly shouted.

Two of them snaked behind her and commanded her to move forward.

"I was just going for a walk!" Polly cried.

They marched her into the middle of their compound and raised their guns and made her kneel. They handcuffed her.

"She was doing something to the wall," said the one who had found her. "She has to be searched for weaponry."

"Send in Thibodeaux. Thibodeaux, you're up."

Thibodeaux didn't look old enough to be an officer. He approached her inch by inch, with dinner-plate eyes.

"I'm going to open your shirt," he shouted.

"I don't have anything," Polly pleaded.

He got down next to her. He was almost wheezing.

"It's okay, I don't have anything," Polly said, to calm them both.

But their common fear did not make them friends. When he knocked her to the ground, black stars popped before her eyes. He pinned her neck with his knee and she sobbed as he jerked open two buttons near her navel. He squeezed the flesh in the opening. He pushed her on her front and used his feet to check her legs for bulk.

"We're clear!" Thibodeaux screamed. "No weapons!"

Polly tried to stand up, but Thibodeaux said, "Whoa, whoa!" and kicked her in the calves.

"Contact RB and say we've got a stow-away," the captain said.

They took her ID and left her there. There was gravel embedded in her cheek. Everything would be all right. They would have to issue an apology. She had the right to freedom of movement. Wasn't that the law? she thought, forgetting she had not arrived in the same country she'd left.

After what felt like an hour, a man in civilian clothing came over and said, "Put her in C," and they took her into a small room with a table and chair, just like in the movies, and an officer guarded the door, blocking the only window. His name tag said *Aguirre.* The other man crossed his arms and eyeballed her, not talking.

"What time is it?" she asked.

The plainclothes man jerked his shaggy eyebrows together. He pointed to an old bedside alarm clock, cast away on top of a filing cabinet. She could just read *21:23* on its face. This Saturday was lost. She had two more Saturdays. A fifty-fifty chance.

There was a television screen on a card table with a typewriter keyboard attached to it. It was a computer. Polly hadn't seen many up close before.

"What is this place?" she said.

"Shit. We ask the questions. Hacemos las preguntas. This is CBP. Customs and Border Protection. I'm an ICE agent. Immigration and Customs Enforcement. Inmigración."

She could have laughed out loud. Clearly this was a misunderstanding. What could they want with her? She wasn't a drug dealer or an arms smuggler.

"Can you explain why you were on CBP premises? Why did you charge our wall?"

"I didn't. I was just going for a walk."

"Where were you trying to go? Why are you here? Your lodging is on the north side. You're a long way from home."

"I was just getting to know the town."

"Why don't you just tell me what you were looking for, exactly?"

Polly hesitated. But what could be wrong with telling the truth?

"I was looking for Twenty-Fifth Street."

"So you were trying to escape."

"No, I was looking for a hotel. The Flagship Hotel? Do you know where it is?"

"You were trying to get to the Twenty-Fifth Street Port."

"I was looking for the hotel."

"There's no backtracking now, honey. Where were you headed? Mexico? Tampa?"

"I'm sorry. I don't understand."

"You were trying to get to the port to hitch a ride on a boat. Don't waste my time."

"Why would I do that?"

"You tell me. We get an escapee every few weeks, when, if you ask me, it's easier to finish the bond than get out of here undetected. Take you, for example. You go on the lam, only to walk right into the CBP field office."

She knew the longer she paused, the more it looked like she was trying to make something up. But she had to find a way to phrase the question so she'd get the information she sought. She'd done nothing wrong.

"I'm sorry to bother you, but could you tell me if there used to be a hotel on this site, called the Flagship, where the port is now?"

"Excuse me, sir," said Aguirre. "Look at her record."

"What for?"

142

"She's not H-1. She's O-1."

The agent frowned. He studied her ID.

"We've never seen an O-1 escapee before. You've got a good deal, in relation. Why would you try to stow away?"

"I wasn't. I was just trying to find the hotel that used to be on Twenty-Fifth Street."

"I don't care if you're H-1 or O-1; you're not an American. You can't leave."

"What do you mean?"

"Come on. You heard all this when you signed up."

"You're not a citizen anymore," Aguirre said. "You left before the formation of America, ipso facto you can't be a citizen. You're here on a visa."

"Thus, there are two terms of your visa that overlap with our area of concern," the agent continued. "First, you are only employable by TimeRaiser. Second, you are required to stay within the jurisdiction assigned until you finish your bond. Once you finish your bond, you can apply for resident status. Then you can get on any boat you want."

Outside, someone was blowing a whistle. She still didn't know where the Flagship had gone. This was now the wrong concern, but the extent of her trouble was too big for

143

her mind to compass.

"You're saying I can't leave, and I can't work for anybody but TimeRaiser, and I'm not an American, until I finish my bond?"

"I don't know about that last part. You don't automatically become an American once you finish. But, yes, you can't be an American and enjoy our rights and freedoms while under bond. How much is there on your bond? You people usually have it tattooed to your foreheads."

She was seated, her soles planted on the ground, but she felt like she was falling, and she wrapped her feet around the legs of her chair.

"Thirty-two months," she said.

"Don't you make another run for it. Even if you slip the Galveston border, which you won't, you can't go far. You can't use your LifeFund anywhere but at the PX."

Frank was an American. He could make it to the pier. He wouldn't know she couldn't.

"The question for me is: What do I do with you? I could arrest you, but TimeRaiser hates that. Waste of man-hours." He sighed. He poked his computer. "I could let you go, with an escort. TimeRaiser's happy, I don't have to do as much paperwork, you don't have to go to detention."

Aguirre left, his boots on the stoop shaking the trailer. The agent was writing numbers and letters in each box of a form, a code Polly couldn't understand. It took an age for his pen to make its way from left to right and top to bottom, but he'd said he wasn't going to arrest her, so once he was done, he'd let her go. He opened a drawer and took out a stamp. He stood up and crossed the room, finding an ink pad in a basket on the floor. Delicately he rocked the stamp across the pad, then pressed it to the page. He put away these implements. He filed the form. An ache burned in her cuffed hands and her shoulders throbbed from being locked in one position. He turned to his computer. A white dot crossed a black screen and then returned to the beat of a beep. He was playing a game.

This was a test to see if she could be obedient. She wasn't going to fail it just because an agent was petty. Maybe they had renumbered the streets and the Flagship still waited, farther down the beach. Later, when it was safe, she could feel as bad as she wanted about this easygoing cruelty. There was a water stain on the wall and she stared at it until shapes wheeled out of the shadow.

In 1981 she had waited until Frank was asleep in his clinic bed, and then she had gone to the TimeRaiser office alone. The clerk had explained things using words like "amortization" and "proration," as if she should know what they meant, and she was too proud to ask for an explanation, and in too much of a hurry, before she changed her mind. The clerk had pulled out an adding machine and pelted her with numbers: $5.25 hourly pay, $6,279 for her portion of the passage, $660 for room and board, thirty-two months to work off what she owed. Babies were crying and telephones were ringing, and she wanted to get back before Frank woke up. When she told him what she'd done, for a long while he only stared at the electric sockets over his bed. There were bubbles in his plastic isolation tent, distorting his expression. "Just stay," Frank said.

But she couldn't stay, because she'd seen the other patients with blood coming out of their eyes. She couldn't stay because, one Saturday night, when they first met, he'd opened the door and said, "Why can't spending time with you be my full-time employ?" She couldn't stay because it could not be that she would never again watch him put on a shirt. Because when Polly's mother died, they had let her sit with her mother's body for as long as she wanted, and she remained for a long time, holding her mother's scarf. There would be no more birthday cards, no more cooking lessons, no more Fridays, no more hugs in the middle of the night. Because Frank had found her ex-boyfriend Chad, and somehow — through threats or bribes, she did not know — Frank got Chad to give back her mother's furniture. And then, for a whole month, until Polly could get a bigger storage unit, Frank had kept the furniture in his apartment. Chairs, so many chairs. Because for anything between Polly and Frank that ever went wrong, any missed phone call, separate holiday, misunderstanding, unhappy night, Polly would tell herself, Never mind, there will be other times. It can't be that this is all there is.

The agent only remembered Polly when she fell asleep.

"Hey! This isn't the Best Western."

He called Aguirre back into the room.

"If we see you again, we're charging you with trespass, we're charging you with illegal exit, we're charging you with terroristic intent. You understand?"

Aguirre took her to a police van. He looped the chains bolted to the floor through her handcuffs. She could no longer feel her right hand. When they were on the road, he opened the grate between the cab and the cage and said, "I'm from Galveston. There did used to be a hotel on the sea where the port is now. But it was destroyed by a hurricane in '93."

She couldn't keep it tamped down anymore; panic geysered up. She would try anything. Maybe Aguirre would help her.

"I have to get back to Twenty-Fifth Street. I just have to meet someone, I'm not trying to get on a boat. Maybe, next Saturday, you could let me in?"

He was silent, then he started shouting.

"Christ Almighty. That's what you get for being a nice guy. You better pipe down before I take you back to holding. You made your bed, now lie in it."

He was right. She had signed the papers, she had agreed, and now she only had herself to blame. She had done it all without understanding the weight of what she was doing. Until this moment, the choice she'd made had kept its true, perverse nature secret: it was irreversible, and only comprehensible after it was done.

MAY 1979

Frank's father left Frank's mother for another woman, and then he came back. If you didn't know, you could never tell. Mrs. Marino sits at the edge of her chair, soberly conducting the distribution of food to her three sons and their women, a procession of wooden spoons and pounded meat and sturdy iceberg leaves. She is the king and her boys bring offerings to her round dinner table: comical tales of the week, requests for job advice, their dates. Mr. Marino sits back and admires, now and then sneaking a touch of her shoulder or the nape of her neck, as quiet as Polly. The rest of them all talk at once, but conversation doesn't suffer, because they can somehow listen as they speak. They are robustly normal, the kind of family Polly used to see through living room windows on Sunday nights as she walked home on her own. Frank can see his own life in other people's rooms, like a call

149

and response, a sound reassuringly returned.

But maybe there are a few hints of his parents' troubles. When Johnny starts a story about a lady customer from the roofing company he runs with his dad — the mistress was a customer — Frank knocks over a water glass. By the time it's sopped up, the subject's changed. Maybe it is strange for a fifty-something to paw at his wife at the table. And it is odd how someone as sensible and solid as Mrs. Marino is so obsessed with happy endings. She is consumed with getting Carlo, her oldest, married off.

"You remember Sylvia?" says Carlo. "From Lackawanna. Studying to be a nurse." He and Frank are sharing a cigarette in the bushes, out of sight of the back door.

"Big" — Frank glances at Polly — "hair?" Polly rolls her eyes.

"Mom and Dad wanted to have lunch at the new seafood joint that opened near my work. I asked Sylvia to come, to cool Mom's jets, stop her nagging about wives. Instead, Mom calls over the waiter and tells him we want to see the wedding package! I don't even know the girl."

"Good hair, though," Frank says.

This alone isn't that strange; plenty of

mothers offer unwanted assistance to single sons. Mrs. Marino is sweeter on Polly than she is on the other girls — Johnny's wife, Pia, and Carlo's revolving crew — even though they seem more Mrs. Marino's kin, always wearing dresses and good at telling stories. She gives Polly extra leftovers to take home, calls her "my love." The first time she does this, Frank gapes. Polly guesses she gets this treatment because she is a motherless child — the one perk. But then there is the Oscars thing. Once, while they were making small talk about Polly's weekend plans to watch the Oscars, Mrs. Marino snapped. They were setting the table and Mrs. Marino slammed down a salad plate so hard Polly jumped.

"After last year, I'll never watch the Oscars again."

There had been a controversy at the last ceremony: Vanessa Redgrave's speech, the word "Zionist." Polly was confused. Mrs. Marino was a Catholic. Her hobbies included swimming and Tupperware. She had never mentioned the Middle East.

"Only a bozo would like that movie. Artsy-fartsy, and in the end the couple doesn't even get together! Nasty, pointless show, and they gave it Best Picture!"

Now Polly knew what she was talking

about, but she didn't understand. *"Annie Hall?"*

"Don't even say the name." Another plate slammed, narrowly avoiding destruction.

"Ma?" Frank came in, dishrag in hand, to make sure they were all right.

But perhaps the greatest clue of their marital unease is how curiously, worryingly frenzied Mrs. Marino is about the anniversary party.

"Which wedding anniversary is it?" Pia asks innocently, one dinner.

"Twenty-seven."

"Is that a thing?" Johnny says.

"Well, we missed twenty-five." Their twenty-fifth year, Mr. Marino was with the other woman.

"Do you think we should wait for thirty?" Mr. Marino says.

What a dope! Frank will howl afterward.

"Why?" Mrs. Marino says softly. This has the effect of making everyone listen.

"Business isn't so hot this year. I don't know about a big party, dear."

"We're doing it next month, and the theme is Happily Ever After." The round table is eerily silent. "Your aunt is invited," Mrs. Marino barks at Polly. "Does she have a date?"

Something about Donna's love life coming up alongside her husband's dallying fuses the two in Mrs. Marino's mind. She becomes fixated on Donna.

"She's single?"

Polly feels pukish at dissecting Donna's private life before all the Marinos. But Mrs. Marino is the only woman more fearsome than Donna.

"Why isn't she married?"

Frank squeezes Polly's hand under the table.

"So she's divorced?"

Then the bomb.

"I ought to set her up with my brother, Teddy. He's also divorced."

After that, Mrs. Marino is unstoppable. She will impose a happy ending on Donna, forged through Teddy. No meeting can pass without the third degree: What does your aunt do for fun? How tall is she? Does she enjoy the tourism industry? Does she wear pearls? Teddy's ex-wife loved pearls. What a cow. Could you ask her not to wear pearls? I wasn't going to make place settings, but if I don't, I can't seat Donna and Teddy together.

Thursdays, Frank works the midday shift. He stops at Polly's on his way home, in the overlap of their off-hours, and they drink tea at the kitchen table. "Couple of grandmas," Donna says. The first few times, they drank Donna's home brew, but Frank never finished his, though he insisted it was delicious. What do they talk about, all those hours? When Donna goes to take her bath, Frank puts Polly's knees between his. He draws circles on the soft of her wrist, sending goosebumps rippling up her arms.

"I feel so close to you," he says.

She wants to ignore this opening, this invitation to ask him anything, but she can't. She has to save Donna.

"What happened with your parents?" Polly asks. She wants to begin at the beginning and edge slowly towards the party and his mother's monkeying, but already she's grabbed the wrong end.

"What do you mean?" His body talk changes. He leans back, hands jammed in armpits.

"With your dad . . ."

"With my dad?"

"And your mom . . ."

Yesterday's newspaper has been left behind on the other chair. He reaches for it.

Polly tries to persist. "And the other . . . person."

He changes tactics swiftly. He swoops and nips her earlobe. Her neck turns hot as summer.

"Can we not talk about my parents when I'm trying to put the moves on you?"

This is the first thing to be off-limits between Polly and Frank. His brothers are the opposite. They are gleeful and crass about their father's infidelity, to rob it of its power: "You'll see my pops isn't in my wedding pictures; that's when he was shtupping Elaine." But Frank sickens at the mention of the woman's name. He carries his mother's hurt.

Mrs. Marino has a monstrous longing to see love conquer everything, to eviscerate all memory of the year love failed. And Donna is in its path. But asking Frank to tell his mother to stop would be like asking him to make her tell of all those midnights when she couldn't bear her marriage bed, and so she sat at her kitchen table, peeling apples while noiseless tears slicked her cheeks.

Polly sees if she can work it from Donna's end. Helpfully, *Fiddler on the Roof* is on TV Saturday afternoon.

"Do you think it would be nice to have a matchmaker?" she asks her aunt.

"No."

"It might be simpler? Apparently, arranged marriages last longer."

"If my marriage had lasted a day longer, I

155

would've shot myself. No. I would've shot *him.* No, murder-suicide."

The next time Yente is on-screen, Donna shouts, "Nosy bitch!"

Polly cannot sacrifice Donna to Mrs. Marino, because Donna would never be anyone's sacrifice, anyone's white-gowned blonde, screaming demurely. She has visions of Donna the moment she twigs to this meddling, roaring *Nosy bitch!* across the packed and bestreamered party room, Mrs. Marino buckling under a platter of Jell-O salad, Frank never speaking to Polly again.

So Polly lies.

When the day of the party arrives, she calls Frank and says she has been vomiting since yesterday. "I'm so sorry."

Five minutes later the phone rings.

"Oh . . . ? Sure, sure," she hears her aunt say.

"Who was that?" Polly asks.

"Frank's mother. She's insisting I come, with or without you. She says they're dying to meet me, and otherwise there will be too much food. Persistent lady."

On the way over, Polly having made an astonishing recovery, Donna says, "It's so nice of them to invite me. They sound like a terrific family." For a moment Polly brightens. Then she sees Uncle Teddy. He has the

156

look of a deflated balloon — a tall, shape-less man, trying not to take up space. There is the shadow of a stain over the belly part of his toilet-blue shirt, and it's easy to picture him trying to scrub it out but being somehow useless, using 7UP instead of soda water, cursing softly. He is exactly the kind of weak-chinned man Donna hates.

Polly tries everything to keep them apart. She has Donna studying twenty-five years' worth of hallway pictures of Carlo, Johnny, and Frank. She shows her the Venetian tiles in the upstairs bathroom, where and how they might create an addition at the back of the house. Then Mrs. Marino calls her away to toothpick the wieners. She stabs as fast as she can. "Whoa," says Pia. "You're a machine."

When she gets back to Donna, Teddy is saying, "So you see, we're due for a pan-demic. It's not if but when. You ever hear of Ebola?"

"Gosh, I could use another drink," Donna says. Teddy volunteers to get one for her. He turns away and Donna hisses, "This worm keeps following me around," just as Teddy turns back to say, "What were you drinking again?" It's plain as the squashed nose on his face that Teddy heard. But Donna just says, "Shandy." She pokes at the tassels on a lampshade boredly, not noticing or not caring.

"Polly, I need help with the toast points," Mrs. Marino shouts. When she gets Polly alone, she whispers, "You have to leave them to connect!"

Frank is inches away from the canapé tray, athletically mixing a vat of sangria. When his mother turns her back, he kisses Polly's neck. What if Polly has invented his mother's investment in Donna and Teddy? What if of course Frank can tell his mother to lay off? Polly grabs Frank's stirring arm.

"Your mother wants to make Donna and Teddy a thing, but I don't think they like each other, and Donna is kind of a private person and if she gets that this is a setup, she might lose her mind." Saying all of this out loud, she realizes how trivial it all is, how silly she was to get into such a tizzy. Except Frank doesn't laugh.

"Shit. Why didn't you say something? I thought you thought it was a good idea."

The impending doom reassembles.

"I didn't want to disappoint your mother."

Mrs. Marino turns too quickly and knocks a stack of fanned napkins to the ground.

"Shitshitshitshitshitshitshit," she mouths.

"She hasn't been doing so great lately," he

says. "She really needs one thing to go right."

Polly passes the toast points through the kitchen hatch to Pia and gets a glimpse of the living room. Teddy is standing alone, inspecting the bottom of a hanging basket. Donna is talking to Carlo. She fuzzes the top of her crew cut and she brushes his arm. Polly has the terrible realization that Donna and Carlo are almost the same age.

"Donna and Carlo, Donna and Carlo," Polly squawks at Frank. "Do something!"

"Say 'My aunt is going to take Frank to the doctor.' "

"Huh?"

"AhhHhhHHhh," Frank says, and crumples to the ground, his hair in the cat's food. Polly just stands there, baffled. Mrs. Marino comes immediately.

"What's wrong, Frankie?"

"Shooting pains . . . in my abdomen . . . I need a doctor."

Polly snaps to it. "My aunt and I will drive him," she says.

But Mrs. Marino ignores her. "Johnny! Get Carlo to get Sylvia in here!" She's careful to keep the party going. "Not to worry, Father Medeiros! We're just looking for the spoons."

Sylvia undoes Frank's belt.

"Ay, ay — no funny business," Carlo says. Frank groans. His mother shushes him.

"Does it hurt here? What about here?" Sylvia asks. She has a decisive, competent way about her, qualities that are likely overlooked because of her big hair.

"Everywhere . . . everything," Frank sighs.

"Does it hurt when I press or when I release?"

"Both," he says.

"Are you sure?"

He gargles inarticulately.

"You appear to have appendicitis. You might need surgery."

"Frankie." The bustle goes right out of Mrs. Marino. She gets down on her knees next to the cooker. She strokes Frank's forehead. He is her middle son, but he is her heart. Carlo pats his ankle and Johnny hovers in the doorway. Frank is everyone's favorite. He is the most fun and the most tender; what Polly feels is not just a delusion of the beholder.

"Can you get your aunt to take him to the hospital?" Mrs. Marino says.

Donna and Teddy are chuckling together on the couch. Teddy tears a corner from the page of a *TV Guide,* Donna dictates something, and he writes it down, maybe a phone number.

Polly barrels back into the kitchen. She bends to give Frank a cool cloth and whispers, "Donna and Teddy are hitting it off."

Frank sits up.

"Take it easy," Johnny says.

"I feel much better. Let me up." They all scooch back, butts against kitchen drawers.

Frank jiggles his gut. "I think it was just gas."

Carlo throws a dish towel in his face.

"Is it time for us to say something?" Mr. Marino asks through the hatch.

A glass clinks and people gather. Frank loops his arm around Polly's neck. They can't meet eyes. Laughter is swelling in him, his side is shaking. Polly clamps down hard on the inside of her cheek, Frank bites the back of his thumb. His mother is thanking everyone for their love through all the years. Their eyes are tearing, their lungs burn. The good times and the bad. When there's clapping, they take a huge gulp of air. Now, his father speaks. He's not one for long speeches. In a few hours, Polly will learn that Donna was just selling Teddy a vacation package, all-inclusive, to Acapulco. But Mr. Marino says he's written a poem. Frank stills.

"In sickness and health, till death do us part." He pauses to snicker, but when he tries to talk again, he can't; there is a hitch in his voice. Polly feels her eyes water. He manages to keep going. "My life would have been much worse without you, forever you have my heart."

The crowd's stunned hush collapses into catcalls and wolf whistles. For once, Mrs. Marino is silenced. Mr. Marino sweeps her into his arms and smooches her. Everyone applauds.

Frank frog-marches Polly into the bathroom. He lifts her onto the vanity, her bum falls in the sink. He kisses her to muzzle her yelps of laughter. "I love you, I love you, I love you," he says.

Some Journeymen were exceptional at the art of keeping busy. Huffing up and down with brushes and mops, unhooking their curtains to wash them, putting their hair in newsprint curlers, taking their bedside rugs to the roof for a beating. Polly trailed them all day Sunday, helping to haul washbasins and sweep away the soot that gathered at the ends of the hallways where the south wall was missing. Other Journeymen watched her jog past their open doors as they lay in bed in their undershirts. If she kept her thoughts and her body occupied, if she could create a diversion, her mind could rout the impossible, and a solution would materialize. All of the people dusting and scouring and folding held this hope in their hearts: that cleanliness would cure them. This sameness didn't dawn on Polly, and she closely guarded her near despair.

Every few instants, she'd catch the edge

of something terrible: she'd made a bad miscalculation; in this country, she had no credibility or leverage at all. But then the edge would slip away from her. There was no way she could grasp how low her status was and carry on, so she kept letting the thought go.

Polly and Misty helped an old lady named Sue move two boxes of videotapes from beside her fridge to under her bed.

"Where did you get these? Why do you keep them?" Misty asked.

"Once they start making VCRs again, I'm gonna make a mint doing rentals."

"Smart," Misty said.

"You got me. I'm an old softie. Inside this box is the only place now where Hollywood still exists."

Polly had been stationary too long. Gloom rolled in.

"What needs to be done next?" she said.

Frank would say, *It's human to be sad. You can't beat your emotions. Let's lie down.*

Polly ran down the stairs. Misty could hardly keep up.

The girl with the perfect red bob had everyone gathered around her in the lobby.

"This button makes it cold," she was saying. A fat-barreled hair dryer lay in her hands.

"Gorgeous," someone said.

"Linda, that's ridiculous. How much of your LifeFund are you paying to run that thing?" They recognized Sandy's voice. Linda rolled her eyes, but it was too late. Sandy had ruined it. The crowd dribbled away.

"How'd you get that?" Misty said.

"My boss got it for me in Houston."

"How? Why?" Misty gave exactly the spluttering reaction Linda sought.

"I did some extra work for him." It was all the detail Linda would give.

Misty's eyes got so big, they swallowed her cheeks.

"Calm down," Sandy said. "She just did some housekeeping for him. Probably a month's worth. Idiot."

"Do bosses do that?" Polly asked.

"What?" Misty said.

"Get things for us? If we do work for them?"

"It's completely illegal," Sandy said.

Could Polly ask Baird to go to Twenty-Fifth Street?

If she asked Misty to go to Twenty-Fifth Street for her, they would think Misty was a stowaway. Norberto would refuse: he was too married to regulation. Baird might do it for a price, but what could she give as payment? What did he like?

All day Monday she watched for clues. He thumbed through a waterlogged Saks catalogue from '62. He looked out the window. He worried away at his nasal passages with a thumb. By evening she had a bizarre gift list, with just three items: drink, sleep, and the past. She had none of these to give.

She could just ask. *The worst he can do is say no,* Donna would say. Still, she almost didn't ask, convincing herself she could wait until Wednesday. But on Tuesday he was sober. Who knew if that would hold true for the rest of the week?

"I'm trying to find my cousin," she said.

He didn't reply. He was applying varnish to the legs of a vanity bench, using feathery dabs to emulate the stroke pattern of the bench's first maker.

The janitor who came to clean the blood closet arrived.

"This area is off-limits!" Baird shouted.

Each week it was a different person; they must have drawn straws, no one was willing to touch strange blood. Each paused to study the posted *Safe Handling Guidelines,* checking and rechecking their gloves, though every second in the freezer scored the skin. One boy cried. Any one of the

166

blood bags could carry the kind of world-ending germ that had flung them so irretrievably from home.

"It's the cleaner," Polly said.

Baird watched the woman until she entered the blood closet.

"I can't find my cousin," Polly tried again.

He squinted at her.

She dropped it. She could not talk about her quest without jogging his delicate, angry wounds. She sympathized with him so keenly that it did not cross her mind that Baird might carry something else: not grief, but guilt. On a sea of strange, she needed him to be her twin, so from very little evidence, she compelled a story for him that mimicked her own. This also insulated her from his contempt.

Norberto flagged Polly down that evening, as she was passing. "I have something for you." He was eating a bowl of beans and he turned his head away until he finished chewing. "Sorry." He swallowed. "Tell me about this contact form."

"Did you find it?" Her lungs felt too large for her chest.

"No." Norberto said this with no regret, and she felt an irrational fury that flamed anyway.

"It was something they had at my departure," she explained again. "A special form they would send to your beneficiaries if something changed."

"Did they charge you for that?"

"No."

"Small mercy. I don't think it's real. Was it an official form, or did someone just ask you to scribble down details on a scratch pad?"

"No. It was real."

"I'm just asking. No need to get salty."

"Okay. Well." She moved towards the stairwell.

"Wait. I told you I have something for you. Come in."

She followed him past rows of provisions. Likely, it was a form that needed to be signed, or another pamphlet. But maybe it was a letter from Donna, maybe Frank was on the phone.

"I'm not totally positive this contact form is a fake, but I didn't find any trace of it. I looked through your whole file. There's all sorts of garbage: flyers, stuff not even particular to you." He was trying to drum up appreciation. She nodded and smiled to boost his speed. "But I found this." He put a half sheet of paper in front of her. "Tada!"

The paper had been separated using the

edge of a table. Like so many TimeRaiser papers, it looked like a tax form, with all the little boxes. But it had been filled out by a sloppy hand that overran the lines and left most of the boxes empty. Polly had to study it to understand it. *Subject: Polly Nader. Inquiree: Frank Marino. Result: in transit.*

"What's an inquiree? A person being inquired about?"

"No, a person who inquired about you. Wait." He leaned over the table and looked. "I guess that's the wrong word. But the form means someone was looking for you."

"When?" She grabbed the sheet. Happiness called from far, far away.

"See, it's at the top: September 6, 1995."

"They told him I'd be late? They told him I was coming in 1998?"

"That information would likely be restricted. The statute of restrictions expired only when your boss requisitioned you. Do you know when that happened?"

"He said April this year."

"So until April of this year, that information would have been confidential. But as of '95, they would have at least informed him you didn't arrive yet."

In order to take to heart this good news, Polly had to let everything else that had happened become piercingly real. So her face didn't change.

"Is there anything else? Did he make the search in person?" She turned the paper over. She brushed her palms across the unmarked back, feeling for anything — invisible characters, something worked into the grain. She wanted to touch what he had touched.

"I don't know. They forgot to write down his address. Didn't forget to collect his fee though."

She turned back to the front. There was an empty space where they should have written the street where he lived.

"Is this the last time he looked for me?"

"Inconclusive. This is the only search in your file, but like I said, that thing was a mess. They don't keep these records well. He could have searched since April and it's just not in the file. He could be on his way right now. He knows where you are. Or where you aren't, ha ha."

There is an irreversible intimacy to tears, and so until now Polly had prevented herself from crying in front of airport officials, her boss, the border agents, her neighbors, and Norberto, as they gave her one piece of terrible news after another. But she had not been prepared for this kindness.

She could have tensed her knees and held

her breath and clenched her teeth to keep her feelings under. But her jaw was strained from keeping shut so long, and she was receiving a signal from land, of safe harbor. Tears coursed down her cheeks, her eyelids overrun as soon as they emptied. The sobs shook her body and she didn't try to hold still.

Norberto did not ignore her. He did not try to distract her. He did not try to talk her feeling away. He sat with her quietly and he held the truth that she was in pain. All the trapped air in her chest condensed into water and trickled away.

People might say, Seventeen years — that's craziness! He can't still be waiting for you. From a completely objective standpoint, the odds were poor. But in that secret, covered place, below breastbone and sinew and pumping ventricles, Polly always knew he was coming. And now the actual surrendered to the imagined: Frank was trying to find her. He was here, not only in the past, that distant place, but in the present.

This gave her unbounded confidence.

"I need help," she told Baird.

"With the tufted ottomans?"

"Oh. No. It's something personal." She should have worked out the exact words and

171

their order before she started talking. "I'm wondering if there's something you might need."

"What do you mean?" He didn't look up from his work. He was using a loupe to examine the seams of a seat covered in figured velvet.

"I need a favor. So maybe there's something I could do for you, to make it equal."

Without getting up from his stool, he took small, staccato sidesteps until he was facing her. He put away his loupe. "Go on," he said.

"My cousin is coming to meet me, but the place we chose back in '81, it's restricted. Journeymen can't go there."

"What do you mean?"

"It used to be a hotel, but now it's the Twenty-Fifth Street Port. If they see me there, they'll think I'm trying to stow away, and they'll arrest me."

"Why did you choose that place?"

"It was a landmark. We thought it would stay the same."

Baird laughed, a cawing, triumphant sound. "Best laid plans, eh?"

Polly was seized by the terrifying urge to smack him.

"So you want me to go to the port and

wait for your cousin. When is this happening?"

"This Saturday."

"Interesting."

She kept quiet. She would not let even a breath out, for fear of tipping this in a bad direction.

"There is something I need," Baird said.

Polly nodded.

"It's a little unorthodox."

"All right."

"I left something somewhere. But it's mine. But I can't take it back without looking . . . stingy. Can you get it for me?"

"What is it?"

"An envelope."

"What's in the envelope?"

"A book. Nothing illegal."

"How come you can't get it?"

He didn't say anything. He chewed his cheek.

She wanted it to be an innocent reason. Things can sound illicit without being so; the rules are unfair, as she was just learning. She supplied him with one.

"Is it something you gave someone accidentally? And you can't take it back without it being awkward?"

"Yes," he said. "Yes." He clapped his hands. "What time is the rendezvous on

Saturday?"

"You might have to wait for a while. Maybe you could go in the afternoon."

"And stay until . . . ?"

"The evening? Until it gets dark?"

"Right. You didn't know your schedule for this Saturday, when you made these plans in . . ."

"1981."

"Lord — 1981?"

She didn't want to hear Baird say how Frank was probably dead, like he had the day they met. She squeezed her jaw between thumb and forefinger. She could trace the shape of the teeth pressed against her flesh.

But Baird said, "How exciting. It's like *An Affair to Remember,* but with cousins." He giggled.

Polly was no fool. Donna would say, *If it seems too good to be true, it is.* Baird was trying to butter her up. But Polly could do the same.

"Your timing is impeccable," Baird said. "My envelope is in the site office, but for a week only."

"But how will I get it?"

"On Saturday there will be no one there. You just have to slip in, grab the package, and slip out."

If it seemed too risky, she could turn back.

She could time it so that he would've already left for the beach.

"Deal?" He stuck out his hand.

"Deal," she said, and shook.

After lunch on Saturday, Baird said, "Well, you better get going."

"Where?"

"The plan. It was your idea!"

"Are you leaving now?" she asked.

But he was in the middle of refinishing a rocking chair.

"No, I'll go as soon as you return with my envelope."

She strained to keep her expression neutral. What could she say? How do I know that once I return you'll keep your word? She couldn't say that, and unmask the ill will between them.

"But that will push everything back. You won't get back until after the last shuttle. If I wait until you return, I won't be able to get home."

"I thought I was to wait until nightfall anyhow. I'll come to your place."

He continued his work, nonchalant. She was defenseless in the face of such uncaring. He would win this. Her only refuge was her belief that most people, most of the time, were decent, even him.

175

"I'll go now."

"Good. The office will probably be empty. The envelope is made of cotton. It's mustard yellow. You can't miss it. It's in a basket of files, on top of the cupboard. I saw it there yesterday."

"How will I get in?"

"Climb through a window. You're small. You can fit."

"What if somebody sees me?"

"Well, don't get seen," he hissed. He armed her with a bucket of cleaning supplies, with rags and a jar of vinegar water to use as "camouflage," and sent her out the door.

The office was in the back corner of the hotel. Its door faced a utility road and a tossing green sea of kudzu-coated neighborhoods. There was no one around. But how could she know a guard wouldn't appear in time to see her legs sticking out the window? She couldn't just stand here either; there was no way to look like she belonged. She had scraped-back, scraggly hair and her cheap coveralls had already paled at the cuffs. It took no time to become an outsider.

She got to the window. It opened horizontally. She pushed the lip. It did not budge; it was locked. A guard came round the corner. She put her hand on the doorknob and nod-

176

ded at him. He slowed to study her. With no other choice, she turned the knob. The door opened; it was unlocked. It was only after she stepped into the office that she realized there were people inside.

The man and woman looked nothing like the others who peopled the site, who were small and sun-worn, with cagey posture. The man's back was squared to the heavens, his face emanating a wheat-field glow. The woman had clean hair and a white shirt — not beige or age-tinted yellow, but white.

"Yes?" the woman said.

"I'm just . . ." Polly said. The rest of the words were stuck in her throat. She felt the bucket tucked under her arm. "Garbage," she said gratefully.

"Could you wipe down the conference table?" the man said. "It's sticky."

They went back to their conversation.

"So, Harvey Hasty."

"Yes, Harvey Hasty."

"Harvey Hasty of Amarillo, Texas, Time-Raiser senior vice councillor, charged with exploiting the chronomigration machine to send contraband correspondence back to himself. Namely, the winning lottery numbers for last October's Big Game draw."

Polly had nothing to clean the table with. If she made their table smell like vinegar, they'd remember her. She used a dry rag, miming cleaning while she looked around for the mustard envelope.

"How did he get it past the censors?"

"He hid it as a date. He got caught because there's no fifteenth month. What a loser."

"Love it. Crazy."

"But that's not the crazy part."

"What is?"

"Well, there's a legal conundrum as to how to proceed."

"Why?"

"He hasn't committed the crime yet."

She saw the envelope, yellow cloth between slices of paper files. She moved down to the end of the conference table to get closer.

"What do you mean?"

"He's received the numbers, but we haven't yet reached that point in the future when he sends the numbers back to himself."

She was inches away. But how could she pick it up without them seeing?

"HA! Only in America, right? But can't they make him say?"

"Say what?"

She wasn't doing anything really wrong. She was only trying to straighten out an awkward confusion. If she was caught, Baird could explain. The worst would be embarrassment.

"Can't they make him say when he plans to commit his crime?"

"No! They cannot! Do you know why?"

"Why?"

"Because he himself does not know!"

The woman screamed with glee and the man pounded the table and Polly dropped the envelope into her bucket. But the envelope was tall: it could be seen above the rim.

"Did you hear about Genevieve Silver?"

Yet she was invisible to them, because she was where she belonged, with the rags and bucket. If she could get to the door, they wouldn't even notice she'd left.

"She got into investing. She stockpiled potato plants."

Polly shoved the bucket under her arm.

"How do you stockpile a plant?"

"Well, exactly."

Polly shut the door behind her.

Safety kept receding: it didn't arrive, as she thought it would, when she returned to the laboring zone, where the hotel's innards were exposed like a dollhouse, and workers stepped like storks from post to post, across an unpoured floor, sun hats under hard hats to keep skin from burning. She did not feel safe by the service entrance, nor did she feel safe in the stairwell or on the third floor. Only when the smoking envelope passed from her hands into Baird's did she feel an interval of relief.

He squeaked with joy. "I can't believe you managed it," he whispered. He peeked inside, then slapped the flap shut.

Baird was transparent. All at once, it was glaring that whatever was in the envelope was not at the heart of a misunderstanding between friends.

But Polly could not care. "Will you go now?" she said. She should have made a backup plan in case he said no, now that he had what he wanted.

But he put on his straw hat. He tucked the mustard envelope inside a newspaper from June of '75 and jammed it under his arm.

Suddenly, Polly wasn't ready. She should have come up with a story for Baird, to explain why he was on the beach, if anyone questioned him. She should have described Frank in more detail. She should have found a way to get to the beach herself.

"If you keep flapping at me, I won't go," Baird said.

She watched Baird from the window until

he was nothing but a beige dot, and then the beige disappeared into the brown. Under the window the thick, hot wind whipped up swirls of dirt that danced each other across the broken courtyard.

She had washed and combed her hair this morning, but the soap wasn't very good and her hair was still flat with grease. She knew Frank would say she was crazy to worry, that he didn't care, but she couldn't stop patting her cheeks and her undecorated face. For a while, every time she heard a shout from the grounds or a door open somewhere, she would start, thinking it was him. The waiting was like ice on a stripped nerve.

She got to work on a wicker throne for the Mauna Kea suite, one with a fist-sized hole in its seat. She found the roll of round reed that matched the chair and soaked a length in a bath of vinegar and water. When the reed was ready, Polly sat on the floor and immobilized the throne between her legs. Typically, she'd use a sawhorse, but she wanted comfort; the chair was something she could touch. She used a pair of diagonal cutters to remove the broken weavers. Despite their dilapidated condition, they were tough, cemented together by some unidentified substance. The chair struggled against her and beads of sweat clustered in her eyebrows, but she got the broken bits out. She rested her head against the scrollwork. Then she set to feeding the new reed into the gaps. But the reed wasn't bending as it should; it wouldn't allow itself to be fed smoothly into the spaces where it was needed. Hadn't she soaked it long enough? She examined the reed. She looked at the chair. The reed was a quarter millimeter too wide. Normally, Polly was meticulous. But sitting in sickening silence while she waited for a new batch of reed to be ready was unthinkable. She forced the reed. She yanked it through with needlenose pliers. And just when it seemed like things might rally, when she had the reed gripped and halfway fed, it snapped in her hands. Polly and the chair tipped over in opposite directions. The chair landed on its back, rocking helplessly on its rounded edges, its little wrapped legs in the air.

She stood up. She found the right reed and put a length in the bath. She waited at the window. Before, she'd watched ships stop short where the waters surrendered their depths, and trawlers rush to receive their merchandise — like a giant trapped in a crevasse as tiny beasts flooded to strip its bones. This was before she knew that Frank would wait there. And still she didn't see them coming.

She took the last shuttle home. There was only an hour till Norberto locked the doors. She stayed on the stoop, listening to the dust pooling in the wrecks, gazing at roof-tops until the edges of the buildings blurred into night. She pictured Frank and Baird turning the corner, one small and one tall, and every time she looked and didn't see them there, she imagined them again, like rewinding a video. If she replayed the image enough, it would stick to the piece of world containing that corner, and become real.

Baird turned the corner. Polly waited for Frank to show behind him. She waited, and she waited, and she was still waiting, even after Baird had passed the whole block and was standing beside her.

"You didn't find him?"

Baird shook his head.

"Did you walk up and down the whole time or did you stay in one place?"

"I found a good spot by the parking lot, where I could see all of the pier and the whole beach. There aren't many people down there, just dockworkers. It wasn't dif-ficult to see everyone."

"Maybe he was there but you didn't see him."

"Everyone had something to do. It's a commercial site. No one was just hanging about, waiting."

There was nothing she could say. It was different when she didn't know if he had come or not. But that search he had made, only a few years ago. Could Baird have missed him?

"Now that I've done this for you, you won't tell anyone about the book, right?"

She didn't know what he was talking about. "What book?"

"This one." He shifted so his jacket fell open to reveal the mustard envelope. "If you tell, you're implicated too."

"I wouldn't tell."

She didn't want to talk about this. It mattered so little.

"I'm sure he'll show up eventually," Baird said.

"You are?"

"Yes. Why not?"

Still, Baird didn't leave.

"Do you want to see something?" He was opening the envelope. "But first!" He gave her a pair of white gloves. He removed a skinny hardcover book from the envelope. She tipped it so she could see its writing by the light of the lobby. The cover was gray and mottled, like the surface of the moon.

A scrolling red ribbon carried the words *The Herald 1953.*

"What is this?"

"Humes High yearbook."

"I don't understand."

He opened the book to the middle. It fell open flat, having displayed this page many times. In faded blue ballpoint, an inscription read, *Best of luck to a swell guy. Elvis.*

Baird started to cackle.

"What is this?"

He turned to another page. He tapped a picture of a teenage boy with narrow shoulders, a pretty face, and a spit curl on his forehead. *Elvis Aron Presley. Major: Shop, History, English.*

"This is . . . Is this . . . ?" Polly sputtered.

"Elvis Presley's high school yearbook! Now, now, now — don't drop it."

"You lied to me!" Polly shouted in whisper. "This isn't yours! This is worth thousands!"

"It is mine." His laughter stopped. "It's mine!" He tapped another student photo: a boy with eyes and a mouth like parallel lines. *Leonard Ruleman.* "This is my Leonard."

"He went to high school with Elvis?"

Baird shrugged. "Someone had to. Did you see the way they handled this? Just jam-

185

ming it in with the weekly paperwork. Serves them right."

"Why wasn't it in a safe?"

"They're rewiring the east wing. Everything that was stored under temperature and humidity control is temporarily housed in the site office. I told you: this week only."

"But how did they get it in the first place if it's yours?"

"Well, I gave it to them. I shouldn't have." He sighed. "It was part of my bid to redo the hotel. This is a dog-eat-dog world. I had to have something really special. So I threw this in, for the Las Vegas Hilton suite. And I won the bid, and you got a job, so it worked out for us both."

"What if they notice it's gone?"

He didn't answer.

"Why did you make me steal it?"

"Listen, have you ever lost someone you loved? We're not counting your cousin."

"Why not?"

"He's not dead! He could still come back. You're young. You don't know." He wrapped the book in its mustard sleeve. "When someone dies, there's no one to share your memories anymore. They become like secrets. A secret life. No one knows you lived it, but you. I didn't want it to be that way." He knocked on the yearbook, now pressed

186

to his chest. "This is proof. It's not a secret. It all happened." He scowled. "Sounds stupid, doesn't it?"

Norberto tapped on the glass door with his keys. "I have to lock up now."

"We're having a business meeting," Baird snapped.

"I still gotta lock the doors," Norberto said.

Polly went up to her room. She changed her clothes and ate a bowl of beans, though she wasn't hungry. She brushed her teeth. She got into bed.

This was not the way this night was supposed to go, passing like all the other nights since she arrived, her life unchanged. Other people shared that same kind of madness that made you do terrible, witless things, just to be close to love. This could make her feel better. But still, by her own reckless design, she had only a single Saturday left in September, one last bullet, and no way to get to the beach.

The Demographics Center was in a battered strip mall that sat on the highest shoulder of the seawall, defenseless against the bleachy sun and sprays of sand, in a no-man's-land between hotels. The windows were filthy with sea salt and mud, and Polly passed it by more than once before she realized it was her destination. She arrived as early as she could, walking from work because the shuttle would not make unauthorized stops, but a hand-drawn sign saying *closed* hung inside the dirty window.

So she waited a few days, and on Thursday, Baird got drunk and fell asleep before 1600, and she slipped out early enough to make it before the center closed. Again the Demographics Center looked dark and empty, but this time when she pushed on the door, it gave with a screech. She entered a sweaty office, furnished with school chairs and desk lamps on the floor.

"Forms are on the table," said an ageless lady reading a paperback behind her desk. "Sobre la mesa."

"I have a few questions," Polly said.

"Mmm."

"How much does it cost?"

"Which?"

"Putting in a search for a person."

"An individual or a group?"

"Individual."

"Two hundred and twenty-seven dollars."

Polly turned to go. She couldn't even afford a search for Donna, let alone Donna and Frank.

"You don't want a form?"

"I'll have to come back in a few months. My LifeFund is low."

"You can borrow off of it."

"I can?"

"They let you go into overdraft. Give me your card. Let's see if they'll approve it." She swiped it and the machine sang. "It went through. No going back now."

"No, no, I didn't want to pay yet, I just wanted to inquire."

"Sorry, too late. Fill out a form. Pencils are there."

Polly stared at her, disbelieving. "Two hundred and twenty-seven dollars is almost my whole passage payment for the month."

"So sorry. Can't reverse the transaction. You should've said before I swiped." The woman stared back pugnaciously.

"But you have to reverse it. I just can't afford that."

"I don't have the permissions to do that. If you have an issue, you'll have to contact the regional financial office."

"How do I do that?"

She tapped a sticker on her desk: *Time-Raiser Financial, Southeast Texas, 7311 Hillcroft St., Houston, TX. Hours: Mon–Fri, 1000–1600.*

"Is there a phone number?"

"Yes, but it's always busy. I'm not happy about it either. It's me it inconveniences the most."

If she could only search for one of them, she chose Donna. She would see Frank on Saturday. It was not permitted to think otherwise. All these fail-safes kept heartache and yearning sequestered. They sheltered her, and she was unprepared for the reality of writing her aunt's name one letter per box; how paperwork makes loss actual.

"The last-known address is Buffalo?" The woman tapped the page with a pencil, dirtying the form. "So they left the territory and then you lost track of them?"

"The territory?"

"Yes, the territory."

"Sorry. What territory?"

"The one we're in. America."

"Oh no, she was never here." Though, Polly didn't know that for sure.

"How was she employed by TimeRaiser, if she was never here?"

"She wasn't."

"Well then, we have no record of her. You didn't see the logo on the door? This is a TimeRaiser office. No connection to Time-Raiser, no record."

Polly stared down at the address sticker on the desk.

"Can I apply for a refund by mail?"

"You can try."

"Can I borrow a piece of paper to write down this address?"

"Come on. There's no one else you need to find?"

Frank. Frank. Frank.

"I don't know for sure if he worked for TimeRaiser. He received TimeRaiser health benefits. From someone else. From me."

"Oh yeah, that'll do. Fill out another form."

"How long do I have to wait for the result?"

"Two to five weeks."

"Five weeks? You don't just look in a

directory?"

"We can put a rush on, for an extra forty. Gimme your card; let's see if they'll approve it."

"No, thank you."

Polly wrote Frank's name on the form, one letter per box. This search would act as an extra measure to make it more certain she'd find him on Saturday. This time the cosmos would reward her for taking nothing for granted. This eased the pain and the panic of so much money.

Back at the PX, she wrote a letter to Donna at their old address. Her pencil stuttered over the page. She did not know what to write.

> Hi Auntie, I finally arrived in September this year. I'm doing ok. Will you write to me so I know you are ok and if you know where Frank is, can you give him my address? Love Polly

Like so many letters written home from a borderland, her note was short and carted only information, because anything else was too much for language to carry.

She had to pay Norberto for a return address too, a PO box, but she never received a response, though she did not stop waiting.

On the shuttle on Saturday morning, Polly balanced an enormous paper bag on her knees. Inside was a sleeping bag, a flashlight, and a jar of navy beans in tomato sauce. She'd borrowed the first two from Linda, the girl with the red bob, in exchange for all the cosmetics Polly had brought from 1981. She was ready to say, It's supplies for my boss, to anyone who asked about the bag, but no one did. Baird didn't either. He had been quiet all week. He was an intensely self-conscious person — furiously correcting himself when he misidentified the origin of a chair — and maybe he was embarrassed. She was glad for this. It would be awful to talk to someone who understood how she felt. Only indifferent listeners tighten the seal that keeps sadness inside.

Though she looked for any opening, she was unable to leave the Hotel Galvez until sundown, but she didn't fuss. This was her last chance, all that was left, and she wouldn't scorn it. She took the route of two Saturdays before. She put the flashlight and beans in her pockets and abandoned the paper bag. A beach wind carried it away, over the road and the rocks and the sand

and the water, all of it the same dun color. Somewhere the sun was setting, but you couldn't see it through the clouds. There was only the sense of light withdrawing from the sky. The road straightened, and once she saw the customs station behind the garbage moat, she walked the rest of the way almost inside the juniper hedge until her destination: the small abandoned construction site. The work had ceased not long ago; tire treads in the mud road were yet to be erased by the rain. She scampered across the garden of rebar, seeking cover in the concrete skeleton of a chalet, a three-story monster that anchored its row. She confirmed from all four directions that no one had seen her and no one was coming.

Most of the ground floor was taken up by a great mound of dirt. She was relieved to see the construction company had put in the staircase before they left. She passed a stack of doors and wooden posts like pick-up-sticks on the second floor. The third floor was vacant and still, forgotten even by vermin. Four cut-outs for windows left the room with more void than wall. As she'd observed two Saturdays ago, the sea-facing walls had been left open, maybe for the installation of a terrace. She looked out, a bad feeling between her ribs, but she saw her plan was going to work: you could see from the parking lot to the tip of the Twenty-Fifth Street pier from here. Her heartbeat calmed.

She counted twenty-six figures in total, most clustered around a shipment that had just come off a boat. She studied each head, one at a time, and when none was Frank — too tall, too small, wrong race, wrong gait — she began again. The heads kept moving and some got the once-over three or four times. She tracked one who half looked like Frank, until a floodlight's arc showed him to be a stranger. When she was finally sure Frank wasn't already there, she trained her eyes on the archway between the parking lot and port. Her back pinched between her shoulder blades. Night was dropping. The figures trickled away in groups, riding out in the beds of pickup trucks.

She was thinking of the story *The Time Machine.* When she was ten or eleven, her mother had bought her a copy with greenish ghouls on the cover from a bin in a beach-town store selling secondhand everything. All she could remember was the moment when the time machine breaks and the traveler is hurled forward into futurity. He sees a trillion sunrises and sunsets, until everything goes red. He is at the end of time. There is nothing but ashy beach and giant, slithering crabs with palpitating mouths and pale, jerking antennae. He remembers the sounds of his world, birdsong and teatime, and he thinks, All that is over. The machine is broken and the whimsical horrors he was just passing through become permanent.

No, she was remembering wrong. The machine wasn't broken. Because the book ends with the traveler going home. She was alone in this.

She placed her hands on the sill of a glassless window. She had a ritual she'd invented for whenever panic surged. She studied her hand, the scar on her left index finger, those short bones, everything normal and recognizable, the dusting of hair on her knuckles. Polly had a childhood memory of a wooden plaque with beveled edges on a neighbor's kitchen wall. The plaque said that God had accounted for every hair on your head. She specifically remembered the word "accounted," though Polly did not believe in God, even if she deeply wished to.

Now she could hardly see where the land ended and the sea began. Three officers emerged from the moat, weapons strung around their waists. Polly stepped back, but not one looked in her direction. Two went ahead, sweeping their flashlights, and the third paused. The sound of a chain slapping against the fence, then being secured with a lock, echoed across the empty.

That was it. It was over. The wind blew, muggy like breath.

This couldn't be right. She went from window to window to see if he was on any of the roads, lost, like she'd been the first few times. She wanted to call his name, again and again, until he appeared, stepping into one of the splashes of light dotting the pier, sliding out from under a jetty, running up out of the water. This was the longest she'd ever gone without saying his name.

Down the seawall road, a light bobbed in the distance. It was just a trick. She'd been following the flashlights with her eyes and now she was seeing things. But the guard saw it too. He'd been squatting against a storage shed at the gate; now he stood up. It was a pickup truck. There was no one in the bed and she could not see how many in the cab. She listened, desperate to hear the sighing of the engine slowing down, but the sea was too loud. Please, please, please.

It was going too fast to pull up at the port. It would zip right past. It was close enough to illuminate the guard's face. He was Thibodeaux, the boy who'd pushed her face into the gravel.

She'd put it out of her mind that that had ever happened. Now she could feel his knee like a fist at the back of her neck, and his fingers scrabbling at her skin. She went cold and sweaty, like she had a fever. Saliva puddled in her mouth, warning of vomit. She slumped, as though someone else was piloting her body. But she needed to see, even just the sight of the truck passing by. She put her head down, just for a second, to clear it. When she looked again, the truck was in the parking lot.

The driver's door opened. A man stepped out. Too few steps from the cab to the gate to analyze his gait. His body was blocked by the car. "Turn around," Polly said. The man was speaking to Thibodeaux, asking a question. The guard shook his head, no. "I'm up here," Polly said. "Turn around, turn around." The man was going back to his car.

No.

How fast could she get down there? She'd never make it in time. She ran down the stairs anyway. If they arrested her, Frank would bail her out. But she was four steps down when she felt Thibodeaux's knee against her neck again, a ball of bone mashing her face into the gravel, suffocating her.

There was no railing and she was going to fall into the dirt. She heard the faraway sounds of shouting. She climbed back up on hands and knees. She got to the window. Another guard was jogging to the gate. The man was still there. "Turn around, turn around."

The second guard reached the gate. He was handing something through the bars. The driver had to step forward, reaching through light, and finally she saw his face.

The years could have made him fatter and grayer. It could still be him.

Then she saw what he'd come for: a small duffel bag. He had not come for her.

The stranger got back into the cab. The taillights glowed red, then white. The guards leaned on the gate, chatting. The truck rolled backwards, swung left, and went back the way it came.

She stood at the hole in the wall for a long time. She trailed every car that came and went — a cargo truck, a minibus, a station wagon — but nobody else stopped. Midnight seemed an arbitrary time to stop waiting, so she didn't. Once she took more than a few steps away from her post, it would be certain Frank was lost, so she stayed put, even when her feet shrieked, even after it had been ages since the last car, and there was nothing left but the fingernail moon.

It really had happened. He had come. Just before dawn, he'd pulled up the mud lane in his old blue Celica. He wound down the window and shouted her name. He took the stairs two at a time. His brown curls. She was just living the moments in a muddled sequence, waiting for him still, taking the morning shuttle back with the night managers and the laundry workers, cheeks swollen from tears, when he'd already arrived. He lifted her off the ground. He held her inside his sweet, briny, sighing heat. He was not sick, or tired, or aged. It was like back at the start.

Polly could not manage how poorly she'd predicted how it would all end. Her mind warped under this weight, and defense mechanisms wobbled out of the warping. The less evidence she had, the more she believed Frank knew exactly where she was, and he was coming to bring her home.

She kept going to the discarded construction site by the port, until September was three, four, five Saturdays past, and then something else happened. Future dates of all kinds acquired mythic qualities. Frank would find her before her mother's birthday, before the end of daylight saving time, before the handwritten expiration date on the dairy products in Norberto's PX. She needed to own the milk for this predictive power to work. So she went down to the store and waited until Norberto was out giving someone directions. And then into her pocket she slipped a pat of butter that had been floating extravagantly in a vat of ice water. Milk would have been too big to conceal on her body. The butter set the wait at ten days. She bought tokens to feed her fridge's coin slot, so the butter didn't go rancid before its time. She stayed in her apartment as much as possible, in case Frank showed up. She left her window open all night so she would hear if someone rattled the front door.

Her mother's birthday passed as it always did, the clocks changed, the butter expired and was deserted in the hot fridge. But ads for a movie appeared everywhere, with a release date in bold type across the poster's face. The date was posted in the elevator, in the foyer; the driver even hung an ad in the bus. It was the first movie made since the founding of America, and Mel Gibson had traveled from 1983 Hollywood to make it. Norberto started a collection jar in the apartment lobby so they could rent a TV set for the night of the broadcast.

This was the date; this was the one. Frank would come, by the day of the premiere. She got a copy of the poster from Norberto. Whenever she felt the slightest tremor that she'd been tricked and Frank was seventeen years dead, she took the poster out and gazed at the digits, and they soothed her.

Moody Plaza buzzed with a sense of communal celebration as the broadcast day drew closer. Every evening Norberto stopped to tell her something: there was enough in the collection jar that he might be able to make potato chips; he was wondering if they had enough chairs; did she like Mel Gibson?

The day of the movie, her neighbors jammed the lobby. They stood in bunches in the dark, happy and shy, even though they'd listened to each other snore and fart and cry for months. Polly elbowed her way to the stairs. Desperation thrummed in her chest, and her hands went cold.

She kept the lights off in her bedroom and she threw the curtains open. A boat setting sail blew its horn. The sky was the color of a lightbulb right after you shut it off. The movie had begun. She could hear her neighbors making noises as one organism: a gasp, a pause, then laughter. Would Frank have trouble getting through all the commotion?

She lay completely still until doors started opening — the sound of residents coming back, the movie over. When the shuffling stopped, she got up. She took the movie poster down from her wall, folded it, and put it in the garbage.

Norberto was still in the lobby organizing folding chairs.

"Wasn't it great?" He looked elated.

She went outside. The weather was changing. All along, she had known Frank wasn't coming. It was she who had invented his vast, urgent movements. In the end, there was only Polly.

1979

On Sundays, Polly wakes up at Donna's. She does her laundry and she waits for the clock to flip *10:30,* when she'll go to Frank's. One Sunday, Polly wakes up at Frank's, and she watches his even breathing, its rhythm like the tides. That Sunday, at his grandpa's cabin, they open their eyes at the same time, and see a deer at the window, its breath on the glass. For breakfast they have the toast he butters with a half inch space for holding, or they have bacon and eggs at the diner on the corner by her house, or they eat muffins in the car on their way somewhere, and for months after, she finds carrot crumbs in the puckers of the seat. They go grocery shopping for garlic and lemons and tuna, for Frank to make pasta. They go shopping for a birthday beanbag chair for his goddaughter. They go to the beach and he drowns her hands in cup after cup of sun-hot sand.

They go to the movies to see *Star Trek* and *Moonraker, The Black Stallion, Norma Rae,* and *Time After Time,* and he lets her hold his hand with her popcorned fingers. They drive to New York City to watch the Phillies play the Mets. They drive to the Cheektowaga flea market and she loses him by the antique vases, but he turns up near the hooks. They talk about music or what they did this week. They talk about his mother, they talk about why Polly and Donna act like office mates. They talk about the regulars at his work, they talk about the old ladies where she works. They talk about how to do things: how to change a tire, how to make gnocchi, how to darn a sock, how to do a headstand, how to chop wood. They talk about how they love each other, how long and how much. She says, Tell me why you like me again. The sun and the shadows lie in cross-hatches across his legs. He says, Because you're good. She wants to know, Good at what? He says, You're a good person. She laughs and asks, Is that slang for sexy? She presses on — What do you mean, good? He says, It's not like you're a protest singer, but when faced with a decision, you always do what's just and right. It gives me a sense of security. She laughs again, perplexed now, because this is not the answer she's fishing for. But after, she'll decide she likes this better than if he'd said, You were meant for me. It's a sensible answer, almost the kind of thing she would say. They listen to records. They drink coffee. They play cards. He unwraps her skirt and she undoes his jeans. He takes off her socks with his toes and she bites his cheek. Sweat pools in the diamond made by the meeting of their chests. They do this in the morning or they do this late at night or they do this for all the afternoon. And when she reaches the point, at the burst there is an explosion of time, and all of the moments they will ever have together occur at once: the first, the four hundred and eighth, the three thousandth, the last. The sun goes down at five p.m., or seven fifteen, or it keeps shining till nine. The sun sets and they lean on his kitchen counter and drink screwdrivers. The sunset makes oily rays across the windshield and she unfolds his visor so he can see. The sun is dropping behind the bank of supermarket cash registers and the middle-aged man in the lineup, with nothing but a basket full of Coffee-mate and Hungry-Man dinners, tears at Polly's heart. The sun sets and Frank is Polly's entryway into the ordinary world, a way to live among the people who always know the day of the week, people who never eat dinner alone at McDonald's on a Sunday night. For dinner they eat fish and chips, or a very large salad, or at the Lebanese diner, or he makes a pizza, or they go to his parents' and in the folds of the tablecloth he touches her knee. After dinner they lie in bed and watch headlights flush the ceiling. After dinner they try to guess the *Sunday Night Movie* playing at his neighbor's, coming through the wall. After dinner he does the dishes and she scrubs the tomato seeds heat-bonded to the stove. After dinner they take a bath and listen to the radio and count the tiles in the floor. She sleeps with her arm around him, she sleeps with her hand on his thigh. She tucks her hand into his waistband, she sweeps her thumb across his eye. He puts her hand in his pocket. He frees her hair from her collar. He wipes a tear from her nose. He gets the fuzz off her lashes. He does the zip on her dress. He kneads the knot in her spine. He kisses her shoulder, he kisses her temple, he kisses her mouth, he kisses her eyes. He kisses her cheek, he kisses her thigh, he kisses her elbow, he kisses her eyes.

"Good morning!"

On a November Monday, there were no seats on the shuttle and the windows were opaque with morning moisture, giving the feeling of traveling inside a packed plastic bag. Polly couldn't see that the bus was about to lurch around a corner, right when she took her hand off the grab pole to pocket her ID. She was thrown, face-first, into the coveralls of a nearby woman. The woman grabbed her shoulder and righted her, and Polly stumbled back in a deluge of apology, held fast to a pole, and faced the window. But right before she regained her balance, there was a moment where the proximity of another person's body, that human warmth, made relief wash through her. This was the happiness of touch, and in that instant she was like a plant standing up, as water makes clay into mud.

"Did you ever go to the Demographics

Center?" Misty asked while her sister snoozed across the aisle.

Here in 1998, Polly had made a swift habit of hiding all her wishfulness, and this was nothing new; long ago she'd learned the importance of acting practical from Donna. But messy-haired Misty, who was easy friends with everyone, was openly, daringly hopeful. Polly had to tell Misty all her expectations, because Misty was the final and only source of external confirmation that Frank was coming. Misty said just what Polly wanted to hear: "I'm sure it will be great news." Polly gazed upon the back of Misty's frizzy head like it was a beacon. Misty believed.

A few days later, on the way home, a man sharing her bench said, "Say, you're the new one, the romantic. Did you find your missing beau yet?"

"You must have me confused with someone else," Polly said in horror.

"No, you're the one, I know. Misty told me about you." He chuckled. "I sure hope, for your sake, he turns up!"

She laughed too, in confusion and mortification. Afterward it disgusted her to remember her response. She wished instead she had said, *What's that supposed to mean?* — both as a comeback and an actual question.

On Sunday, Sandy said, "Did you hear back yet? Hope for the best, prepare for the worst!" and Polly wished for death.

She started to hear condescension in the morning hellos. Poor dear, they thought. How can anyone be that young, to believe in a love that endures? All her neighbors thought her uncritical, naive, as if the only way she could have arrived at a different conclusion from theirs was by not truly thinking things through.

If she'd been there longer, she would have learned that everyone was always interested in everyone else's searches — not because they didn't believe, but because they dearly wished to. Everybody was looking for someone.

Polly returned to the Demographics Center five weeks after her first visit, preparing herself to hear that she'd have to wait another month, or a year. She was unnerved when the woman produced an envelope labeled with Polly's name and number and said, "Probably not good news."

"What?" No matter how unfeeling Polly tried to be, she could not keep up with the disappointments.

"Small envelope. Probably not good news."

Polly ripped the contents in two trying to

get the thing open. The torn paper was a stingy slip, only large enough to contain her details and the message *Frank Marino: No results found.*

"What does that mean? Is he dead?"

"No. It would say if he was dead. It means that he's not in the country."

"In the country?"

"In America."

"Could he be dead and not in the country?"

"The results don't preclude that."

Polly searched for another question that could get her the answer she needed.

"But could he be unlisted? He's here but they don't know his address?"

"Well, in that case, it would say 'unlisted.' Though, you know, now that you mention it, I don't entirely comprehend the difference between 'unlisted' and 'no results found.' But I do know that 'no results found' means 'out of the jurisdiction.' Most likely, let's say ninety percent likely, it means 'out of the country.' Bottom line: they don't know anything about him. But it's worth paying just to know, I always say."

It was a scam. It meant nothing. There was no reason to feel anything about this information — other than shame at her own foolish believing. But Polly asked Sandy how to get to Buffalo anyway.

"You have to take the boat. It's very expensive. Over a thousand dollars."

"A thousand five, easy," Misty said.

Polly waited until Misty was ensconced in conversation with someone else on the shuttle, and then she asked Sandy, "A boat? Why a boat? Where does the boat go?"

"You can't fly," Sandy scoffed. "Too dangerous."

"Why is it dangerous?"

"That's how diseases are spread — instantly." Sandy snapped her fingers. "And you can't take a train or drive: the railways are defunct; the roads are garbage. You have to sail, from Galveston to Miami, from Miami to New York, and then I guess up the Hudson River and through the Erie Canal."

"What's wrong with the roads?"

"You hear this all the time from rookies. It's like you all think it's an easy thing to clean up a disaster. The pandemic was one thing. But consider the infrastructure. People just left. What happens when all the little people who keep the world running disappear? Roads, bridges, highways either flooded, exploded, or collapsed within ten years. Why do you want to go to Buffalo?"

"Just curious." Polly kept her gaze out the

window.

"They found him, didn't they?"

Polly ran down possible replies: I don't know. None of your business. He's here. But she was too deflated for subterfuge. "They said, 'No results found.' "

"But TimeRaiser knows everything in America. He must be elsewhere." Sandy said this in her righteous way and Polly concentrated on the comfort of "he must be" until it eclipsed the shock that he had left without her.

"Where could he have gone? Buffalo?" Misty rejoined the conversation.

Polly ignored her.

But Misty wanted to talk about it. Later, in the hallway, she brashly brought it up again. "Disappointing results, huh?"

"I wish you hadn't told everyone about my search."

"Sorry," Misty said, surprised, and then in a cutesy voice, using *w*'s in place of the *r*'s, she said again, "Sorry!"

Polly's face didn't soften.

"I didn't know it was a secret. You know, it's really crowded in the United States. Cold. Expensive. You're better off here."

"Don't tell anybody about my results, please."

But she must have, because then Polly

began to see something new in everyone else: a tilt to the head when they addressed her, a softness in the eyes. Pity.

After that, Polly avoided all her neighbors.

On sober days, Polly and Baird worked together like cogs in a clock, exchanging wrenches and pliers instead of words, a language in tools. He only had one record, the soundtrack from *Cabaret,* and he played it at least once a day, but it was one of Donna's favorites and Polly didn't mind. He would hum along, sometimes even giving in to song, forgetting Polly was there, crooning along with Liza Minelli about how this time was bound to be better.

On drunk days, he mumbled tears, he unbuttoned his coveralls to his navel, he told aimless, slurring anecdotes about Before. Once, he crouched down to take a closer look at a child's rocking chair, and as he leaned forward precariously, she saw a urine stain the size of a dinner spoon, high on his thigh. She had not been able to get the image out of her mind.

She had thirty months to go until her bond was up and she could go home to Buffalo. It was only a couple of years, she wouldn't even be in her late twenties by the end of it, and it was a plumbless lot of days.

Every unit of time was a border she needed to breach. Work took care of the daytime and, if she was tired enough, the evenings, but then she still had Sundays to cover. She would have given anything to have something to do on Sunday, with its pale walls and the daylight never changing on the ceiling.

Polly knew herself, and she knew that she was not a brave or remarkable person. Someone else who was not Polly would've been able to think up a brilliant scheme to speed through her bond. Someone else might know how to run away and survive in the swamp, how to eat weeds and navigate by the stars. Donna might have been able to, after all of those action and adventure TV shows she loved. Polly did not know what had happened to Donna.

One beautiful Sunday, Norberto gave Polly a book of crossword puzzles. She was at the swaps board, scouring it for new messages.

"Are you looking for something in particular?" he asked.

"No. I don't have anything to trade. I just like to read them."

"I see," he said kindly, and she reddened.

"Do you like this sort of thing?" He tossed her a blue-and-orange book with *Puzzles*

Vol. 1 in bubble letters on the cover.

More than half the puzzles had been completed in chunky, confident letters. Halfheartedly she picked at an unfinished one. But then she turned the page and kept on going, until she looked up and it was almost Monday.

The next Sunday she went back to the store. She waited ten minutes while Norberto explained to the woman ahead of her how candles were made, and while she was waiting, she decided she'd even pay money for *Puzzles Vol. 2,* even if it meant she had to stay in Galveston a few more days.

"Sorry, dear," Norberto said. "That was the only one. You shouldn't have finished so fast."

"Oh." Her gullet tightened, like a cable tied to a weight. She looked down at her copy of *Puzzles Vol. 1.* "Do you know the name of the three-word, ten-letter Thailand town that borders Burma?"

He shook his head energetically. "I hate those things."

Loneliness tackled her, compacting her until she had no more breath. She sat on the curb. She laid her cheek on her knees and imagined Frank. She could see him at the intersection, hopping the curb, crossing the block with his dear, swaying gait. She kept closing and opening her eyes, but each time there was only the empty, pummeled street. Norberto came out and regretfully told her she was creating a hazard.

In late November, a whole week went by when Baird wasn't drunk once. He became consumed with their quarterly review, which was coming up in a few days. "You shouldn't be so complacent," he snapped at her — though every morning she arrived before him, and every evening she left after. "If I go, you go." The logs became outlandish. There'd be no entry for days, and then there'd be three in a row, announcing fantastical feats. The morning before the review, she intended to work through lunch, as she always did, to avoid her thoughts and the endless accounting of days; but when he saw it was her mandated lunch hour, and her, still in her corner with reams of reed, he shouted at her to go before he got written up for a code violation.

She handed her tiffin carrier through the kitchen window, and the server filled it with gray black beans and some wan-looking broccoli. No one liked to eat in the unlit, stuffy mess hall. There were penalties for any meals left unfinished, and if they ate in the mess hall, their tiffin cans were checked

217

at the door before they could leave. No one knew what the penalty was.

Everyone ate on the rim of rocks along the seawall, rocks in as many colors as skin. The scorch of summer had ebbed into a phase of gentle, sunny days, like a sixty-day May. The littlest rocks were perfect for stacking, and dozens of rock piles, like wee russet people, gazed nobly out to sea. A group of young adults from North Carolina held debates.

"What would you do if you were super-rich and you could time travel for fun?"

"Where would *you* go?"

"I'd rob a bank and get away to the future."

"Wouldn't that just give them time to figure out you did the crime?"

"I'd travel till Brooke Shields is legal."

"That's now. You're a perv *and* you can't do math."

"I'd live forever."

"What do you mean?"

"If you had money to just go forward and forward, you could still be alive in two hundred years. You could be a witness to the rest of time."

"But we wouldn't know anybody there."

Just as the invention of air travel had made it easy to go, but no easier to leave, the invention of time travel made time easy to pass, but no easier to endure. The philosophers left before she finished her lunch and she had no more distraction. She had to stare at the sea and think about Donna.

The day before she left 1981, she had called Donna to tell her she was going. Someone in the apartment complex had a working phone, and Polly paid for the call in sanitary napkins. The phone was in the kitchen, crusted in cooking grime. As she talked, she scrubbed the plastic with her thumb, the grease coming off in little black rolls. She preferred to remember the grease over what Donna said. Donna said, "You're a strong girl, you'll be all right." Her tone was bright, cleansed of emotion. It was the last time they would hear each other's voices, and instead of saying what she wanted to say, Donna had said what Polly wanted to hear.

Back at the workshop, Baird was drunk. He had his back to her, but she could tell from his sagging posture, and because he was sitting in one of his green leather chairs from the Starlight Roof. He was turning the pages of a book and sighing wetly. She went back to sanding an altar table for the Shangri-La suite.

Close to an hour later, he was asleep sitting up. The book fell out of his lap with a slap, and she saw that it wasn't a hotel glossy. It was Elvis Presley's yearbook.

"You can't have that here," she shouted. "Are you nuts?"

He almost fell out of the chair. He grabbed the book, plunging for it like she'd tried to snatch it.

"Yes I can," he said. His look of hatred fixed her in place.

She was livid. He had put her in such pointless danger, but more than this, his vulgar daily performance of brokenhearted- ness became, in that instant, intolerable.

"You did what you could for him. Move on."

It was insubordinate. She shouldn't have said it.

But he didn't care. He staggered up, tot- tered, then righted himself against a chair rack.

"No I didn't," he said.

"What do you mean? You couldn't save him."

"Why not? You think I didn't have it in me?"

"No. Because they wouldn't admit you."

"What are you talking about, Nader?" He sat down and rested his elbow on a saw- horse. A whiny tone came into his voice, common to children and lushes.

"You said they wouldn't let you go for Leonard. Because you were two men? You told me that the first time we met."

"I never said that." He laughed. "Who said that? That's not true. TimeRaiser didn't care. I could've been wearing a fruit tiara and they would've said, 'Right this way, sir.' It's business."

Shock turned her rigid, like she was coated in glue.

"But I didn't save him! Because I didn't want to. I didn't want to, and that's that. It's just the kind of guy I am. I would've liked it better if Leonard had said so. Instead he said that he understood. Terrible! It was terrible."

She went back to work as if he hadn't spoken at all, her whole body burning.

He kept facing her. She could feel the weight of his need, as heavy as hands, beseeching her for reassurance, or at least for witness. But in a moment, all the sympathy she had made for him mutated into rage. She refused to turn her head.

He stood up. Very deliberately, he made his way to the couch and he lay down.

Why should she care what he'd done? It was even possible that what he'd actually done had been mangled by memory, what truly happened lost forever. Yet a seasick, tilting feeling persisted. If she had been at home, with her routines and the oven clock in Donna's kitchen and *Laverne & Shirley* on at eight, it wouldn't have mattered. But she had none of her old polestars by which to find her bearings. She knew no one here except for him, and she knew him not at all. What she had thought was a mirror was another room.

Or what if she was just like him, left behind, trapped in another time, twisted and horrible?

She couldn't even look at him. When it came time for her to leave, she didn't wake him up. She'd go in early tomorrow to make sure he hadn't left the place in chaos.

But in the morning, a bus broke down and blocked the service road, and everyone had to be diverted, and she was late. She ran all the way from the bus stop to the workshop, hoping that she'd beat the review committee.

Even before she reached the top, she heard their voices. It was the woman with the clean shirt and the man with the good posture from the office, who hadn't seen her steal the yearbook.

"If you can change the Committee of

Adjustments meeting, we can go to Permissions earlier," the woman was saying.

"Got it. Done."

Polly stayed put halfway up the last flight of stairs. They had not seen her; she could still turn back. But she couldn't skip work.

Baird burst out from behind the plastic curtain.

"Cassie, Michael, so nice to see you again!" He walked towards them, his arms outstretched, like a magician. "Come see the new mirrors I resilvered!"

Polly ducked, unable to make a decision.

"Polly! Come!" Baird shouted.

"Is that your assistant?"

"Indeed," Baird said. "Ask and Time-Raiser will deliver!"

There was nothing else she could do. She tried to enter naturally. She was afraid to make any moves, to swallow.

But they looked right at her and did not react.

Cassie said, "Well, let's get a look at your logs."

Baird ignored the request. "Polly has a very interesting story. She's from 1981."

She could see that he had tried to tame his hair with a wet comb, and for the moment it was lying submissively against his scalp.

"How many years did you travel?" Michael said. "How old are you in actual time?"

"In actual time?" Polly said.

"Your actual-time age. What year were you born?"

"1958."

"What's that?" Cassie said.

"The big four-oh this year!" Michael announced.

"And you look like, what, twenty?"

"I'm twenty-three," Polly said.

"No you're not," Michael said. "You're forty!"

"It always makes me giggle," Cassie said. "TimeRaiser: miracle anti-aging solution. We should change our marketing strategy."

"She's older than me," Michael said, "and she looks like my daughter!"

"But I'm not forty," Polly said, but quietly.

"So let's see the workshop," Cassie said. "We have to be getting on."

"She even has an old-fashioned name," Baird said.

"Polly. Polly," Michael said. "Do you know that old children's song? How does it go? You know the one." Puzzlement crossed Michael's face. Then he said, " 'Polly Put the Kettle On'! That's it! How does it go again?"

"It's just that one line, repeated, I think."

"How does the tune go?" Baird said. "Sing it for us."

"I don't think so," Polly said.

"But you must! It's a lovely tune," he said.

By now she understood that he was stalling. She couldn't think why.

"It's a lovely tune," Baird said again, and she saw that it would be more awkward to continue to resist than to surrender.

She opened her mouth and sang, in her thin, reedy voice, "Polly put the kettle on."

"That's it?" Baird said.

"Polly put the kettle on," she sang again.

Baird tapped the table like a conductor. Cassie showed a folder to Michael. Polly's voice wavered.

"Polly put the kettle on."

Cassie and Michael started discussing a slip of paper. Polly stopped singing. But Baird frowned and made angry gestures at her to continue.

"And let's have tea."

Baird applauded. "Encore," he said. "Come on."

"Polly put the kettle —"

"That's fine," Cassie said, and put out a restraining arm.

"Great!" Baird shouted. "Let me show you the antique mirrors I resilvered."

225

Dank misery descended on Polly. Why had she gone along with that?

Baird was showing the mirrors. "You'll notice that, while the glass is now like new, I actually worked to preserve some of the bumps and bruises on the frame. They're part of the life of the piece, you know, and we must respect that."

Polly had actually been the one to resilver them by herself.

He toured them around the room — showing them the wee drawers in the gentleman's valet, the swivel base of a papasan chair, a trestle of lamps from across the ages — speaking in a strange way, drawing out his vowels like an aristocrat. He explained in minute detail how to weave a lace cane seat, but at the end of it all, Cassie said again, "Now let's take a look at your records."

"Okay, then," Baird said. He turned to the curtain and Cassie and Michael followed. "Oh, you should wait here. The workshop is in disarray, a touch hazardous — don't want you to trip."

"In that case we should take a look. You should be following workplace safety protocol," Michael said.

The workshop looked like Baird had started five projects at once. Cuttings of fabric slathered the floor, sawhorses were scattered in all directions, jars of varnish lay lidless. Polly could tell from the state of the couch he had slept there last night.

"Oh, dear," Michael said. "I'm going to have to go over the seventeen-point safety check."

"I'll take a look at the log myself," Cassie said.

"Let me get it for you," Baird said.

"I see it there," she said, crossing to the stand where he kept the records.

Finally, Polly saw why he had been trying to delay them. The mustard-yellow envelope with the yearbook inside was lying with the logbooks.

There was nothing Polly could do. If she lunged forward and plucked the yearbook out of the stack, Cassie would notice. Baird pretended to be drinking in Michael's every word, but in his nervousness he kept unbuttoning the buttons on his front, his hair now drying into vertical fuzz. Polly leaned against a drafting table, windless. Neither could look away from Cassie, bent over the logs and a black spiral notepad she'd pulled out of her pocket, but nothing showed whether or not she'd seen the yearbook.

Then it all came to an end. Cassie slapped her notepad shut.

"These numbers are weeks behind target. In addition, there are disturbing discrepancies between the logs you've kept and the independent logs. We thought, with the addition of an assistant, that you'd be weeks ahead of where you are."

"Oh yes, well." Baird rocked on the balls of his feet. "Sorry about that."

"We'll need to have a meeting," Michael said to Baird as Cassie put back the logs. "Wait for the memo."

Cassie straightened the logbook, lining up its spine with the other books on the stand. She reached out and fingered the yellow flap. The silence curdled. She turned to Michael. "What's the plan for lunch?" she said. "Have you spoken to Susan?"

Polly and Baird watched Cassie and Michael cross the courtyard.

"It's fine," he said. "She didn't see it."

"She touched it!"

"Nonsense! She would've said something." He sat down in a wicker throne and bit his thumb.

"What if she's just coming up with a plan?"

"No, I know her. She would've confronted us right away."

But Polly could not get a hold of herself. What if she got arrested? She remembered

228

Thibodeaux's hand stripping her belly, and she started to cry.

"Put a sock in it, Nader."

"What will happen next?"

"I don't know. Nothing. Go cool off."

She went to the sink to splash her face, but she could only put her face in her hands and weep.

"Land sakes, Nader! What is wrong with you?"

The weight of the stories she carried was too much, and her muscles buckled. She told him about Frank, who was not her cousin. She told him their plan to meet every Saturday in September, and how hard she had tried. Everything she wanted to happen, and what actually did.

Baird sat up straighter. He was entirely engaged, leaning forward, his elbows perched on his knees.

"Is he dead?" he said.

"I don't know. They said he's in another country."

"But there's still hope if he's not dead. If he left the territory, there should be a record."

"Where? Where are there records? I've been asking and asking." Though she had never quite asked Norberto if there were records of departure.

"This is very interesting," he said. He was buttoning and unbuttoning his front again.

"It is?"

"You should go to the Strand."

"The Strand?"

"Red-light district. You live in the Moody building? It's right around the corner. That's part of its appeal. It's not coastal. It's inland, in the ghettos. Great cachet. Attractive to vacationers and Americans looking for a thrill."

"Why would I go there?"

All this time, she had kept her sorrows from him, when in fact this kind of story gave him lurid pleasure.

"It's a type of liquidation station. Journeymen selling whatever they have, to draw currency from vacationers. There's the flesh trade, and gambling, but also information. Some Journeymen, if they work in transportation, they have passenger manifests. Or hotel registers. You can pay to have a look at a specific register. If you know he left, say, in July of '83, you can pay to see the pages of outgoing trips from the port of Galveston that month. Everyone is looking for someone. Do you want to go?"

"Of course."

"We'll go tonight! I'll meet you there. Let's say eight p.m."

"Does it cost a lot of money?"

"To get in?"

"No, to buy information."

"Of course it costs a lot of money. Are you crazy? It costs big money."

"But I don't have money."

"Well, find some money, girlie! You can't give up. That's the problem with people these days. That's why it's '98 and the country is still in the toilet. If I were you, I'd just hit the road to find him."

"I can't do that."

"Can't, or won't?"

"Can't! I'm bonded!"

"What?" Baird said. "What's bonded?"

Polly got off the evening shuttle at Moody Plaza, but she didn't go in. She walked north, following Baird's directions. Two cars that had crashed into each other head-on about fifteen years ago still blocked an intersection. To their left, west, there lay the Strand, an avenue of old-timey buildings, tram tracks, and cobbled pavement, like the movie set for an old western with honky-tonk pianos. She had been here once before, in 1980. The street had been kept clean, no trees growing out of the sidewalk.

She sat on the curb, next to a decapitated parking meter, in front of the cast-iron storefront where Baird had said to meet. A retail sign had survived the years of hardship: *Col. Bubbie's Strand Surplus Senter.* Its archways and windows were bricked over, save for one glass door, painted black, with lines of light passing between the frame and glass, glowing brighter now that it was getting dark.

It must be about ten minutes past their meeting time. Polly was antsy. She got up. The street dead-ended at a massive art deco building rising out of the road, like a ship's prow. Its sidewalk, steps, and awning were blanketed in black birds, all talking at once. She got too close. The edges of the crowd screamed in their high-pitched language. Polly fled north, to the ferry terminal. Little whirring bird heads still stared in her direction. She put more distance between herself and them. Here the city was interrupted by the sea. This sea was only a slight gray strip; another body of land sat across the water, less than a quarter mile away. But it was still the sea, in its glitter and its moves, and in the smell in the air like an old envelope, something left in a drawer and forgotten.

In her heart, the past was not another time, but another place that still existed. It was just that she had taken a wrong turn. One day, she would figure it out and she would go back to the house where she had lived, and it would not be lost to the violence of time, the roof caved in. It would be just as she had left it, and she would look up at the front of the house, and see the light on in the bedroom window.

She went back to Col. Bubbie's, but Baird hadn't shown. She still had forty minutes until Norberto locked the doors. She didn't need Baird to go with her. All this time, the answer had been right here, minutes from where she lay her miserable head.

Polly opened the door and stepped into a vestibule hung with soldiers' helmets and canteens. A bouncer waited in the corner — a towering rectangular woman. Polly stared, unsure of what to say.

"Coming in?" the bouncer said.

"I don't have . . ." Polly said, stopping at the noun because she didn't know what she needed to get past. She wasn't dressed right; she didn't even own anything for a night on the town.

"First time?"

"No. Yes."

"First time is free," the bouncer said, and parted a black curtain that hung behind her stool. "The bar is on the first floor, the entertainment is on two. Enjoy yourself."

Instead of a lounge, through the curtain

was a lengthy passageway clogged with military gear and drinkers. Where there might be light fixtures, there were flashlights clamped to the tops of clothes racks, and between the thin spotlights you had to look out not to trip. She could tell by how new their clothes were and how clean their necks were that the crowd was mostly American. When she said "Excuse me" to get past, they didn't budge. But the walls had give, being mostly made of flak jackets and camo pants, and Polly made her way along the folds. The passageway ended in a bar. Racks of tin cups and unmarked bottles of clear liquor lined the walls. Beyond was a staircase to the second floor.

She let the crowd push her back into a swinging display of gas masks. What was the plan? Even if she were to find a passenger manifest or whatever else Baird promised, she had no currency. Though there were other things a girl her age could offer.

Tangled in the masks, the hair on her arms and legs stood up so straight, it was as if her skin were peeling away from her body. All she wanted was to cross the road and go back to her room.

But it had only been a few months — weeks, really — since she had last seen Frank. It was little enough time that they could still resume their life together. All this could just be a disastrous, forgettable blip. It was not too late for their story to end differently.

Maybe she could find someone nice, and perhaps it would only be once, and couldn't that be managed?

She could just go look. She didn't have to make a decision.

She came into the light of the landing. She took one step, and then another, and then another. A man and his friend teetered around the corner and down the stairs and walked right into her.

"Hello," the man said. "Come for a drink." He put his arm around her and snuggled her down the stairs, his friend on the other side of her. The men had bulbous heads and white teeth. Their arms behind her back were like a cordon, and the only way out was down.

At the foot of the stairs, she tried to unwind from the first man's hold. But he tightened his grip at the same time as she tensed to bolt.

"Don't worry," he said into her neck. "I can pay."

Her almost-resolve evaporated. In another life, this never would have happened to her. This was terrible and ridiculous. But the men marched her to the bar and ordered drinks in tin mugs, keeping her between them. She could run. But what if they followed her? Her mother's advice on how to deal with unwanted male attention faded in and out inside her head: *Politely and firmly remove his hand.* She looked around for help, but no one would make eye contact.

She looked at the one who had offered her money and tried to picture doing the thing with him that, seconds ago, she thought she could do. He was gulping down his drink, his lips glistening like slugs. The smallest muscles in her body vised shut.

Down the bar, a commotion flared. The bartender wanted a drunken patron to leave, and security was ambling forward with the intention to eject. The pushing of the crowd unhooked a display, and helmets came tumbling down like pots and pans. People scattered with hands over heads. Polly was about to take this chance to run, when she saw that it was Baird who was causing the problem.

He was draped over the counter, his right cheek pressed in a puddle. From this vantage point he saw Polly. At first he did not appear to know her. Then the fog of liquor cleared. He saw the men beside her and the look on her face, and some kind of calculus clicked in his head.

He sat up and said, "You two, leave her alone."

Throughout the hubbub, the men had stayed by the bar, ignoring the splattering of citizens around them. Now the first man looked at Baird.

"You're not talking to me," he said, a statement.

"Stop bothering my employee."

The friend looked confused. "We didn't know she worked for you."

Baird squinted, like he was examining a fissure in a table leg. Then, without warning, he lunged forward, grabbed a bottle from the bar as he traveled, and cracked it over the big man's head.

People screamed as alcohol and slivers of glass sprayed everywhere. The two men vanished. Baird was clinging to the inside edge of the bar while a bouncer tried to detach him.

"He's had too much!" a patron cheered.

For such a thin man, Baird was solid around the middle. Hard as the bouncer pulled, Baird looked unconcerned. When the bouncer slapped him across the face, Polly shouted, "He's an old man!" though Baird was gazing up with delight.

"You know him?" the bouncer said. "Get

him out of here before I beat him to a pulp."

Polly shoved into the crowd, dragging Baird with her. Warm blood was leaking from somewhere on his face onto her arm. The crowd was returning to the bar, dragging her back like an undertow, and she gripped the walls to propel them forward.

The bouncer in the vestibule was staring at a corner of the ceiling with her hands clasped over her knee. She looked upon Polly and Baird woefully as they tumbled into her space.

"Wait outside. I'll get you a car," she said.

Down the stoop they went, to the black silence of the street. Baird collapsed gracefully onto the curb and she dropped beside him. The door completely muzzled what was inside, but the bawling from the bar still rang inside her ears. It was minutes before she could hear the still of the night.

She couldn't have been in there more than a half hour, but her nerves were singed. When she thought about what she'd almost done, she felt like she'd swallowed a bag of marbles.

"I'm not a bad man, Nader."

She was startled by his voice and its softness. His face was blotted out by the shadows of the street.

"Of course not," she said.

"But I always put myself first. Forgive me, Nader."

Slowly, oxygen eased back into her lungs.

"You rescued me tonight," she said.

To her surprise, he gently took her arm.

"It was my fault Leonard got sick. I used to make him go out, to get groceries and things. I've always been afraid of germs."

In the end she could never resist being nice to him. It was his piteousness and his bluster, as if he were a swaggering toddler.

"I'm sure you made the best choice you could."

Out of nowhere, like a creature from the deep, headlights flickered and a car pulled up.

"I'm very sorry. I really am."

"Where to?" the driver asked.

Polly helped Baird into the car and shut the door. Baird stuck his hand through the open window.

"Good-bye Polly Nader," he cried to her, on the sidewalk.

"I'll see you tomorrow."

But he repeated his farewell, his earnestness unsettling. The taxi moved away with his hand still wagging out the window, clutching sightlessly for hers. Two high-heeled American women pushed past her on their way to the bar.

Night clouds hung in the sky like phantoms. When she turned the corner and the front doors of Moody Plaza came into view, she almost cried with relief.

It was then that she realized, with abrupt clarity, that this, here, now — this was her life. Home was no longer at Donna's, the little pink house in Riverside. Home was her room on the fourth floor, by the ferry terminal, where the boats blew their horns. Pain stalled her. She went stock-still, as if by stopping all activity, she might yet be able to reverse to just a few moments earlier, when Frank was still her most true life.

She tugged on the glass double doors. They were locked.

She knocked lightly, hoping someone who wasn't Norberto would hear and let her in without making a report. But Norberto's face appeared behind the glass, big and pale like the moon.

"Do you have to charge me for after-hours entry?" she said.

"I'm sorry," he said.

It took him ages to fill out the paperwork, and when he was finished, he did it all over again so she had a copy, even though she insisted there was no need.

"Trust me, you want a copy of everything.

You know I don't believe in all of this."

"Sorry?"

"I don't think these regulations are fair. Are you kidding? I do what I can to combat the basic injustices, prevent undue distress, but there are major limitations on what I can do. I can't lose this job. I've almost saved enough for my next venture. It's a daily struggle to balance my own interests with the guys who are higher up the ladder and the guys who are lower down."

When he finally unlocked the stairwell for her, she was so tired, she could hardly stand.

"Tomorrow is another day," he said.

"GOOD MORNING! IT IS 0645 HOURS AND TODAY IS FRIDAY, DECEMBER 4, 1998! THE TEMPERATURE IS 69 AND RISING, SO GET OUT YOUR SUN HATS AND SANDALS! THE ASSIGNMENT FOR POLLY NADER TODAY IS: REPORT TO HENRY BAIRD AT HOTEL GALVEZ. YOUR SCHEDULE IS: AT 0730 HOURS, PROCEED TO THE LOBBY FOR PICKUP."

Baird didn't come to work. Even by lunchtime he hadn't arrived. She wondered if he hadn't made it home. But, returning from the rocks after lunch, she saw his outline faintly in their window.

She got in line to have the gate guard

check her ID against his list.

"Okay. Okay. Okay." His voice droned as, one by one, he let the workers in. He took her ID. "Hang on," he said. "It says that I have to call."

"What? Who?"

"Wait over there." He pointed to the shred of shade by the side of the guardhouse. "Quédate."

You let me in every day, she wanted to say. As the line of workers coming back from lunch trickled away, she kept waiting to see Baird in the window again so she could wave to him. He could come down and vouch for her.

Then Cassie came out. Long, clean strides from the main building. When she was steps away, she removed a pink slip of paper from her clipboard and held it flapping in her hand as she advanced.

Memorandum
Re: Polly Nader, Termination

Polly Nader has been dismissed on account of charges of grand theft. Supervisor Henry Baird reports the party removed and concealed a high-value artifact from the workplace with the intention of sale. On account of this flagrant violation which

242

contravenes the TimeRaiser code of eth-
ics, the committee has ruled that the party
no longer be employed at O-1 visa status.
The party is downgraded to H-1 status ef-
fective immediately and must report to
new lodgings at earliest ability.

"This is not true." Polly's voice shook.

"We found the yearbook in your workshop.
You didn't remove it from the management
office?"

"No. Yes. But Mr. Baird asked me to."

"Was it his idea to go to the Strand to sell
it?"

"I didn't do that."

"You didn't go to the Strand?"

Polly paused for a second. "No," she lied.

"We have a photo of you there last night,
entering alone. Security camera." Cassie
pulled a black-and-white printout of a
photo from her clipboard. A dark smudge
loomed in the foreground. It took a moment for Polly to decipher it as the bouncer.
After that, she was able to make out the
entryway to the vestibule, and her own
body, distorted in the middle, where the
printer had tripped and imprinted her legs
to the side of her torso instead of under it.

"This isn't what happened. Baird told me
to go to the Strand."

243

"A moment ago you said you weren't there at all."

Polly looked up at the window. No one was there. Her arteries were filling with cold water. "Oh my God," she said. "He set me up."

Cassie's eyes knife-flicked from the clipboard to Polly.

"You could contest this." For the first time, Cassie sought eye contact. "To speak candidly, there have been prior concerns with Mr. Baird's performance. If you have information, it would not fall on deaf ears."

Polly leaned against the guardhouse, her legs no longer trustworthy.

"But we'd have to formally charge you and let the courts decide who is right," Cassie continued. "You'd have to be shifted to a detention center to await trial."

"How long would that take?"

"I'm not an expert. Not too long. Months, not years."

"And if I'm found not guilty, can I leave?"

"Of course. After you complete your bond commitment to TimeRaiser."

An earlier version of herself might have revolted. Kicked in the gate. Ran up the stairs, three at a time. Grabbed Baird by the collar, by the hair, and screamed and screamed until he told the truth. But all

244

roads, except obedience, led to prison. She knew how they treated their workers, those who lived in the containers, people who were free. How did they treat the prisoners?

Polly pressed the heels of her hands to her eye sockets, making ghost lights reel in the dark. She put down her hands. Everything was the same: the guard's empty face, Cassie's white shirt, the sea. She had lost the luxury of rage.

"Never mind," Polly said. "It was my fault."

Frank takes two days off work to help Polly move to Massachusetts. He was the one who found the college program for furniture repair and restoration in Worcester. She devised so many reasons why she couldn't go: it was six hours away; she'd just got a raise; Donna; Frank. But then she applied without mentioning it, always one to keep doors open, and when she revealed she'd been selected, he had to quickly reconstruct his dismay into pride.

They play with the car stereo, they eat Kit Kats, they listen to the final Agatha Christie on tape, and the reality of just how far six hours is sets in. They unload her boxes into her one-room rental, and she goes to get meatball sandwiches for dinner. He offers to go instead, but she says, "I have to get used to doing things on my own."

It takes the cook an age to make the sandwiches. The knives are stored at the opposite end of the counter from the bread, the cheese is in the back, he's run out of foil. All the while, the last night of their way of life drips away. She's gone forty minutes. But when she returns, Frank's made a bed out of sofa cushions and pillows and a woolly sweater. He's combed the unkempt front lawn for wildflowers, and he's arrayed honeysuckle, foxglove, and Queen Anne's lace in soda cans, coffee mugs, and a roll of toilet paper. He is sitting on the floor, at a dining table constructed from cardboard boxes.

"You romantic fool," she says, and kneels to tuck a dandelion behind his ear.

He doesn't say anything. He catches her hand on its way down and presses his lips into the bowl of her palm. He doesn't take his eyes off her.

"What?" she says. She feels nervous. She doesn't know what to do with intensity. "What are you looking at?"

"I couldn't stare at you before you were mine."

"Did you want to?" She plays along, but like it's a joke.

"My heart would start to race at five p.m. if I thought you might be coming by. I wanted to stare into these brown eyes all day. These cherry cheeks. Those other cheeks."

She giggles, looks away.

"Stay here with me," he says.

She looks back, and she is caught. By his eyelashes, and his beautiful mouth.

"How lucky we are to be able to look," she says.

"I've never fully exploited this advantage."

He hooks his fingers in her pockets and he slides her across the floor, into his orbit. Their movements are deliberate, languid, as if they have an embarrassment of time. He unzips her jacket, each pair of teeth parting one at a time. She counts the hairs on his belly, the ones that meet to make a trail, and she follows them down, down. They rock together, as slow as they can bear. The sofa cushions come apart and they lie in the dip.

He asks her what she would like to eat on their wedding day.

Others would shout, Are you asking me to marry you? and squeal and call their mothers, all reasonable replies. Polly says, Meatball sandwiches. She looks at him through half lids, sly.

What else?

Stuffed peppers.

Cheese balls.

Really? Cheese balls?

Cheese balls. What about dessert?

Lemon cake.

Sounds perfect.

She will borrow Carlo, so Donna doesn't stand alone. They will have to let Johnny play guitar at the reception, there's no way around it. Their guests will blow bubbles instead of throwing rice, rice is bad for birds. They will put wildflowers on every table, but instead of toilet rolls they'll splurge on vases. They will have something of her mother's there — her bicycle or her rocking chair. They will have a September wedding, so their anniversary doesn't change. They will have a baby, a girl with chunky legs and curly hair, and then one more: it's a package deal, if you have one, you have to have another. They will live in a house with yellow walls and wooden floors and light.

In another universe, this timeline becomes actual. In their universe, the vial breaks, the virus spreads, the borders are closed. Frank gets sick. At first he says it's just allergies, This Texas pollen is savage. He'll sequester himself in the other room, just so he doesn't disturb her sleep. But in only twelve hours his skin is a different color and his strong shoulders look to have shrunk. She must be imagining this. Every time there is a lull between coughs, she thinks, Please let this last. And then the rasping starts again, each heave like a lash to the face. He won't let her touch him. They airdropped flyers with instructions on how to make a virus-containment gown and mask from household materials; she saved one. She makes these clothes for both of them. They look absurd; she wants to be able to joke, but she can't. They'll laugh at us when we get to the clinic, it's only allergies. There are multiple rings of fencing around the clinic, an inner circle and an outer circle, and an armed guard instructs her to wait between the fences, saying, If he's negative, he'll come back, if he's positive, an orderly will further advise you. There is another person waiting in this no-man's-land: a white-haired woman called Nina. Nina says, I think your fella looked okay, I think it will be okay. A white-haired man comes out of the clinic and Nina says, George, thank God. But an orderly comes for Polly. She starts to cry. Nina takes her arm and says, It's okay dear, a cure is around the corner. But the orderly rushes to separate them, because Polly has been exposed. There are hours of tests before Polly is declared negative. The nurse in turquoise tells her about TimeRaiser. When Polly finally gets to see

Frank, his eyes are yellow and she can no longer deny that he is smaller, his skeleton reversing, towards birth, to a world without him. Outside, she takes two days to make the choice to travel. Inside, immediately, she knows. The meatball sandwiches, the bubbles on the wind, her baby's thighs. All that love. It can't die. It has to go somewhere. Their future will be unthinkably different from what they imagined, and in other ways it will be exactly the same: she will give her life to him.

In the blue light of the evening, between the cushions on the floor, Polly and Frank fall asleep.

Because Polly was new, she had to take the top bunk. It was days before she could sleep with that sheet of steel ceiling a foot from her face. She slept with her head under a pillow, in case of cockroaches. With the night chill there were hardly any, but the threat of feelers in the mouth was enough.

Container 4A1 slept twenty: five bunks on either side, head to foot. Never was there a time when you didn't hear speaking or breathing or spitting. The closest to privacy you could get was to stare at the wall. Once, they had put up sheets between the bunk beds, like cubicle partitions. Everyone liked this and some even gave up a blanket to make their wall. But one day they came back from work and the sheets had been removed. A notice was left, saying that items hung from the ceiling were considered a fire hazard.

Everyone kept their few clothes and bedding and toothbrushes in bags tied to the bed railing, but bag straps snapped and dumped their contents. Things carefully collected went missing right away. No one could keep order. You couldn't move without brushing wet plastic or cardboard. The air had a mealy smell, like metal and raw meat. Strange hair was in your mouth. They were haggard from the effort of peaceful endurance.

Most people would have been able to manage a day, two days, in the containers; someone stoic, like Donna, would have done fine with a week. It was not the conditions but days of conditions, tied together. Like the threads of a rope rubbing the same ring of skin again and again, until all seven layers are gone.

Container 4A1 was closest to the highway, no protection from the elements and the lookie-loos. Deeper into the compound, better conditions could be found. Some sold months or years to TimeRaiser to live better. No containers had plumbing, but some had electricity — lights and radios to cut the time. You could pay for any number of upgrades. Electricity, longer water hours, bedding, space heaters. A long, thick trench between the regular containers and the electrified containers prohibited freeloaders on the edge of light or music.

Twelve minutes' walk away, in an abandoned brewery part-condemned for asbestos, damp like a hole in the ground, crisscrossed by fallen catwalks and tumbled titanic piping, women made tiles for the bottoms of swimming pools, for decorative sidewalks, for bathroom floors in beautiful places in other worlds. Most of the workers made new tiles, working together at long tables in what used to be a brewhouse, each section completing a different part of the tile's cycle: mixing, glazing, cutting. When they realized Polly didn't speak Spanish and couldn't keep up with the calls, they assigned her to the bespoke line. She worked alone in what used to be a freezer — a windowless, timeless box — cutting old plates into minuscule tiles. Floral plates, glass plates, blue-and-white plates, souvenir plates. The line's first client was Gulf Pearl Vacation Homes, who wanted a bohemian flower-power touch for their new phase of chalets.

On her first day, she had to buy sixty dollars' worth of tools — a pair of nippers and a pair of callipers — so she could cut the tiles to their perfect size: round, square, rectangle, irregular. The big tiles were fine, but the mini ones, sometimes a quarter inch in diameter, could drive her to despair. Even the foreman, who hardly ever came by, once paused to watch her struggle with the intricate pieces. "Customers assume we have a machine do this," he said. After the tiles were cut, she sorted them by shape, color, and size into bins, like filling a drum a drop at a time.

She would rather have worked the lowest jobs. She would have rather harvested swamp cabbage, wading out in coagulated waters as snakes writhed around her knees, knowing that, if the stagnant, bubbled surface was burst by the head of a gator, she wouldn't make it back. Up north, they bought the greens in capsules, two dollars a pill, as an immune-system booster.

She would rather have shucked oysters and come home with bloody hands, stinking of the rotting sea. Polly would rather have done anything than spend every day as she did, alone in the tile-cutting box, in the unsafe place of her mind. A tangle of hotspots and land mines wreathed around the thought of what to do beyond the end of her bond: a yawning steppe of life, to be filled alone.

The only salve was if she could get into a rhythm. Grab the edge of the plate on *DON'T,* clamp the nippers on *THINK,* cut on

AB-B-OU-OU-UT, toss the tile on *IT.* Four hundred of these made up one hour. It was a blessing she had no more Sundays. There were no limits on how many days the H-1s were assigned to work.

The women said to each other, "Don't worry: only a few more weeks and it'll be April." Or "We could be in Missouri." The cold was enduring. It got into their beds. At the showers, naked and wet in the February dark, they felt like only bones, with no more flesh. But the cold was not the true problem with the shower pit. The problem was that Polly had seen the pit from the outside.

She could think of nothing worse than Misty or Sandy catching her inside the pit, their faces gazing down, their lips mouthing, *What a shame.* She would've showered in the dark, but the water barrels were only filled twice a day, and once the water was gone, the only option was to sleep covered in the glue of your own juices — which is what Polly did, until her skin started to burn and itch. So she bathed as fast as she could, sickening tremors running up the inside of her rib cage, like she was robbing a house, ready to bolt. Sometimes the bus came. She'd run, without rinsing, the soap dribbling down her hairline and into her eyes. She'd wait by the ladder to her bunk bed until the bus was gone. She would've waited on her bed, but then she'd get the sheets all tacky, and laundry was high-priced.

One evening this happened and, while she waited inside, her eyes crying from the soap, she had an epiphany. All the times she had seen the women in the pit from the shuttle, she had thought, Those poor things, and partly what she was thinking was, Thank God that couldn't happen to me. But meanwhile all the women in the pit were thinking, How could this have happened to me? This was very funny, this gash between the expected and the actual, and she started to laugh. The women lying nearby tried not to stare.

By the time Polly got back to the pit, the water drum was empty. She dabbed the inside with her towel, but there was not enough wet to wipe the burning off her skin.

"Take this," someone said. "Please."

A woman who slept in 4A1 stood over her, holding out a bottle of water.

"I always fill a bottle before bed. Take it."

Polly poured out a drop, not wanting to take more than the woman planned to give.

"You can have it all. No hay problema," the woman said.

When Polly went in, the woman was waiting at her bed.

"Do you want to look at my book?" The woman held out an exercise book. "I collect inspirational sayings."

Polly had to turn the pages of the yellowed exercise book gingerly so as not to detach them. Each saying had its own page, with illustrations. *Life has many chapters for us; one bad chapter doesn't mean it's the end of the book.* Rain clouds and rainbows drawn beside *Life isn't about waiting for the storm to pass, it's about dancing in the rain.*

"Very nice," Polly said. The woman looked Chinese. She was under five feet tall, with wide-set eyes and a wrinkly neck.

"How about this one? It's good if you're a new arrival." She opened the book to *Every end is a new beginning.* "If you have a favorite one, you can write it down." She held out a pencil.

"No, thank you."

"Go on, take it."

"No!" Polly shouted. She hated this woman. She hated her for so conscientiously collecting these sayings and printing them out in her big, stupid script, and soppily sharing them with other needy-looking people.

But the woman only shrugged.

"Too bad," she said, and went back to her bunk.

Polly's bunkmate who had, till then, always been pleasant said, "Stuck-up brat."

Polly climbed into her bed. She was shaking. I'm not stuck-up. If you had gone through what I've gone through, you'd act the same way.

But her neighbor had likely gone through everything Polly had, and worse. Yet now Polly could hear her sleeping, her breathing even and sure.

Polly was not sure of anything. It'd taken only months to break the unit that she and Frank made. It was this fact — not the time machine, nor captives that lived in shipping containers — that called into question every other fact of her life. How love could neatly and unremarkably stop; that was more impossible and terrible than traveling through all of time.

Sometimes in the mornings, when she was trying to leave for work, if she sat on the bed to put on her socks, Frank would crawl up behind her and wrap his arms around her waist. "I'm a deadweight," he would say. "I'm a barnacle and I won't let go."

To get to work, Polly walked twelve minutes from the container field to the brewery, from Forty-First Street to Thirty-Third Street, along the parched tongue that was

Church Street. After sundown, she could see the glow of the resorts on the horizon, on the other side of the miles-long midden of broken doors and dirt. She was at the bottom of a moat of darkness, circling a castle of light.

They got their three daily meals at work. They got beans, pickled vegetables, usually cabbage, and every now and again a piece of dried fish, so salty it stung your tongue. "It's only temporary," they all said to each other. Sometimes the women brought in vegetables to share. Someone lived near a squash patch or some cucumber plants. The day after her tantrum, a bag of carrots was circulated. They took one each, marveling at their barky sweetness. Polly saved hers to give to the woman with the sayings, wrapping it in an old cloth before she put it in her pocket.

Once a week they cleaned the showers, using thick-bristled brushes to drive soap scum and hair out and under the walls. When Polly saw the woman with the sayings heading to the showers with a bucket of brushes, she turned to her bunkmate.

"Diana, are you on shower duty this week?"

"Mm-hmm."

"I'll do it for you."

Diana had already donned the communal galoshes. She looked at Polly suspiciously. She shrugged.

"Your choice," she said, and removed the boots.

"Hello," the woman said when Polly entered the pit.

Polly handed her the carrot.

"What's that for?" the woman said, and dropped it in her pocket. "I'm Cookie."

"Polly."

"Mucho gusto. What do you do?"

"Tile factory. You?"

"Just got promoted to topiary. I'm learning the standard shapes: spiral, poodle, double spiral, Michelangelo. When did you arrive?" Cookie turned on the hose and water glugged across the pit.

"Last September. You?" Polly asked.

"October '97."

"Is your bond up soon?"

"Almost halfway. Twenty-four more months. How much longer you got?"

"When I started in September, it was thirty-two months, because I had a good job. But I made a mistake and got demoted. They restarted my bond at forty-four months." She said this quick, like trying to swallow something without tasting it. "I'm going backwards in time."

261

"That's too bad." Cookie handed her a broom. "What year did you leave?"

"1981."

" '81! Never met someone from so early. You must be real adventurous."

"Maybe just dumb."

"Nah. Where you from?"

"Buffalo."

"Buffalo. That's a ways from Mexico."

"Yes, it is," Polly said, confused. "Are you from Mexico?"

"No. I'm from 1985 Oklahoma. Before, Vietnam."

They started their scrubbing. Old soap squatting in the pores of the pavement foamed in gray clods.

"Why did you mention Mexico?" Polly asked.

"I thought you were from Mexico. You're not from Mexico?"

"No."

"Guatemala?"

"Buffalo. You're not from Mexico? You speak Spanish."

"Well, I pick up words here and there from the other girls. You ain't Hispanic?"

"No. I look Hispanic?"

"People might think so."

"I'm not."

"What are you?"

"Caucasian."

"Only Caucasian?"

"My father was Lebanese, but I didn't know him, and nobody ever said I looked anything but Caucasian. I don't know why everyone here speaks Spanish to me."

"Everyone? Like other Hispanic people?"

"I don't know." She thought of the women she worked with in the tile factory, and of Norberto. "No. Other Caucasians."

Cookie laughed. "It's because you're a laborer." She had reached the edge of the pit. She leaned against her broom. "What did you do before? Before you traveled."

"I was an upholsterer."

"What's that?"

"I fixed furniture."

"Oh yeah? Can you make furniture?"

"Sort of. Mostly I make old furniture new again."

"Is that high-end work? You made a good living?"

"I was just starting out, but people can do okay."

"So you looked white until you went broke. That's funny."

"I don't think that's right," Polly said. "It might be because I have a tan."

Cookie nodded knowingly. A thick gold chain, like the kind Carlo wore, had been

263

knocked outside her collar by the vigor of her scrubbing. She noticed it there and tucked it quickly back under her coveralls.

"My son's," she said, patting the chain beneath her collar. "We arrived from 1985 together, but right away he was taken to work construction in the Gulf. I got transferred down here to be close to him, but I can't find him. Though maybe he's not here. Could be in Corpus Christi." She rubbed the underside of her chin. "Everyone has a story like this," she said, as if to anticipate dismissal.

"You don't have any leads on where he could be?"

Cookie shook her head. "Where to even look?"

"Did you try the Demographics Center?"

"What's that?"

Polly straightened in surprise. She had knowledge to offer someone else.

"You'll have to go into debt. It'll extend your bond," she said, one to give bad news first.

Cookie shrugged. "Lay it on me."

Polly explained how the center worked.

"But this is amazing," Cookie said.

She explained when it was open and how Cookie would have to bargain for time to go.

"Amazing . . . amazing!" Cookie said.

"It's no big deal," Polly said.

She drew Cookie a map on the back of a piece of paper taken from her book of sayings, so that she wouldn't get lost.

"Simply amazing," she said, and Polly felt uneasy. What kind of disappointment was she setting this woman up for?

"They might find nothing. They found nothing for me."

Then she wished she hadn't said this. She sounded like Sandy. She didn't want to be old and craggy.

But Cookie's delight was resilient.

"You have to find a good attitude. Look and hope that your missing person comes back, but your life cannot be based on that. Make friends. Make plans. Move on. If you pause your life until your missing person shows up, you will never be happy."

"You're not going to go to the Demographics Center?" Polly was disappointed. Her offering was no good.

"Of course I'll go!"

The next week Polly was walking the final stretch of Church Street, when she saw a clutch of women gathered around Cookie in a slip of sunshine beside 4A1. One by one, each of the women handled the receipt the Demographics Center had issued Cookie. They chattered in Spanish and Vietnamese, but Polly caught some English.

"Just a few weeks and they can tell you where he is?"

"So fast!"

"But it cost you two months."

"If we start a cundina, I can do a search."

"There she is!" Cookie cried. "The one who showed me!"

"Ahhh," the women said all together, and when she reached them, they started to clap.

Polly giggled, terrified. The air was infused with unhedged expectations. They looked at her, maybe waiting for her to say something, and she did not want the first words out of her mouth to be negative, but the temptation to pad them in case of a fall was excruciating.

"Look at your face!" Cookie shouted. "She's worried we'll be disappointed. Shoot for the moon! Even if you miss, you'll land among the stars."

They laughed and squeezed her into the circle and patted her shoulders. They handed her the receipt so she could look too, and by the light of their excitement it did seem like a harbinger of possibility.

How nice it was to be in that circle of warm bodies, released from the misery of possessing only solo concerns, like a din you hear only when it stops. A narrow world opened.

"Who's that?" Cookie said.

A man was by the container door, twisting his baseball hat in his hands.

"It's Norberto," Polly said, even though she couldn't quite believe it.

"Hello," Norberto said. "How are you? Can we talk?"

"I'm so happy to see you," Polly said, surprised by how true this was, and by the warm feeling she got from seeing his familiar, nervous face.

"Can we go somewhere?" he asked as the other women eyed him.

She took him away from 4A1, under a tree, by the trench. He put his hat back on his head and scratched his forehead under the brim, so that his hat sat uneasily on his crown.

"I have an idea that I think could be good for both of us," he said. "I have a proposition. I live on the Bolivar Peninsula."

Her warm feeling gave way to nerves.

He didn't say any more after that. He watched a big blackbird on a close-by branch make noises like a small machine starting up.

"What's your proposition?" she said eventually.

"I thought you could come and live with me."

"Me?"

"I thought it would be more comfortable for you."

Now, when Polly was scared, she no longer lashed out. She shrank behind a shell of politeness. "That's very nice of you."

"It's not charity. I would get your rent instead of it going to TimeRaiser. It's like billeting."

She wanted to know what the catch was, but she was afraid to ask outright.

"What about my job? Would I work for you?"

"No, you would keep your job here. You'd just live at my house."

He hardly made eye contact, but she couldn't remember if that was irregular. The bird carried on its engine sounds.

"Is that a no?" Norberto said.

"I should think about it."

"I thought you would say yes right away. You would have your own room. Isn't that better than this?"

"I need to think about it. But it's nice to see you." Though, this was no longer true, because he had become unfamiliar all over again. "How is Moody?" she asked.

"Good. More tenants now. More work."

"That's too bad."

"No, it keeps me busy. You're all right?"

"Yeah. People are nice."

She took a few steps back towards the crowd, as a way to end the conversation.

"There's something else. Let me tell you the truth."

He beckoned her to come back, as if what he had to say was confidential.

"I need your help," he said. He looked around. "Come behind this tree."

"What for?"

"I just have a question."

She shook her head. In her memory, he was her height, shrunken by his halting manner. But in real life he was at least a half foot taller. She stayed where she was.

He was undeterred. He improvised. He stepped close and whispered, "There is something called a family credit, okay? If I had a baby, I'd get a big bonus. Like a monthly increase. There are bonuses for re-population if you're American."

All she did was press her tongue to the floor of her mouth and take a breath.

But he saw it and said quickly, "You don't have to have sex with me. It's not like that."

"What is it like?"

269

"We just have to pretend like we're having a family."

"Pretend?"

"It wouldn't be that hard. We like each other enough, don't we?"

That uncanny laughter from the week before came out of her again, but he kept talking.

"And you don't really have to be pregnant. To prove you're pregnant, you only have to give them a urine sample. I can get some urine. From a pregnant lady."

"You're crazy. That would never work. There'd be no baby at the end."

"It would be good for both of us. Mutually beneficial. That's why you should come live with me."

"Why are you asking me?" She wanted to upset him, to jolt him into seeing how wrong his request was. "There are hundreds of desperate women. I hear you can buy them on the Strand."

But when she succeeded — he got as far away from her as he could without moving his feet, and a wretched, cowering smile covered his face — she felt regret.

"You look like someone else," he said.

"What do you mean?"

He had the hat in his hands again, gripped so tight he might rip the seams.

"My ex, Marta. You look like her. I have lots of photos of her, and we could use them as proof of an established relationship."

"I don't know what you mean."

"Look, no one knows what my ex's name was. Nobody knows that she isn't you. They're cracking down on the repopulation program. Too many frauds. But if we get married — it's a formality, it doesn't have to mean anything — and if we have old photos on top of that, plus the urine, we'll be a shoo-in.

"Think about it. When they come to verify our pregnancy, we show them the photos, say that it's you and me in the photos, instead of me and her, and you and I knew each other before, and then we got separated, and then by chance you moved into my building, and then we got married. Destiny. It's a romantic story. It will go great."

"You've already worked it all out."

She moved back, but he matched her steps. His whispering entered frenzy.

"If I can get the bonuses, plus your rent, I could get together a down payment to buy a storefront. A lot of the Journeymen, when they finish their bonds, they stay here and keep working. They need somewhere to shop. You know, to buy housewares, clothes.

271

The PXes ain't gonna cut it. I've been collecting stock for years. I'm going to open Galveston's first Kmart."

Polly walked away.

"Wait," Norberto said. "I could give you some of the profits. We could live separate lives. We don't even have to sleep in the same room. We could be like roommates."

"When were you going to tell me your real plan? After I had nowhere to go?"

"That was wrong of me. I apologize. But I didn't do that. I told you the truth first — now."

"I thought you cared about trying to achieve your interests without taking advantage of the guy lower down the ladder."

He pepped right up. "I do! That's why this is the perfect plan. It doesn't rock any boats, it's good for me, and it's good for you. You could have a room! With a door!"

All along such a bashful guy and you turn out to be a crackpot. But Polly didn't say this out loud. She just went back to the crowd.

"You're looking for someone," Norberto called after her. "When you arrived, you were trying to find someone. If you help me, I'll help you find him. Tell me his name!"

"I'm not looking anymore," she called back.

■ ■ ■ ■

At the showers, Cookie let Polly cut in line.

"What was that? What did he want?" Cookie said, pushing Polly ahead of her.

"He wants me to move into his house."

Behind Cookie, one of the women from the circle shook her head and clucked, like she was part of the conversation.

"He's your boyfriend?"

"No."

More clucking.

"This is Mary," Cookie said. Mary was a forty-something black woman with a concave face like a crescent moon.

"Why does he want you to move in with him?"

"Some kind of scam."

"Don't do it. You must be independent. From men."

"I wasn't going to."

"Hey," Cookie said. "Sleep with one eye open."

"Okay." Polly had no idea what she was talking about.

But it became clear, a few days later, when Cookie shone a flashlight in her face before sunup.

273

"Wake up," Cookie whispered. "Come on."

"What time is it?" The dark looked darker than it usually did at rising time.

Cookie put her hand over Polly's mouth. "Come with me."

There were four of them gathered outside the door to 4A1: Cookie and Mary, and another two women Polly didn't know.

"I can't go with you," Polly said. "I have to go to work, and I can't get fired again."

"Shhhh. It's five a.m. What time you gotta be at work?"

"Seven thirty."

"We got lots of time. We're just going for a quick walk."

"But where are we going?"

"Just come."

They crossed Church Street and left the lip of Polly's twelve-minute world. They walked south in single file. Soon they were in the unsettled city, the torrent of jungle and broken buildings that had taken most of the island. Polly followed the bobbing lights of the other women's flashlights.

At first she was on edge, but Cookie kept turning around to beam at her, and a stillness came over Polly. She was briefly stepping outside of the monotony of her everyday, and some point in her past life when

274

she had taken moonlight walks was converging with some point in her future life when her time would be her own.

For the first five minutes they followed a lane of caramel-colored, churned-up land that looked as if it had been formed by a meteor skidding to a stop. Then the terrain changed and they were crossing old, mutilated concrete. They stopped to squeeze their dynamo flashlights. The flashlights were always the first things to go missing from the emergency kits in every container.

"This was Broadway. This used to be the main thoroughfare," Mary said. "That was a cemetery ahead of us."

Polly couldn't see anything beyond a combine in the middle of the street. It had crashed into a palm tree which, in the years since, had calmly grown around it. Everywhere, roots had plowed up the concrete in huge shanks, shoved wherever the plants decided. You could not see more than ten feet ahead. They passed what looked like the remains of a crash-landed spaceship.

"The old Chevron station," Mary explained.

They turned off what had been Broadway. The pathway narrowed until bushes grew around and over their heads, entirely blocking out the sky. The only sound was the intermittent *click-click-click* of someone shaking a flashlight. Rats darted, streaks of squeaking gray between their feet. Polly kept her shoulders to her ears, afraid that poisonous things above might drop down her collar. Lengths of the trail were submerged in reeking water, with only thin margins for passing over without getting wet. Polly's hands were sticky from clinging to the sappy branches.

Polly imagined fantastical things at the end of the trail: an underground city run by self-subsisting runaways; a hidden port with ships going anywhere but here; a storage locker packed with all the things she missed — peanut butter, orange juice, pork chops, television. She tried to stop these wild fantasies so she would not be let down.

The leafy tunnel came to a dead end.

"Careful, careful," someone hissed, as the woman at the head of the line apprehensively parted the branches. They stepped through the hole, letting go of the boughs delicately once everyone was through.

They were in a clearing, one formed so sharply that a straight wall of broken foliage and debris rose on the left. To the right, there were the remains of once-splendid houses. And overhead, like giants, live oaks stretched their arms to make a total canopy.

The porch roof on the first house was propped up by a piece of plywood leaned against the facade, only held in place by gravity, which seemed an oversight. The next two buildings had no roofs. The fourth's porch was missing, and in its place an interior staircase led to the door. They trooped down the sidewalk, a springy pavement of cardboard and tin. Number five had once been a fourplex, until the roof descended and made it a bungalow.

Cookie turned to Polly and put her finger to her lips.

"Don't wake them," she said, and Polly realized that people lived here.

A drying mop hung from the sill of one window, and at another someone was using a Bob Marley blanket as a curtain. There were three more houses before the clearing stopped, but all were uninhabitable in their own different way: a slumping roof, a missing exterior wall, lichen covering one whole side of a house, like a skin disease.

"We can look in the window of number five. They just finished it, no one is living there yet."

They shone their flashlights through the windows. Corridors extended on either side of a central stairway. The whole floor was dotted with posts — PVC pipe, rods of rebar somehow bound together, a thick, sturdy branch — to stop the ceiling from coming down. There were no doors: the doorways canted too much to accommodate them. They could see into a front bedroom. It had a wardrobe covered in plastic sheeting and nice things to cover the walls: strips of floral wallpaper bleached clean, an old bedsheet hung like a tapestry, torn-out pages of magazines from the '70s.

Cookie spoke as if the place were a mansion.

"You should have seen what it looked like before. It's amazing."

She swept her flashlight over the front yards. The squatters had vegetable gardens, lumpy gourds springing from a mini pergola of chair legs lashed together. Maybe this was where the squash at work came from.

Cookie beckoned them on to number six, whose door was swollen shut. Part of the roof was missing, giving the house a lopsided, crazy look. It was light enough now that they could shut off their flashlights. They stood in front of the living room window and looked in. Scabs of paint peeled off the walls. Dust lay on the floor in sheets, like loose leaves torn from a book. An armchair looked eaten through with acid. But the ceiling was still elevated and one window even had glass. Streaks of dawn came dappling through the hole in the roof.

"Furniture breeds mold, and, man, is it a pain to get it out the door. You can't pick it up without it collapsing in your hands. But I think we can do it if we put our minds to it," Cookie said. "What do you think? You want to move in? My friend founded this compound. She says we can have this if we want it."

"Why do people live here?" Polly asked. "Is it free?"

"No. You still pay rent to TimeRaiser. Can't get out of that."

"But why? This is TimeRaiser housing?"

"If we want to stop paying rent, we have to officially inform TimeRaiser. Then Time-Raiser would raze this place. You pay rent like protection money. This way, TimeRaiser leaves us be."

"So why live here?"

"Isn't it obvious?" said Mary. "Autonomy!"

"Imagine. You could have your own space," Cookie said. "They use rain barrels to collect water, so you could shower whenever you wanted. You could go to sleep when you wanted. You could cook!"

"Why did you invite me?" Polly said.

"You know things. Like the Demographics Center. You can make furniture."

She'd been no one because nobody knew her, but they had given her a new identity, and her cheeks tightened with the urge to cry. She looked up at the Spanish moss, drifting from the boughs like beautiful blue ghosts.

"So what do you think? Are we in or are we out?"

"In," Mary said.

"In," said the other two.

They all looked at Polly.

"Moving in here is no big deal," Cookie said. "After what we survived?"

Polly looked into the house. Off the living room, a doorway led into another room they could not see. Maybe a kitchen, maybe a bedroom. Polly imagined sitting in that room and hearing the birds and the ladies whistling outside. She imagined looking out the windows of the house. What would it be like to look out a window and not hope to see Frank? What would it be like to look out a window and not even have him cross her mind?

"Let's do it," Polly said.

"Really and truly?" Cookie grabbed Polly's hands. "You won't regret this!"

Cookie should have used another word. Instantly, Polly was made only of regret and fear. She couldn't live out here. What if he couldn't find her?

Back into the tunnel of brush they went. She mirrored their movements. When they scaled root bulges, like stepping-stones across the bog, she followed them up. When they yawed hard to the left to make way for a low-passing bat, she rolled with them. They packed the mud down with their feet and she used the pathways they had made. She could not back out now. They had taken her as their own.

On Broadway, the sky was lightening in preparation for the sun. If she waited for him and he let her down, she would not survive it. Who would not choose to preempt such pain?

The other women sang softly as they walked, and by the time they got to Forty-First, Polly lifted her voice just above audible when they sang "The Piña Colada Song."

"Today is a gift. That's why they call it the present," Cookie said as they crossed Church.

"Who said that?"

"Anon," Cookie said. "Me!"

"Who's that man?" Mary said. "Did we get caught?"

"What can they catch us for?" Cookie

281

said. "Walking?"

Even from a distance, Polly could spot Norberto's nerves from the stoop of his shoulders.

"It's Polly's stalker," Cookie said. "Let me deal with him. You go inside."

"That's not necessary," Polly said, but Cookie was already running across the dirt road, shouting at Norberto like he was vermin.

"Scoot! Get lost!"

"I only want to talk to Polly! I got some information for her!"

The women of 4A1 clustered around the doorway to watch. Cookie put two hands up as if to push Norberto. She was so short, her hands were almost overhead.

"No, it's all right." Polly stepped forward as Norberto's arms popped up like a boxer's.

"You get lost!" Cookie shouted. "Stop preying on innocent girls!"

Then Norberto did a bizarre thing. He shouted, "Frank Marino! 113 Grape Street, Buffalo, New York!"

Polly had been hanging on to Cookie's arm to keep her back from Norberto, but she let go. Cookie stumbled forward and almost fell.

"What did you say?" Polly said.

"Frank Marino, 113 Grape Street, Buffalo, New York."

Polly rushed to Norberto. He was holding a sheaf of papers in his hand. She glanced down at the papers and saw her name. She slapped him, without knowing why.

Mary grabbed her hand. "Don't! Don't!" Mary said. "If he's an American, you could be arrested."

Norberto's hat fell off, and then hastily, he sat down in the grass.

"Isn't Frank Marino the man you are looking for? I found him for you."

"Who told you his name?" Polly sat down in the grass too.

Cookie hovered. Then she turned away. She began focusing her efforts on getting the other women to go inside.

"I never told anyone his name," Polly said. "Except in the contact sheet, and you said that didn't exist. Wait. You got it from the Demographics Center search I made, didn't you?"

"It was in your file. Remember? The little piece of paper with his inquiry from '95."

Her confusion frightened her. She shouted to cover it.

"But where did you get that address? Did you make it up?"

"No. He looked for you again. He did

another inquiry, in October '97.'"

"You said there was only one search, in September '95. You're trying to trick me."

"It's not a trick. I wouldn't try to trick you. I'm not like that. See — here." He handed her the paper-clipped sheaf of forms, and pinned to the very top was a black-and-white photo of Polly, her eyes wide from the flash. It had been taken in 1981, the day she left.

"I thought if I did you a favor, you might do me one. I could show you how our interests line up. I have a corps brother who works in TimeRaiser admin. I asked him to do a search for your inquiree's name, see if an address was floating around. There were three hits. The one we knew, the 1995 search, but the fellow also looked for you in '93 and '97."

"He looked three times?"

"*Inquiry submitted. Frank Marino.* There's his address. It costs money to make an inquiry. Three, four hundred dollars. But he did it three times."

"Why wasn't this in my file? The file you had on me."

"Because nobody cared to keep track. But I did."

"When were they going to tell me?" Polly cried. "When were they going to tell me he was trying to find me?"

"I'm not positive. You probably have to ask."

"I have to ask for information I don't know exists?"

"I don't know. I don't know! But I've already helped you, see? Even if you do nothing for me, I've helped you. I got no reason to keep information from you. I'm not TimeRaiser."

Everyone had gone back inside. It was just the two of them in the grass.

"Don't crumple the pages," Norberto said. "It's TimeRaiser property and it'll look fishy if the pages are crumpled." He took the papers from her hands.

"How come you can have tenants? Cookie says we can only live in TimeRaiser housing. Are you lying?"

"I got a landlord license from TimeRaiser when they were giving them out in the early days, before they built the worker housing. I'll show it to you."

Polly thought about Cookie's book of sayings. How Polly wanted the sayings to be true; how Polly wished that letting go could be mastered within the length of a line. But the sayings were directives without instruction. They told you what to do with no information on how to do it.

285

"If you stay here, you'll be bonded till kingdom come. How many more months do you owe now than when they signed you up? It'll only get worse."

She didn't say anything. He placed the folder back in her lap. There was her own face from 1981, on the other side of time. The corners of the forms flickered in the wind. There was her name and, below it, there was Frank's.

"If I live with you, I'm not paying rent. I get to keep the rent money in my LifeFund so I can finish my bond."

"All right." Norberto exhaled like a trumpet.

"Okay," she said.

In preparation for the wedding, they went through Marta's old clothes. Polly tried on the dresses, to see if any fit, for the ceremony. The more Polly looked like Marta, the more they both could sell this.

Polly pulled on a yellow dress with bitsy purple flowers. The colors were foul. When she stepped out, Norberto handed her a brown belt.

"In the photo she wears it with this," he said.

She looked at the snapshot in his hand. Marta was leaning back from the dinner table, her head tipped to the side, smiling ferociously, as if she wanted every tooth in the photo.

"Tip your head," Norberto said.

Polly did.

"Hand on hip."

She put her hand on her hip.

"Can you smile?"

She smiled as wide as Marta.

He stood in front of her as he always did in these moments, with his palms in midair, like someone trying to straighten a picture frame.

The first time he had given this kind of instruction, her chest had closed like a fist, and she had steeled herself for the press of his hands. But he'd done nothing. He just stood there with palms out, looking at her, but not at her, the creases in his forehead getting deeper and deeper.

Sometimes he would say, "Well, what if . . . ?" and ask her to move her hair or stand in different light. But every time he would finally say, "Not quite, but good enough." Eventually, she felt disappointed too. She too wanted a kind of magic to exist, where the way someone curled their hair behind their ear could turn time, and something lost would be returned.

Norberto sat down on the bed. The clasp on Marta's suitcase had seized; they'd had to hammer it off. Now the components of Marta's life spread out like a blast radius: all shades of jeans, gardening shorts, notebooks. Absentmindedly, Norberto rubbed the vinyl of a green backpack, then pushed it away. Polly had been living with him for a month now. The wedding was the day after tomorrow.

"Was Marta Hispanic?"

"Chilean."

"Do I look Hispanic?"

"Are you?"

"No. But my father was Lebanese. People think I'm Hispanic here."

"You could be."

"People keep speaking Spanish to me." She paused. "My friend — that short lady at the containers? She says people think I'm Hispanic because of my . . . situation. When I had status, I looked white, but now I look Hispanic."

"Who said this?" Norberto frowned.

"Cookie."

"Cookie sounds racist," he said.

"I think she meant other people are racist. Americans who assume I'm . . ."

Still frowning, Norberto crossed his legs and shook his foot, coiled. Polly trailed off.

"How did you develop these photos?" she said. "Is Kodak still around?"

"There's a guy around here. It's his hobby. He scavenged the photo-development kiosks in Galveston and built himself a darkroom in his back shed."

"Why?"

"Way to pass the time. He traded photo services for food."

289

"So you can get photos developed, but you can't mail a letter?"

"Yes. Like I said already, a thousand times."

Norberto had insisted there was no postal service. He'd said that the stamp he'd sold her for her letter to Donna, the PO box, the whole thing was a scam. "Why else do you think you never got an answer?"

Polly couldn't believe this. "What kind of scam is that?" she asked. "Just to make five dollars a pop?"

"Factor in PO box rental, Journeymen sending letters everywhere, searching for their families," said Norberto, "and you'll make a million."

Polly had decided to mail a letter to Grape Street anyhow.

"Money down the drain; more useless days on your bond," Norberto tutted, but he took her letter to post at the PX, and registered a new PO box for her at Moody.

Every evening they motorboated across the bay to get home to the Bolivar Peninsula. Here the landscape was neither abandoned nor impeccable. "There were never many living out here," Norberto explained, "so when they left, it didn't make much difference."

Norberto's house was up on stilts, and

that first night, Polly had tripped climbing up the porch in the dark; but when he opened the front door, the sunset poured out. The house was in the way of the horizon. Sunlight found its way around the columns of painstakingly stacked goods.

"This is clothes," Norberto had said, pointing to a line of steamer trunks, packed four high. "This is firewood, obviously. Has to go in here because the shed has a leaky roof. Newspapers, here." The bundle was the size of a sofa. "I scavenged a library for copies of all the major events: end of Vietnam War, Nixon resigns, first lady prime minister elected. They'll be worth quite a bit one day." There were fans and lamps, although his house had no electricity. "I used to sell them at Moody, but TimeRaiser got wind. Now I'm keeping them for the store."

The couch looked homemade. The kitchen sink was stacked with stereo receivers and the fridge was filled with toys, but there was an unobstructed view of the sky through the kitchen window. There were no pastel chalets or jetties cleaving the sea. There was nothing built, only things that had grown; no human etchings, only grain-colored sand and dark water for miles.

When Polly confessed she wasn't coming

with them after all, Cookie said she understood. "But you be careful, dear," she'd said. Polly promised to visit their house and help with the furniture anyway. Cookie said she'd let her know what day to come, but then she never did. Polly was cruel with her own feelings at this loss. She scolded herself that this was the sadness of choice: she was lucky to feel so blue.

At head office, the clerk consulted with three different supervisors to verify it was not against regulation for Norberto to charge one dollar's rent. They tried and tried to find a ruling written against it, but eventually they had to concede it was within Norberto's rights. They recalculated her bond to completion in thirteen months. Polly got up at four a.m. every day to make it to work on time. Norberto said that, after her bond, she could live with him for as long as it took to earn her boat passage north. Maybe she could make it to Buffalo in time for their anniversary. The fifth for Polly, the twenty-second for Frank.

Now Norberto lit the kerosene lamps and put some water on the woodstove to boil, and Polly put her coveralls back on.

"Will you tell me about your life? Like how you got here?" she asked him.

Norberto squeezed his lips like he was eating something sour.

"Not necessary," he said.

"I need to know some things about you. What if they ask?"

"They won't ask at the wedding."

"Will they ask after?"

He spooned what he called coffee into a pot — a black dust of ground-up chicory root. For a filter, he had a woollen sock. He drank it straight, to save the cost of milk and sugar, but he put sugar in hers. While she was making tiny evil tiles under the blinking lights, she could forget she was human, but for the thought of the evening and a cup of coffee laced with something sweet.

"What happened to Marta?" She sat across from him in a kitchen chair and he sat on the couch. In the little time she'd lived there, this formation had become their routine.

"This is a big house, right?"

"Sure." Polly couldn't really tell. Most of the rooms were filled with home goods.

"It's five bedrooms, in great condition. TimeRaiser even offered to buy it — for a new venture: rustic vacation rentals. Anyways, in the early days, before Moody or the container system, we rented out the rooms."

"Okay."

"You see the dunes, between the house and the sea?"

"Yes."

"Do they look natural?"

"Sure."

"They're man-made. Part of the hurricane-protection system. One of our tenants, he was an engineer on that project. Marta fell in love with him."

"When did she leave?"

"Two years or so? Oh no — it's 1999 — three years. Who's counting?" He laughed bleakly.

"Do the neighbors know? Are the neighbors supposed to think I'm Marta?"

"Don't worry about the neighbors. We're tight. No one's going to rat us out."

Blackbirds, the ones she now knew as grackles, tapped on the roof.

"How did you get here?" she asked.

"Where?"

"Here. Are you from here?"

"I got here by boat."

"Where did you come from?"

"I'm from El Paso."

"Will you tell me your history, from the beginning?"

"My history? Like, my great-great-grandfather fought the Texians at the Alamo. Then —"

"No, just tell me what happened once the pandemic started."

"You should talk to Mrs. Howard, down the road. She'll talk your ear off about surviving, foraging for mushrooms and ferns and flowers, decurrent gills and compound leaves. Hot," he said, rippling the surface of his drink with his breath. "Why don't you tell me your story?"

"I have no story. The story is that I was with you until '81, then I traveled, and now we're together again. After we're done with you, we'll have to make up a story for us."

"True." He stared at his mug. "I was eighteen when they started evacuations. We were sent to Albuquerque and I lost my family. Got separated right away. Parents and younger siblings."

"How did you get separated?"

Heavy bones slid under the skin as he clenched his jaw.

"It's okay. Never mind," she said.

He nodded curtly. "I joined the corps. You get to move around, I thought I could find my family. But the policy changed from evacuation to containment and we started closing borders. It was awful. People would be trying to cross, to find someone, but you couldn't let them through.

"When the central government collapsed,

some of my corps brothers kept trying to keep the peace, even after we were disbanded. But I didn't like the work. I did find one of my cousins eventually, trying to cross a border. He knew what happened to my family."

"What happened?"

He shook his head.

"I'm very sorry."

He shook his head again, like an animal trying to shake something free.

"I was in Alabama then, by the mid-'80s. You know, it doesn't have to be this way. Before, hundreds of years ago, people lived in sync with each other, and animals, plants, all that."

"They balanced their interests?"

"You got it, sister. Do you know how Singapore survived?"

"Singapore?"

"The pandemic barely grazed them. One: they gave the good pharmaceuticals to all citizens. Everything was free. And two: they sent boatloads of medicine, also free, to the nearest islands with the largest surviving populations — Sri Lanka and Taiwan."

"Are they communists?"

"The opposite! They needed trading partners, so they kept their neighbors alive. Cooperation can be self-interested. But not here. In the '80s, people'd strip a corpse to survive. It was awful. I couldn't even tell you." It was work to get to the next sentence. "So I wanted to get away. Most people were going east, towards the settlements. I went the other way. Down. That took a few years."

"A few years?"

"I walked most of the way. For a while I drove for Great South Bus Lines."

"What's that?"

"A bunch of crooks who stockpiled gas and ran a bus service for criminal prices."

"Why did you work for them? Weren't you trying to get away?"

"To get away, I had to work for them. Story of my life. It got us as far as San Antonio."

"How did you get here?"

"We walked, and then I helped a guy repair a boat, and he got us here."

"Who is 'we'?"

"Me and Marta. Found the house together. Don't know what happened to the former residents. If this was my place, I would have stayed. Who could you catch the flu from here?"

"How did you meet Marta?"

"On the bus line. Love at first sight." He said this mechanically.

"What year was it by then?"

"How many questions is that? I should cut you off. We met in 1988. It was 1991 by the time we made it here. TimeRaiser took control of the area in 1993. Marta saw it as a chance to make our way back to 'civilized' life. That was when things went bad between us."

"Why?"

"We felt opposite ways about TimeRaiser. I didn't know she didn't like the way we lived. Truth is, they were the happiest days of my life. But, for her, I went back to corpse stripping, and then she left me. What do you think of the couch?" he said abruptly. "As an expert."

The couch was made of two-by-fours and a headboard. The cushions were hand-stitched.

"Very resourceful."

"It was Marta's doing."

"After Marta left, why didn't you quit working for TimeRaiser?"

He took a big swig of coffee. "You know what I hate?"

"What?"

"Being poor. No choice but to follow orders. Better me superintending than some sadist, right? Not really. But if I do this, I can get my store. I'll be autonomous.

"I remember what it was like to not be poor. Smelling good. Food that doesn't taste like dirt. Toilets that aren't holes in the ground." He set his mug down hard and the scrawny table wobbled. "That's what she said when she left: 'Can't shit in the ground no more.' I never minded it, till she said that." Then he laughed to show that all of it, his life, was of no importance to him.

Polly helped him change the subject. "Are those records for sale?" He had covered a row of records, three feet long, in plastic sheeting, painstakingly pulled taut to show the spines.

"They were here when I arrived. They're probably ruined."

"Did you test them?"

"It's not like we can go to RadioShack."

Finding the plastic alone must have cost great effort. It was easy to imagine him on his dimpled knees, tenderly wrapping the records, cursing each time the plastic slid out of place.

"You've kept them so well," she said.

He looked proud. "It's for my nostalgia department. Prepandemic artifacts will be in high demand. Hey, you could work with me! You could restore furniture. A one-woman purveyor of nostalgia."

She slid to the end of the sofa to see the

record spines. Norberto talked about how he'd lay out the store. It was important that the cash register be near the front door. He visited a Kmart once that had a cash register near the back, and the flow of the place was all wrong.

"Where will you live when you have your store? Will you still live out here?"

"Heck no. I'll live above the store. I'm gonna have running water, and a duvet."

The records were in alphabetical order, even to the second letter: Joni Mitchell before the Monkees. One album had its spine to the wall.

"This is the wrong way." She tried to figure how to flip it without disturbing the plastic.

"Marta's favorite band. Toto. Don't like seeing it." He sighed. "You know what I like thinking about? All the songs that didn't get written. Or the movies. Everything that was planned for production, then — whoosh — never happened. Musicians on the verge of making the song of a generation, who never got to. Boz Scaggs. Marvin Gaye. Could he have made a comeback?"

"You like thinking about that?"

"Not 'like.' But I like having the records. I like imagining all those follow-ups are still coming. It's still 1980. There's still time."

She remembered how excited he'd been for the Mel Gibson movie, how he had tried to talk to her about it.

"Maybe there is," she said. "It's not over yet."

The woodstove pinged as the fire died inside. She rubbed the permanent cuts on her fingertips, where splinters of plate and glass had slipped under the skin.

"Let's go for a walk on the beach," he said. "It's what lovebirds like us do. Am I right?"

"Ha! Ha!" Polly said.

He took her hand to help her cross the boot-sucking mud between the house and the shed. He discussed how he'd prolonged the life of their galoshes by rubbing them with animal fat.

On dry land, she took back her hand. But he said, "D'you think we should try to get physically comfortable with each other?" He reached for her hand again.

They passed the leavings of a chicken-wire fence, long downed by the wind. He talked about its removal: it would be an undertaking; it ran all the way to Crystal Beach Road. Polly tried to imagine he was someone or something else, that his hand was an empty glove or a magazine. She imagined her hand was not part of her body. There was a smarting in her chest, like when you try to stop coughing, and instead you choke.

"Okay," he said. "I counted to 120. That's probably enough." He took his hand back.

They scattered, yards apart, the only two people on miles of beach. The sea smell could be unbearable: salt choked, fish flesh. But tonight smelled like the inside of a shell. The moves of the tide hypnotized. She was startled to find Norberto beside her.

"Marta and me always meant to get up and watch the sunrise. But there was always something else to do. And the sunrise is right here, you think. There'll always be another one."

"If I get another day off, we could watch the sunrise, if you like."

"Tomorrow you and me will go to me and Marta's favorite place. Re-create a moment. Then Monday we'll sign the marriage papers. You booked the afternoon off, right?"

"Yes. The foreman will let me do one extra hour every day after, until I make it up."

There was nothing on the horizon. Only the flat line of forever. There should be birds.

"After the signing, we wait six weeks, then we file an application for family support."

"But how will you prove there's a baby

when there's no baby?"

He paused awhile.

"There are people you can hire to help with the whole process. Like a fixer. They tell you how long to wait, they help you with the papers, they supply you with what you need."

"How did you find this fixer?"

"He found me. Friend of a friend. He figured me a perfect candidate for this scheme."

She wished she hadn't asked. She should've known he hadn't cooked this up himself.

"But it's a good deal. Most fixers take a percentage. He takes a lump sum."

"How do you know most fixers take a percentage?"

"Because he told me." He turned stormy the instant the words came out and he heard how naive he sounded.

Polly said nothing. If they stopped talking now, they could forget this conversation, and things could still turn out all right.

"Try this," he said. He put his hands on her shoulders. She tried not to cringe.

"Step forward. Stop." The tide pooled around her boots. She moved out of its march.

"No. Don't move." He stepped away

sideways, right leg behind left leg, like a dance.

"What are you doing?" she called.

"Don't look at me. Look forward. What do you see?"

She wanted to go inside and pretend to sleep, so she could be alone.

"What are you talking about?"

"What do you see in your peripheral? No, don't move your head. Just look forward."

"I don't see anything. Only water." They had to shout over the noise of the surf.

"Exactly. If you get close enough to the water, you can't see behind you. You can pretend you're on a beach, anywhere. Somewhere else."

The sky had gone dull. Polly let her eyes blur sky and water and ground. She could feel Norberto's beady gaze on her, so she held her eyes to the horizon to satisfy him.

But he was right. She could have been anywhere.

There was a time when Polly and her mother went to Canada every summer, to a cottage on the lake. Her mother would sit on the deck with her friend while Polly played in the water with the other kids, but they were rowdy and someone would always get kicked in the face. So Polly would swim alone to where the buoys marked the point of Go No Further, nothing there except the sun bejeweling the waves. But the best was when her mother would swim out to her with a black rubber tube. "Get on," she would say. "I'm a taxicab: Where do you want to go?"

Polly let the world behind fade. She let an image form slowly, working from background to foreground. She replaced Norberto's house and its spindly stilts with sunshine, then jagged woods, then the green-glass cabin, then the stripy deckchairs. Only then did she imagine her mother in a polka-dot swimsuit, holding the tube overhead, tiptoeing across the pebbled bank, coming to get her. Her mother's skin and her mother's voice, and the rocking of the lake.

But Polly couldn't keep the pieces together. If she got the body right, the muscles and the freckles on her legs, she couldn't see her face. If she held on to the face, the body disappeared.

She whirled around. There, still, was the house on stilts. There, still, was Norberto, timidly off to the side.

"What happened?" he said.

"It didn't really work," she said thickly.

He squeezed her shoulder. That was the moment when she stopped, once and for all, being afraid of him.

She asked him what he had imagined.

"The same place. But a different time," he said. "I guess that makes it a different place."

The next evening, after work, they met on the Galveston side of the Bolivar Roads, to catch the motorboat back together. On hot days the sky pressed down like a chloroformed cloth, but today it was high and clear, its colors crisped by the breeze.

Norberto led Polly down a dirt path cut between the towering fields, following the shoreline. A hill appeared, a curious-looking thing. The ground didn't slope up to make a base; it looked airlifted from elsewhere. It was not a hill at all. It was a broad two-story building, with overgrown shrubs and ivies and grasses growing like ankle-length hair.

"Battery Kimble," Norberto said. "World War One gun fort. Covered with dirt, for camouflage."

Forgotten by the forces that had put it there, the fort was enjoying a second life as a garden. Beyond, the sea began without warning. The earth was a fishbowl filled with dirty water. When Norberto reached where the sea began, he stepped right off the edge, jumping down to an algae-slick platform, then stepping from it to a rowboat.

"Come on," he said. "Before we lose the light."

She got into the boat and it wobbled and tipped, but she managed to sit. All the twigs in the sea had gathered here. Norberto dragged the oars through the thick stew and the boat set off, the two of them face-to-face, cutting east, parallel to the coast.

"You can't go south," he said. "That would fling us into the sea."

The world spread out to her left and the water spread out to her right.

"Thar she blows," Norberto said, pointing behind. "The pearl of the South."

She twisted around and gazed back at Galveston, at the eastern end, where the land doubled back in a blunt edge to meet the northern coast. The tip was dotted with palm-leaf roofs and white sand, trucked in from who-knew-where. Through the sea haze, it was a rotten brown.

"Under normal conditions, it would take decades to build up an island this much. But we got it done at cut rate, in four years, thanks to the Journeymen."

Polly thought of the people on the buses and the split-open skin of their hands, and Cookie looking for her son. Frank had never portered parts, or climbed a truck to secure a bundle of rebar the length of a man, under the beat of the sun. He was in Buffalo by 1993, filing a search for her. But what could've taken you away?

"We can stop here." Norberto threw a line that arced perfectly through the air and hooked itself onto a crooked post, one that appeared to have no purpose until he tossed the rope.

"This is Marta's place?" They bobbed along at the end of the rope.

"Yup."

The sun was slipping and the sky was every kind of blue, the water eerily calm for a sea.

"If I'd asked her to marry me, I would have done it here. She used to say, 'This is the end of America.' Even though Galveston is right there."

"You weren't married?"

"No." He swallowed. "There was no one to marry us. I wish we were married. She might not have left. The paperwork might have slowed her down."

"Were you going to have a baby?"

"I really thought so. I thought he would be big by now — 1999."

She could almost feel the quickening of tears in his chest. She asked another question to help him quell it.

"So, what's our story? How did we meet?"

"How do you want us to have met?"

"On the buses?"

"No, I didn't start work there until '87. Before '81, I was in Socorro."

"Socorro? Is that in New Mexico? Okay. We were high school sweethearts."

"But you were in Buffalo."

"But they don't know that."

"Don't they?"

"They never asked. Family history, mental health, vaccines, but not where I was from. They don't care about that."

"Huh. Okay, we were next-door neighbors. We grew up together."

"We used to talk over the fence."

"Yeah. Over my little brothers' bunny hutch."

"We got separated. You went to the corps. I decided to time travel."

"When I picked you up from Houston, I couldn't believe it was you."

"What was I wearing the first time you saw me?"

"I saw your reflection in the bus window first. Little face. Your old green coat."

"What did I wear on our first date?"

"Wrangler jeans, with a crease. I wanted to know how you got that crease in."

"Where did we meet up?"

"At the stump, next to the old water tower. What was I wearing?"

"Navy jacket. Curly hair."

"What did we do?"

"We went to the park. You brought beer in a plastic bag, and when you hugged me, you almost clocked me in the head."

Norberto laughed. "That sounds like a bad first date."

"No. It was nice."

"No beer. I woulda been too young."

Every now and then, the current would tug the boat and the rope would tauten and sing.

"I got you something," he said.

"What's that?"

He took something, a box, out of his pocket. "Catch?"

She envisioned it sailing into the Gulf. "Hand it over."

They leaned in gingerly. He dropped the ring box in her hand. It held a band of gold.

"I found it in Marta's suitcase. I think it was her mother's. Didn't know she had anything worth money in there. Anyways, I thought you should wear it. You know, so it looks legitimate."

She didn't know what to say. She put it on. She had to work it over her knuckle.

"My mom told me once that all the gold in jewelry is recycled," Norberto said.

"Meaning?"

"Jewelers get gold in sheets, and they hammer them into rings. But, to make the sheets, a supplier melts down old jewelry. So all the gold in the world is just circulating, going from one person to another. The first person to wear that gold in your ring died a thousand years ago."

"Creepy."

"But then nobody really owns the gold, right? It belongs to the universe. Makes me feel better about being broke."

"You could say that about water too."

"Obviously water belongs to the universe."

"No, all the water in the world is just circulating. Maybe you've met this water before."

"I see. Like that water, there. Maybe I drank that when I was five."

"Or this water." Polly cupped some in her hand. "Maybe Marta used it to wash her hair." Had she crossed a line? But Norberto simply leaned over and took some water in his own hand. He examined the shimmer closely.

"Maybe Frank Marino peed this," he said.

"Gross." She dumped her water. "Now

311

it's gone. Can't even mark the spot where it fell."

She had done this before. As she was forming the last words of her sentence, she realized she had done this specific thing already, spoken of the unmarkability of water — but with Frank. Now she was doing it with someone else.

She was stricken. She had betrayed Frank and she didn't even know, until it was done. She stared at the hull of the boat, the fiberglass formed in a pattern like ice makes on glass.

But what could she do? She looked up. She kept laughing in the evening light, which is what people do when monstrous epiphanies surface in their minds. You cannot put life on hold to have a moment of grief, so every second, half the people in the world are split in two. This is what they mean by life goes on, and the worst is that you go on along with it too.

Polly put on the ugly dress with purple flowers. Norberto dressed up too, in a white short-sleeved shirt just long enough to tuck into his cargo pants. "Sorry," he said. "I couldn't find one with long sleeves, I can't get to the trunk on the bottom." She could see his puny nipples through the fabric, and she felt such a dreadful tenderness for him that she thought she might be sick.

The signing office turned out to be in the building that was shaped like a ship, at the end of the Strand. They followed the signs until they were in a tight corridor, only two bodies wide, with brown walls and brown carpet. All of the doors had the TimeRaiser logo on them. "TimeRaiser does the contracts for government services," Norberto explained.

The agent said, "If it's only the two of you, we can do it right here. If you have guests, then we'll go to the boardroom." They were in a windowless office only big enough for a desk and two chairs. She wondered if they should have brought guests, to make it look more real.

"No," Norberto said. "This will be fine."

And Polly realized they were really going to marry each other. She dug her nails into the bouquet they'd picked as they waited for the motorboat, until green blood showed on the stems.

"I don't have the right forms. I'll be back." The agent had to squeeze to get out the door.

Norberto turned and looked at her like he was readying to give a pep talk, but she said, "I'm fine." She patted his hand. "Neither of us thought getting married would be like this."

She meant for him to laugh, but he only said, low and very serious, "It means nothing, it's not for real," as if she might be thinking otherwise.

She nodded and then disappointment for the way her wedding day turned out came over her like a spasm of pain, and she squeezed her eyes shut.

Yesterday as they floated in the Gulf, she had asked him what memory he wanted to re-create. Marta used to sing to him — "Georgy Porgy" by Toto — but the only words he could remember expressed he was the center of her universe. He stopped speaking. He pulled the oars into the boat and pressed his knees together and balled his hands in his lap and knit his shoulders. Every muscle a blockade against the sadness and the tears. She had tried to comfort him as best she could, telling him that, the next day, he could pretend he was marrying Marta, he could even call her Marta, they would say it was a pet name. It would be almost, just like, marrying Marta. The sun was in Polly's eyes, and then he was weeping so violently that the boat shuddered, and she was afraid that if she stood up to put an arm around him, they would flip. He could only say, "In my mind, I am always in this boat with her. Time ended here and everything that's happened since, I can't believe it's real."

The agent banged the door open against their chairs and they jumped and they clutched each other's hands like schoolchildren. They agreed to the terms and signed the paper. The agent said, "Do you want to kiss each other?"

He watched them put their lips together, very carefully.

"Best of luck," he said to them, shaking their hands with both of his own. "Really."

On the motorboat home, Norberto planted himself starboard and leaned out as far as he could without riling the boatman.

"When you were in the rowboat, what could you see? Tell me when we reach the place where what we see is exactly what you saw from the rowboat."

"Why?"

"I always sat with my back to Marta's point of view."

The boatman drove fast and the horizon kept changing, the flat sea giving way to spiky coastline. She tried to call up what she had seen yesterday over his shoulder as he cried. There was no drop from the shore to the shallows. Just water, without the

315

ceremony of a cliff. The coast on their left zigged and zagged, and then made a sharp right turn into the Gulf.

"Almost there," she said. "Almost, almost . . ."

While the rowboat had floated on the whim of the waves with only the rope to rely on, she had seen what Marta meant about it being the end. That right turn of coast cut off the rest of the country so completely that, even though she lived on the beach on the other side, if someone said there was nothing but outer space beyond, she could have believed them. You'd think the end of America would be some forlorn place, but it was wide-open and beautiful. It was otherworldly and reaching, like the sand was stretching out its arms to touch somebody.

Then the motorboat lined up just right with the land, and Polly put her hand on Norberto's arm and said, "Here. Right here."

They stood single file and watched as the end of the world came into view. It stayed for only a second, and then the seascape shape-shifted, and what Marta had seen disappeared.

316

APRIL 1980

Frank has always liked to collect things. Baseball cards, stamps, coins. Once, when he was a substitute history teacher, he gave every student a penny, and asked them to look at the date on their coin and relate the most important thing that happened in their life that year. What was their personal history?

None of them could come up with much. They said a lot of "I dunno, I was four." He tried to prompt them. "Was that the year you learned to read? Maybe your parents got divorced?" The students settled into a sullen silence. At the end of class, they all carefully returned their pennies. "No, no, keep them," Frank said, but they wouldn't.

Frank says that collecting is a kind of journaling, a way of keeping track of time. Polly and Frank play a game: Polly takes an album of Frank's baseball cards and picks any card on any random page and says,

"Where did you get this one?" No matter how many times Polly tries, Frank has a story for every one.

"I traded Johnny for this one."

"This one is from the first time my dad took me to a sports memorabilia store. I was in heaven."

"This one, the Rollie Fingers rookie card? We bought it together, don't you remember? At that Cheektowaga flea market? You were wearing a huge barrette in your hair."

Frank collects other, curious things. He still has the bottle cap from the first beer he ever drank, with Carlo. One night they are having dinner at a pizza place and Frank leaves his wallet open on the red-checked tablecloth, and a ticket stub slides out of a rip in the lining. Before Frank can return it to its hiding place, Polly picks it up.

"Is this from when we went to see *Superman*?"

"Yes," he says, sheepishly drawing out the vowel.

"This is a two-year-old ticket stub. Why do you have this?"

"Not even eighteen months! Not two years. It was the first movie we ever saw together."

"You're nuts."

Later, as they are walking down the

almost-springtime street, arm in arm, Polly says, "How did you know you should keep the ticket stub?"

"What do you mean?"

"How did you know that the first movie we ever saw together wouldn't be the last movie? You keep things before you know they're worth keeping. We could have broken up the next week."

"Then I would have thrown out the ticket stub."

"But say we break up tomorrow. Think of all the things you'll have to throw away. You'll have to go through every pocket of every jacket you own, looking for important ticket stubs and pencils and bits of my hair. You're making things so much worse for yourself." She ends in a laugh, to show him she is only joking around, but her knuckles are nestled into his ribs and she feels his torso stiffen.

"Are we going to break up tomorrow?"

"Of course not, silly." She should drop it, but she can't help herself. She truly wants to know. "But how do you know something bad won't happen, something to make nice memories into bad ones?"

They haven't told anyone about their plans to marry. She wanted to keep it a secret until she graduated next year. She

319

thought that would be more romantic. Only recently has she realized her choice might have had the opposite effect. Another time, he might have answered her question with something like *I'll always have love for you, even if it doesn't work out.* But since Polly moved, their easy way with each other has strained.

"With your lousy attitude, I guess I don't know. You know, some girls might actually find it sweet I keep things."

"Maybe you just stay with me because you're trapped now. It would take too long to purge your life of me." She means this to be teasing, flirtatious. But Frank pulls his arm away.

"Must be nice, to know someone loves you so securely."

She tries to salvage their evening after that, believing she can still turn back the night to before they left the restaurant. But when they get into bed and she slips her fingers under his waistband, he pushes her hand away. It will be another two weeks before the next visit, and it is unbearable that the time to mend this new rift before it sets has come and gone. Her distress comes across as disinterest in his departure.

"I think we have different ways of expressing love?" Polly tells Donna over the phone, when Donna asks what the problem is.

"What does that mean? So why don't you just go ahead and 'express love' the way he does?"

Polly wishes they had a real, concrete problem, instead of this amorphous, teenage disparity.

"I want to be myself with him."

"Don't nitpick," Donna says. "You'll drive him away, and don't you know love is hard to come by?"

Polly and Frank decide to take a long weekend trip together. It is the end of winter but not yet spring, and Polly wants to go to Florida. But Frank says they should go to see the cherry trees in bloom in DC. Florida is nice anytime, but the cherry trees blossom only once a year. He used to go there with his grandma when he was a kid; Polly will love it. She doesn't know why he thinks this.

Everything about the planning process is fraught. Polly wants to come back early to see Donna on Easter Monday; Frank complains about cutting their time short.

"But we're going to take lots of other holidays together," Polly says.

"Are we?" Frank asks in a maudlin tone that Polly can't dignify.

"You have to coddle men," Donna says. "They're weak."

■ ■ ■ ■

"Let's stop for dinner in some lost spot," Polly says.

"We don't have time to get lost or we'll get to the hotel too late," Frank says.

"Let's lie in bed together all morning," Polly says.

"But I made us a schedule so we can make the most of our time," Frank says.

On Saturday morning they sit with their feet wrapped in the hotel covers, drinking coffee and watching *Mighty Mouse,* and for the first time, Polly feels Frank release. "This is nice," he says, and Polly says, "Hm." She doesn't look at him or make a big deal, in case it breaks the spell. But then there is a commercial break and Frank takes their mugs into the bathroom and puts on his shoes.

"What are you doing?" Polly asks.

"We have to go: I booked us on a nine-thirty bus tour. I told you, did you forget?"

"Can't we stay awhile?"

"You don't really want to waste our whole trip sitting in the hotel."

Polly can see Frank regrets these words the moment they hit air, as clear as if he's said it out loud. She goes for the throat.

"What's the rush? Why are you making out as if it's our last day on earth? Am I missing something? Does one of us have a terminal illness and you forgot to tell me?"

"Why are you so sarcastic? You live six hours away! I supported your decision to move, and now I'm the bad guy because I want to spend the little time we have together doing something, instead of piddling it away?"

"I can't live in this state of heightened emotion, as if it's always our last day together."

They talk at the same time.

"It *is* always our last day together. We don't get to see each other every day!"

"It is never our last day together! This is just the beginning."

"We have limited time together. What's so wrong with admitting that?"

"Fine. Soon you and me will be over. The world will fade away. Everyone will die. Are you happy now?"

The phone on the bedside table rings, a sudden, shocking clang.

"Hello," Polly says.

"This is a friendly reminder that the tour bus boards from the lobby in five minutes."

"For God's sake." Polly hangs up the phone. "What are you so afraid of?"

Frank sits down. There is a luggage bench waiting to catch him, but he is going down, whether or not there's anything there. He looks about to cry, and her irritation turns to shame.

She knows the phrase she needs, the thing to say to comfort him, but she can't figure out fast enough how to explain its meaning.

When Polly's mother died, a parade of adults told her that her mother would live on, always, in her heart. Every day she would cut school and go to the woods. She would lie flat on her back, the wide weave of her jacket collecting all the leaves on the forest floor, the sky mercilessly close, and it was an overwhelming responsibility to be the single safeguard of another's continued existence on earth. Frank resurrects this time in her life. His meticulous archiving, as if otherwise everything will disappear, a phobia of forgetting.

After weeks of coming home with twigs in her hair, Donna said to her, "If you're having sex with boys in the woods and you get pregnant, so help me God." Polly started crying, which was regular, and Donna ignored her, setting the table and aggressively stirring, but when the crying continued until Polly's bowl of hamburger soup was cold, finally Donna said, "What is it?

What is it?"

Donna had so little patience for anything foolish. But Polly told her anyway: "If I forget my mom, she'll be gone."

To Polly's surprise, Donna took her hand and spoke in the low, threatening voice she used when emotional. She said, "Once something's been done, it can't be undone. Your mother had a life, and that's not up to you."

It was an idea that brought Polly the deepest solace. No matter what happens, the past has a permanence. The past is safe.

Polly wants to say to Frank, *Once something's been done, it can't be undone.* But he might not hear it the right way. Maybe to him it would sound bleak.

Outside their window, the tour bus is honking its horn.

Their faces are still red when they get on the bus, and they sit like strangers, overcome by embarrassment and sadness. They pass the Washington Monument, the White House, the National Mall, and the Lincoln Memorial without speaking. As they pass over the Potomac River, she puts her arm around him, consoling him in the face of the dissolution that threatens them. When they go under a bridge, just before Arlington Cemetery, Frank lifts the camera and takes a photo of the glass in the moment that it holds their reflection, as they pass through the dark.

They hurry off the bus at the cemetery, because they only have a few minutes before the tour resumes, and Frank promised his mother a photo of the two of them out front, to send to Grandpa. The camera is out of film, and while Frank rummages through their bag for a fresh canister, Polly pops the back of the camera open. Then she yelps and slams it shut again and looks at Frank with wet eyes.

"What's wrong? You forgot to rewind the film?"

She nods.

"It's okay." He pats her arm. "Only the last few shots will be ruined. The rest of the roll will survive."

But that photo of them on the bus was the last on the roll, and now it's gone forever. For the first time, she takes proper notice of all the little white headstones in the winter-hardened ground, so unbearably sad in their uniformity.

Frank is standing on a mound with the camera.

"There's no point, really," he says after a few snaps. "You can't capture it." He squints at her. "It's okay. We won't forget how the photo would have looked."

She can't ask which photo he means, in case he doesn't mean the one from under the bridge. So instead she takes his hand, and there is that painful rush of hot and cold at the same time, the one she used to feel when they first met.

He gets one of the mothers milling about to take the photo for Grandpa, and the photographer is a perfectionist.

"Let's do another shot, just in case," she says more than once as her children look on. Polly and Frank smile until their cheeks tingle. Polly decides she can just do everything the way that Frank wants to. Why not?

"No, no," the mother calls. "Don't look at him, look at me!"

They get on the bus and Polly feels a weight lift. It is so simple — just be nice! Why did it seem so complicated?

"I'm having a nice time," she says to Frank, and his face lights up.

In the afternoon the clouds clear and they go down to see the cherry blossoms. The air is pink-tinted by the invasion of blooms. They are carried along by the crowd, their elbows pinned into their sides by the other long-weekend tourists, nobody able to stop the wash of bodies. A teenager leaps into

327

the air and grabs at a branch. There are gasps of horror as he falls to the ground in a shower of petals.

"Thug!" someone says. "Don't you have parents?"

"It didn't used to be this crowded," Frank says. "Aren't the trees amazing?"

"Yes," Polly says. "It looks like pink popcorn."

"I've never heard flowers described that way before."

Eventually they get hemmed in against a fence between the path and the grass, and they can't see any of the monuments across the water. Frank keeps beaming, apparently oblivious to the discomfort of sharing the sidewalk with three hundred other people. When the crowd forces them to hop the fence and retreat towards the parking lot, Polly says, "Well, what's next?"

"You want to leave? So soon?" Frank says.

"Of course we should stay. Let's sit down."

There isn't anywhere to sit, so they sit on the grass. They try to find an out-of-the-way patch under a tree, but the moment they crouch down, an extended family comes to pose for a portrait. They crowd under the tree to fit everyone in the frame, and the backs of their knees are against Polly and Frank's noses. Then someone runs over Polly's hand with a stroller.

"Okay," she says, and heads off towards the parking lot.

"You don't like the cherry blossoms." Frank follows behind.

"Doesn't the crowd bother you too?"

"Why don't you like the flowers? All girls like flowers."

"That's insulting."

"What? Why is that insulting?"

"I thought you wanted to bring *me* here, not any girl."

"That's not what I meant."

"Fine. I don't get it."

"You don't get what?"

"The flowers. I like them. The first second you see them, you say, 'Wow.' But that car there has a Montana plate. People travel hundreds of miles. Why? The trees don't even smell good."

"Because they don't last! It's special!"

"But no flowers last. It would be more special if they did." She is winding up to further defend her point, eyeing his trajectory so she knows just where to strike, when he moves away.

"Okay," he says.

"Wait." Her thoughts stumble, confused by the sudden shift.

"I'm going to the car."

"Don't be dramatic!" she shouts, though nothing about him is dramatic. She is behind the change of the curve, still gunked in rage, while he's left for somewhere else. The anger has completely gone out of him, and in its absence his shoulders slope. She watches him go, in shock. This has never happened before. He's given up.

He crosses the parking lot, getting smaller and smaller, until he finds his car and gets in. She is afraid that he is going to start the car and she will be left here with the giddy throngs of tourists, but the car doesn't move.

She keeps still on the knoll, blocking the school groups, tour groups, and couples trying to pass. At the edge of the lot, a cart sells souvenirs: cherry-blossom soap, T-shirts, mugs. He can't give up. She's not ready. Panic seizes her. She wants to tell him that the past is safe, no matter what. But she knows, with a stinging pang, that it is the future he is concerned with.

She takes her time walking to the car, so that maybe, when she gets there, he'll be glad to see her. She loops back and circles the same column of cars twice, in case he needs more time.

When she climbs into the car, he is just

sitting there, staring numbly out the wind-shield.

"Listen," she says. "I know what you mean about us having limited time. I'm not stupid. I know because of . . ." She struggles. "Because of family stuff." She can't bring herself to say, *Because of my mother,* not even to him, not even after all this time.

His denim jacket makes a rasping sound as he drops his hand from his mouth.

"Then why don't you act like it?"

She's never realized until now how like Donna she has become, how she has to say anything true in an angry voice.

"It ruins things. It ruins the only mo-ment." She reaches between her knees. "I brought you something."

"Did you steal flowers? You're not sup-posed to touch."

"No, this is better, see?" She brings a bouquet of blossoms out from under the car seat. "They're plastic. They last. Spe-cial." She puts them in his lap.

He stares down at them for a moment. He flicks the polyester petals, but they stay firm, epoxied to the stem. He clears his throat and he starts the engine.

It takes a long time to get out of the park-ing lot; everywhere they turn, a large group is waddling across their path. They get stuck backing out of their spot, turning out of their lane. At the final exit, they get stuck the longest. The tourists seem to think the car is not a car, but a rock to be brooked, as if by a stream. A crowd of twenty seniors cross, each of them slowed down by fatigue, or conversation, or the desire to stop in the middle of the road, and look around.

They gaze at each other without speaking, hearts in their mouths. He tucks the plastic blossoms under the passenger-side visor. He reaches over her; their clothes brush. She breathes in deep his smell, like paper and salt cut with something sweet, like a street in summer after it rains.

The fake flowers remain there for the rest of the car's life. Even when the stalk falls each time someone opens the visor to block the sun; even when Frank's friends complain they ruin the look of the car; even as the two of them take this car and head towards the South, before the year is out.

One June night Norberto didn't come home. At first she didn't worry. Often she took the evening crossing, and he the night. Being married was not such a burden after all, since they only spent an hour together each day. When she got in, she lit a fire in the pit. It was too hot now for the wood-stove. This was their routine: the first one back made the coffee, so their hour could begin the moment they were both home.

She woke up close to midnight. She had fallen asleep against a log, its imprint on her neck. After ten p.m. there were no more crossings; the boatman went to sleep. Norberto would not be home tonight.

In the morning she jumped up and went into the hallway, where he had wedged a cot among the sundry goods, but the cot was empty.

Without Norberto and his place to live, she could not finish her bond in ten months' time. Was he lost somewhere? Was he hurt? He was such a big, soft fool, anything could have happened to him.

After work, she walked to Moody Plaza. She hadn't been back since her eviction. She visualized getting to the store and not finding him there, so that she would be prepared and not panicked when it happened. It was really summer now and the atmosphere was sopping. By the time she got there, she was slick with sweat and her breath stung coming out of her chest.

She was not prepared for the old smell, unchanged though everything else had changed, and she had to work not to see herself crossing the lobby and going up the stairs, that echoed girl, forever lost.

A group of tenants was gathered around a display of preserves. As soon as they saw her, they knew she didn't belong.

"Are you looking for something?" one of them said.

"I need to find my husband."

The people parted, and there he was, at his tidy old desk in the back. But his face was greenish and his eyes were bloodshot.

She went to him. "Are you sick?"

"What are you doing here?"

"I came to find you."

They were whispering, because of the

nosy tenants.

"I'm fine. Go home. I'll meet you there."

"But what's happened? You're coming home?"

"Yes, of course, you moron."

The tenants goggled at him, astonished that their dumpy superintendent had a secret young wife, who he kept so poorly.

She waited for him at the Bolivar Roads, and the first time the boatman departed, he said, "Are you sure you don't want to get on this one?" The second time, he said, "This is the last one, and it's going to rain." She climbed aboard. He had the boat untied when Norberto came running up the dock. Norberto leaped and landed so heavily, the boat sank a foot before steadying, the other passengers toppling and groaning.

"She's been waiting for you," the old man said.

"Sorry, dear." Norberto put his arm around her. His sweat stank like liquor. She moved away.

It started to pour, right as they got in the front door. She put on the kerosene lamp.

"Should I make a fire in the wood stove tonight?" she asked.

"Whatever you want." He disappeared down the hall.

After a day of dread, fury now came

335

strangling up.

"Where were you last night?" she shouted.

He didn't come back. She marched down the hall.

He was in the back bedroom, a tiny box for a child or a maid, moving stock in the dark.

"What are you doing?"

He jumped. The rain pelting the roof had muted the sound of her coming.

"Nothing."

"Are you drunk? You don't drink."

"What does it matter?"

"I was worried about you."

"We have no agreement I report to you every night." The drink sharpened something in him, instead of blunting. "A slave at work and a slave at home. Where do I do what I please?"

It was an accusation that did not belong to them. It must have been said before, in this house, in another of Norberto's lives, dormant in the walls until it was reanimated by anger.

"You called me a moron. In front of ten other people!" O-1s, she wanted to say.

He sat down on a low stack. "Is this a real marriage now?" He acted as if she was the problem one.

His weight displaced the top of the stack;

a pamphlet for a fitness center announcing a grand reopening in July of '79, a children's board book, and a folded letter fluttered to the ground. The letter caught her eye, and then the processes of her mind stalled. The letter was written in her own handwriting.

Norberto started, but she was faster than him. She grabbed the paper, worn at the folds. The first few lines: *Dear Frank, How to write this letter? I'm coming to you.* It was the letter she had written to Grape Street months ago, and given to Norberto to post.

White rage billowed over her.

"What if the letter got to him and you heard he was dead or married or some such?" he said. "There'd be no reason to find him, you wouldn't need to help me anymore. I couldn't risk it."

"Why did you leave it out for me to find?" Her rage, unhinged and unstable, lighted randomly on his sloppiness.

"It felt like a sin to throw it away."

She ran back down the hall.

"Where are you going?" he cried.

She picked up a bundle of newspaper. She lifted a front page that said: *Sadat Visits Israel* and began to tear.

"What are you doing? Don't!"

She ripped it in half.

"I need that!"

337

She split the string that held the bundle, tearing the skin between her thumb and forefinger. The next headline read: *Virginity Tests on Asian Immigrants at London Heathrow.* She clawed the page into two.

"Stop, stop, stop."

He folded himself up on the couch, resting his big head against his knees. He moaned, a sound rising out of his throat of its own accord. It was a terrible noise to hear from an adult. It stopped her. Something had happened. Something worse than this moment.

"Why didn't you come home last night?" she asked.

This time, he told. He had submitted the wedding paperwork as he should have, six weeks ago. He sent it to his fixer, who sent in the whole package for them, with the results of a forged pregnancy test and ultrasounds. He was supposed to hear back from the benefits office after four weeks. He'd heard nothing. He sent notes to the fixer through his contacts, but no response. The fixer had disappeared. In a panic, yesterday, he went to the benefits office himself. They said they had no record of his application. He gave them his middle name, he gave them her name, he even gave them his name spelled wrong. But they had nothing.

"How much money did you give your fixer?"

"Everything I saved since I started working for TimeRaiser."

It took her less than a split second to calculate that she would be all right. So long as he let her stay living here. But he had lost a near-decade. More than her bond, two times over.

"All my photos. I put them in the application. The fixer said I would get them back. But they're gone."

She crossed the room to him. When he moved towards her, she let him kiss her cheek with his mushy mouth, because he had lost everything, and here was something kind that she could do. Then he pressed the plane of his fingers between her back ribs, and her lungs lifted like a lid. All of the memories of love, buried deep in the tissue of her spleen and coiled around the fibers of the muscles that carted her hips, came unlatched. And now she had to wrap her arms around his neck and hold on, because she was being borne forward upon a flood.

It took her a moment to see that he had undone the top button of her coveralls. "No," she said. "No, no, not that."

"It's okay," he said. "Don't worry."

"I don't want to do that."

He kept trying to get at her third button, but the coveralls were poorly made, the button too large for the hole. "No," she said. She wedged her elbow between their bodies and shoved against his breastbone.

"Please, please. It would be only once or twice. You wouldn't have to keep the baby. Once you have it, I could keep it, and you could still go. You could still go home. I can't go on like this Polly. I'm powerless. I got no leverage."

She screamed. She tried to get her knees up so she could kick him in the chest, but he pinned them underneath him.

"This is why I didn't come home. I knew I had to do this, but I didn't want to. I'm not like this. Other guys did this. But I never did. Not in all those years."

She slammed the heel of her hand as hard as she could against his jaw, but he was dense and heavy, and he held her down with no trouble at all.

"I have no choice. If I do this, I'm free." Tears rolled down his cheeks and dripped onto her face.

His knee dug into her thigh. Her eyes were tearing and the light split; she couldn't see. The kerosene lamp was just there, on the kitchen counter. She could reach it. But what if it killed him?

He jammed his forearm against her wind-pipe.

She writhed her hand free and she scrabbled the lamp into her hand and the hot glass seared her palm and she smashed the lamp across his back.

He reared up, screaming. His hair was on fire. She rolled to the floor, smacking her forehead against the coffee table. For a moment the color of everything faded, and then she got up. She fell down the front steps. She ran flat out, not thinking, until she realized if she followed the road he'd find her easily, and she staggered into the fields. There was so much rain that all she could see were the weeds lying down before her as she crushed their bases with her boot. Something was in her hand. It was a rain-coat that she must have grabbed as she fled. She fumbled it over her arms and the hood fell into her eyes for a second and she crashed into something vertical so hard it knocked the wind out of her. Sand was in her mouth. She had run into the bottom of a dune. In her confusion, she had run diagonally. She did not scream. She put her hand over her mouth so that she wouldn't scream, and staying as low to the grass line as possible, she inched up the dune to find out where she was. She was disoriented and nothing was where she thought it should be. But then she found the road, then the abandoned mailbox, and then his house. It was almost a mile away. It was not on fire, but there was no light, not lamplight nor torchlight nor any show of life. She looked for leaping flames. She listened for footsteps slapping through the puddles. She was aware of a choking desire within her that he not die. She wadded up the collar of her raincoat and shoved it into her mouth, and then she screamed. She lay against the dune and waited for signs of life, but when the refuge of rain and night started to dissolve, she had to go.

Summer evenings, the women of 4A1 lined up their buckets in the shade at the back of the containers, out of view from the gawpers on the road, and sat eating turnip slices with a touch of salt, and talking to each other.

Polly appeared at dusk. In the morning she had walked from the dock to work, as she always did, following the way her feet knew. After work she walked the twelve minutes down Church Street, and when they saw her coming, still in her raincoat when the sky was dry, they got Cookie.

"Do you want to tell me what happened?"

Cookie said. Polly shook her head. Cookie pressed no further. She knew what it might cost her to recount it. Cookie rinsed Polly's hand with her bottle of water and Mary bandaged it with some rags, boiled for this purpose. They gave her a gardening glove to wear over her wounds so she could still cut tiles at work.

"Come sit with us. It'll do you good," Cookie said.

Polly could follow Spanish a little now. She knew tú and yo, the basic action words, and the names of places, and she could get the sense of a story from the rising and falling of the voice.

"Why are you here? What happened to your house in the woods?" Polly asked.

"We got raided for sanitation violations. Nothing ventured, nothing gained," Cookie said. But she wrapped her arms around her chest and poked out her chin, mournful as a turtle, her buoyancy tinged blue.

"Maybe there's another house you could take?" Polly suggested.

Mary shook her head. "We won't try that again."

They listened to the story being told. It had something to do with work, a sleazy foreman. Every now and then, Cookie would reach over and pat Polly's hand. But everybody was on one side and Polly was on the other. She had always felt that way, but now it had actually come true.

They folded a tarp up for bedding and put it on the floor between the wall and the last bunk in the row, where she'd be least likely to be discovered. But she couldn't stay long. There would be an inspection soon enough, and if they got caught, they'd all be fired.

She did not sleep for nights, waiting for Norberto to come. After three nights, she knew he must be dead.

All her life before had been imagined. Frank and Donna were people she had dreamed. She could not eat. She could not stop crying, but she could do it without making a face or a noise, and maybe it just looked like she had a cold. She could not stop thinking about Norberto, all alone under the coffee table, burned or blue. His tragic, stupid life, and the evening they went out in the rowboat.

At work, she tried to be a machine, her desires and her employer's desires finally in alignment. Hours divided into jobs, jobs divided into tasks, tasks divided into operations. It was like climbing a rope, hand over hand, out of a hole, leagues deep in the earth. Walking up the catwalk after lunch,

344

she looked out the window and saw Norberto in the weeds on the other side of the fence. She only registered what she had seen four steps later. It took a struggle to go back.

The glass was blown out, the window just a hole in the wall. She stood adjacent to the opening, her back to the outside, and then she rotated very slowly, so that a slice at a time came into view. With every degree pivoted, she thought she'd see his head. He was not there.

There was nothing beside the brewery, just an empty lot with waist-high bull nettles. She must have hallucinated the man.

Yet this vision ruined her ability to be a machine. Now every time she passed that window, she could not help but look, a twitch that spoiled the groove.

Days later she saw him again. Again she plastered herself against the wall and pivoted, and at seventy degrees, she saw his face. He was looking right where she was, but he showed no sign of recognition. She wanted to wave for his attention, but she could not.

He walked away.

She ran — down the catwalk, across the old loading dock, into the empty lot. Nettles bit into her pant legs. She turned and turned, trying to see in every direction at once. Nobody was here. Only that rough sky and the mangy weeds just trying to get by. She was losing her mind.

Any day, someone would report that Norberto had not turned up to work. They would go to his home and find him dead on the floor, burned to death or asphyxiated, and they would look for his wife. She couldn't run away. If she ran, she would have to cross the checkpoints, and that would make it even easier to catch her.

Five days passed, then a week. Then it was ten days, twelve days, and then Cookie found her son.

It was a telegram, by way of the TimeRaiser office, responding to hers. Cookie'd found his address through the Demographics Center. It said he was coming Sunday evening.

On Sunday afternoon around four p.m., those with the day off started to put out the buckets for party seating. Mary presented her prize possession, an old tin platter with a Santa Claus pattern, and they organized mulberries from the roadside bushes and pieces of tomato, and placed the platter on a bucket in the center of the circle. When Cookie arrived from work at five p.m., she clutched her throat and made like she was swooning.

"I want everyone here when he arrives," Cookie announced, "so we can all be happy together."

Polly marveled at this. If she were Cookie, she would not have been able to bear being out in the open. As it was, Polly was overcome with nerves. She had to sit quietly with her back against the wall.

"Do I look like an old woman?" Cookie kept asking. "I've lost a lot of weight. I don't want to scare him."

"Don't even think about that," Mary said fiercely.

Some kicked around a soccer ball. A group of three women screamed every time a vehicle on Harborside Drive approached Thirty-Seventh, starting with a low rumbling when any car, bus, or pickup rolled into view. As the vehicle ate the distance to the intersection, their voices built and built to a scream-pitched peak. Then the vehicle would cross Thirty-Seventh without slowing, and their voices washed away. Neighbors poked their heads out to see the source of this screechy disturbance.

By six p.m. they were starting to fidget. Diana kept time on an overturned bucket while a chorus of the older women sang Mexican folk songs — "Cielito Lindo" and

347

one that Cookie translated as advice from a rock on how to be king of your own destiny, even if you have no money.

By seven p.m. some of the Catholics began to pray the rosary, the burble of their voices going up and down in unison. Mary started a Carpenters singalong.

At eight p.m. some had to go inside, to bathe before lights out. "We'll be right back," they said.

At nine p.m. Polly leaned forward and put her hand on Cookie's shoulder. "Don't worry," she said. "It's still evening. Look. The sun hasn't gone down yet."

Close to ten p.m. Mary was dozing against the container, snoring softly. Only two other women remained: sisters with their arms around each other, talking low. They had put in a search for their mother and were still waiting to hear back. Cookie hadn't spoken in an hour.

Polly's eyes had adjusted to the dark, and the compound just caught the edge of the edge of the glow from the streetlamps on Harborside, but when she saw a figure, like an ounce of the darkness moving, she didn't say anything. She didn't trust herself. With every yard the figure gained, her heart jerked, as if he were her own.

When he was about fifty yards away, she

took Cookie's hand. Cookie was staring at her feet, but at the touch she looked up. She squeezed Polly's hand. The figure kept coming. She squeezed harder, and harder, until Polly's fingers hurt. When the man reached their circle, Cookie made a noise, like a cry imploding, but she didn't get up.

"Ma," Cookie's son said. "It's me."

Mary woke up and shrieked.

The sisters came over and helped Cookie stand.

Cookie held his elbows and stared. Polly had always imagined him as a boy, but of course he was a man, with strong arms and a big white smile.

"When did you get so tall?" Cookie said.

"I've always been this tall. You just forgot that I'm grown."

Cookie started to cry. She forgot how to breathe, inhaling when she should have been exhaling. Her son put his arms around her and she wept into his chest.

"Everything's good now, Ma," he said.

Cookie and her son were going to get a house together in 2001, after their bonds were up, maybe in Texas City, where there was a settlement of ex-TimeRaiser workers. "You should come join us when you finish," Cookie said. "You're single now, right?"

Polly had never told Cookie about Frank. It would be impossible now to explain. There was too much to say. All the things she'd done to get back to his singing in the car, his toes wriggling in the sand, his chuckles in his sleep.

Polly mapped all the places she'd ever been. She picked the farthest point she knew from her mother's house, from Donna's house, from Frank's house. Then she traced the route all the way home, picturing it first from above, then zooming in: the highway, the smokestacks, the headlights feelering the turns, the Mister Donut, the scarred street sign, the wiggly stone in the path, the knob in her hand, the smell of figs in the hall. She could see everything.

On the twenty-first day, her foreman came to her station and told her to report to Head Office after work. She was afraid it might be some kind of trap, some test: if she ran, she'd be proven guilty. She went as fast as she could.

Head Office was almost at the causeway to the mainland. It was a long, low building, alone in a lot they must pay H-1s to keep clear of weeds. It had been a post office once. She had visited it in 1980 to send a postcard to Donna.

Inside, the long counter was still there,

but first you had to give your name to a receptionist seated at a table at the front, and she gave you a ten-page form to fill out. Polly flipped through it. *Last known address before time travel. Names of references. Blood type. Family medical history.*

"Excuse me," Polly said. "Are you sure I need to fill this out? Do you know why I'm here?"

"Everyone fills out the form, regardless of basis for inquiry."

"I'm not making an inquiry. I was asked to come here."

"Everyone fills out the form."

Polly filled out the form. It took fifteen minutes.

"You left blank sections," said the receptionist. "The form must be filled out in full."

Polly took it back and wrote nonsense in the fields for *Paternal medical history* and *Guarantors of identity* and *Financial standing.*

When the receptionist was satisfied with her paperwork, she gave Polly a number. Then Polly had to wait, seated in a row of chairs with others like her, in dusty coveralls, leaning forward so sharply they were barely in their seats. There was no rhyme or reason to the numbers. They were not called in order. Everyone was afraid to fall asleep. She was still there when they pulled the entrance grille shut for the night.

"Don't worry," the guard called. "If you're in, you're in."

When they finally called her number, she shuffled up to the counter and gave her name to a man behind a hard plastic divider.

He took her ID and number and walked to the back. He opened a filing cabinet and flipped through, very slowly. A woman passed by and he struck up a conversation with her.

None of this made any sense. This was not how they would apprehend a killer. But not knowing what this was made it somehow worse, and her legs began to shake.

He finished with the filing cabinet and took an age to cross the carpet.

"Well, congratulations, Mrs. Galván. There's just the matter of the paperwork and then you're on your way."

She didn't say anything. She waited for him to divulge more information.

"Hello?" He waved his hand in front of her face.

"I'm sorry. On my way to what?"

He frowned. "Let me look at your ID again."

He held her ID up to the light. He clipped it to his clipboard and dragged a finger from her ID to his papers.

"Well, we've got the right girl. But you don't know that your bond is over?"

She shook her head.

"This has gotta be a first."

It seemed safest not to speak.

"Who is Norberto Galván? Your brother? Your husband?"

"My husband."

"Mr. Galván paid off your last several months, plus the early termination fee. You're a free agent."

She studied the papers in front of him, reading the figures upside down, making out her name and her ID number.

"I have to get you to initial here and here and here and here. I have your salary payout. All expenses deducted leaves you with $213.81. Would you like that in cash or in your LifeFund?"

She couldn't see properly; the plastic glass between them was scratched. She couldn't ask him if it was a mistake, because he might check and discover that it was a mistake.

"You have the option of signing a contract for another year, to keep your same job. TimeRaiser is committed to retention and would be willing to give you a twenty-nine-cent raise — that's per hour — should you sign up for another year. Are you interested?"

Her hands were clinging to the counter, leaving porcelain tile dust on the Formica. The skin looked inflated below her right thumb where the burn on her palm wrapped around. She counted her fingers, and she counted them again. She said to herself, These are my hands and this is my body. This is me and I've carried me through.

"You really should consider it. What we can also do, now that you no longer have to allocate income towards your passage, is sign you up for a savings plan. We have a great savings plan. I'll put some information about it in your package. And here is some information on vacating your housing and how to find new housing. This is your unsigned contract for the next year. Take a look at it, please; you won't get a better offer. And this . . . What's this?"

He opened a fat envelope and pulled out some folded papers.

"Your husband left this for you. I guess he thinks we're the postal service. Here you are."

It was a visa and a boat ticket to Buffalo, leaving the next evening.

"But why Buffalo?" Cookie wanted to know.

"My missing person is there."

"Well I'll be. Of course. You are a mysterious girl."

Polly wanted to give Cookie her wedding ring, but she couldn't get it off her finger. While Cookie put some things in a shopping bag — a sweater, socks and underwear, some vegetables — Polly tugged and tugged, with no success.

"Don't worry. It doesn't matter," Cookie said.

"But I have to give you something."

At the last moment, when she was supposed to have left for the terminal five minutes ago, Polly borrowed a cake of soap and rubbed it, dry, on her finger. She spat. She twisted and turned the ring, and finally it popped off.

"There," she laughed, teetering on tears.

"But what am I going to do with this?"

"Sell it, towards your house in Texas City."

"Don't be silly," Cookie said, but she smiled, delighted.

They'd only had one or two true conversations, and if they'd met under different circumstances, they would never have been friends. But Polly hugged her deeply until Cookie said, "Time to go."

Polly headed off. She took Church Street for the last time. She passed the brewery and came to a lane to the highway, and then she followed its shoulder. The only thing worse than leaving without saying good-bye to Norberto was seeing him again.

A bus passed her, spitting hot dust in her eyes. She caught up to it at the ferry terminal. Passengers bottlenecked at the entrance and she had to wait to get in. He had bought her a ticket on the cheapest shipping line, but she'd still have all her meals and a berth in a shared cabin. Some of the passengers, wealthy businessmen who must've missed the plusher sailings, were tugging at their shirt collars and rolling their eyes. But most passengers looked like Polly, dressed in their nicest wash-faded clothes, concentrating on the print on their tickets, anxious to smile when spoken to. She was a few doors over from where she'd sat on the curb and waited for Baird, that night on the Strand, a million years ago. The crowd gulped into the terminal, the door coming closer and closer. A child in line pointed out their boat to her mother, a red-and-blue passenger barge, long and low and cast to the precise width of the canal. The horn tooted. Polly was leaving Galveston and she'd never be back.

She clutched the straps of her shopping bag so nothing would fall out, and ran with it slapping against her thigh down the Strand and around the corner, and there was Moody Plaza, like a dusty column of doom, and through the glass door, of course, Norberto was there. He was leaning against the counter, thumbing through a shoe box of index cards. When he saw her, he froze. His hair had been shorn and he looked gaunt, but had enough time passed for that to be possible?

"Where did you get the money?" she said.

"You're supposed to be on that boat."

"Where did the money for my ticket come from?"

"I sold the house."

"But how? To who?"

"TimeRaiser."

"Did they give you enough money? To buy another place?"

"No. But they gave enough for what I needed."

"But where will you live?"

"I live here now. I rent a room."

"What about your stock? Where will you put it?"

"I left it all in the house. They made me lower the price. They said it was going to be expensive to dispose of the contents. It's okay. Don't look like that. It's all right."

"But your store. All your things."

"Stop this now. I don't have another house to sell if you miss your boat."

She had to look to the left of his head. She couldn't look at his face, or she saw it inches away and streaked with panic, his tears in her mouth and the blade of his arm crushing her throat.

"I did the wrong thing." He paused to gather himself. "I did the wrong thing and I had to make it right. That's all there is to it."

"I thought I killed you," she said.

"Did you pack snacks? It's a five-day journey." He put a jar of beans in front of her. They kept the counter between them. They wouldn't see each other again. Their course ended here, with no more chances to change it.

Some tenants came in, fussing around the message board. She wanted it to unhappen. She wanted his face to go back to the face of a brother, of someone she'd loved. She fished around in her paper bag until she felt the hard edge of the baseball cards she'd carried so long. She put them on the counter.

"You should take these. They could be worth something. You can still have a store. You can sell things like this. You can start again."

358

He stared down at the cards.

"Please. For your nostalgia department."

He tucked the cards into his coveralls. He carefully zippered the pocket shut. He jabbed his knuckle into his eye and wetness streaked across his cheek.

"I won't forget you," he said. He pushed the beans at her.

She nodded, because she couldn't speak.

"Come on, now. You have to go."

Everybody went up on deck to wave good-bye to the city, and Polly followed them, not knowing what else to do. She thought she might see something — the headless palm tree that oversaw 4A1, Cookie waving, the window to her room in Moody Plaza, the new tenant within, even Baird in the back of a trishaw, haranguing the driver. But all of that was to the west, and the boat went east, and the island scurried away, uncaring. It became very small, until it was too far away to tell one thing from the other, just like that. She had wanted to leave for a lifetime, and now it was all gone too quick.

She stayed on the deck, until the sun set and the wind rose and the first mate came to lock up for the night.

Once something's been done, it can't be undone.

DECEMBER 1980

It is the anniversary of my mother's death
and you are trying to cheer me up. I don't
even know why I'm crying in the kitchen in
the middle of the night, when it's been
nearly ten years. I'm embarrassed that
you've found me. You are very nice and that
only makes me sadder.

In the morning you try to convince me
that what we really need to do is go to New
Orleans. It's that time between Christmas
and New Year's, and we still have a few days
until our vacations end. You say it's warm
down there as a blizzard pummels its fists
against the window and the wind screams
to get in. In December? I ask. So you make
Donna call meteorology, and she reports
that it is sixty-eight degrees. We have no
money, we can't go to Hawaii, but we can
go to New Orleans, and doesn't that sound
fun?

We pack the car, running down the back

steps with our arms full of potato chips and sun hats and pillows, like we have to get a move on before one of us remembers a reason why we simply cannot go. And then we are off, cutting a line across the country in your old Celica, and I am not sure we'll make it in one piece. I do not know that this is the last time I will ever leave this house. This is where I became myself. I should have gone from room to room touching everything, seizing as much as my memory could hold: the flip clock on the oven, the accordion door always stuck in its track, the dust motes and how they twinkle when I open the blinds. But I don't know.

Somewhere in Indiana we see a semi with its cab on fire, smoke that looks dense enough to touch churning out of the windshield. Life goes on in its depressing way, even when we are happy. At any given moment, someone is being tortured or raped, I say, right now. What a lovely tidbit, you say, and put on the radio. They are reporting on the fallout from a lab accident at the CDC in Atlanta that occurred during a fire drill, but tests on a patient are inconclusive and doctors are hopeful. You change the channel and a soft-rock singer is warbling over plonking keys that he can't unlove his lover, no, no, no. It's sappy but it works. For the rest of my life I could just be on this road with you, and I'd be happy.

As we go, we see the ground change from gray to green, and by the time we get to Nashville the air is so much softer. We stop for the night in a motel with crusty carpets and gum stuck to the underside of the night table, but I go along with it. You slide your arm under my neck to pillow my head against the lumpy bed and you say, Oh, do I love you.

The next day, the road again. We've been driving for ages, and as the sun is setting, you start saying that New Orleans is right around the corner. After you've been saying this for more than an hour — It should be here, I saw the sign — we finally stop at a lonesome gas station. A teenage attendant with an unreal accent tells us that we're in Lake Charles, almost Texas, and we overshot New Orleans by three hours. You can't believe it — you almost want to call the operator to confirm — and even the attendant tries to cheer you up, saying that a lot of people get confused at Slidell interchange. If it's all the same to you, he says, we're close to Galveston, which in his mind is a nicer vacation spot than New Orleans, a more appropriate place to take your pretty wife, and it's only about an hour down the road. We know nothing about Galveston, save for the song. Why not? I say. We're being spontaneous, aren't we?

The attendant lied. Galveston is at least two and a half hours from Lake Charles, plus all the stops at other gas stations to make sure, but finally, after midnight, we roll over that causeway and you say, How cool, just the sea, the stars, and us.

We pass a hotel, an amazing monster, built right on the pier, the silty sea sloshing under its footing. Two forty-foot mermaids flank its logo, their nipples pointing the way to its name: Flagship Hotel.

I'm turning the car around, you say, there's no way we're not staying there. Our room smells just a little like a wet dog. Everything is mauve.

The next morning we walk around the Strand, this kooky, old-timey street, where we buy some taffy from a candy store with glass counters, even though neither of us likes taffy, because this is what people come here for. The curbs are three feet high and there are tracks in the street where you can take an antique trolley up and down the main drag, ringing its jolly bells. There's hardly anyone around and I feel that all of this is here just for us.

We ask our waitress what else there is to

do in town. (You drove all the way from Buffalo, she says, just for Galveston?) You could take the ferry to the Bolivar Peninsula, she suggests. The beaches are nicer there and people say you can see dolphins on the way over, though I haven't yet.

I have never driven a car on a ferry before and we're amused by the novelty. When we get to the other side, we're both awed by the emptiness. There's no development on the beaches, and when we get out of the car, we see no buildings, no people, just the wavy sand and the full sea, the wind making whorls around our feet. So much space, it hurts the eyes. The air smells different here, wet and pulpy, and it sparks some memory in me, but I can't place what it is. I just feel nostalgic, as if I'm being visited by a moment from a past life.

It's too cold to swim or sunbathe, but it's sunny, with fluffy clouds, and warm enough to sit and watch the surf. We eat our potato chips and I pull you onto me and I don't even mind that my privates are exposed to the elements. The wind trapping sand in your eyebrows, the hills and valleys of your face.

So soon, we have to get the ferry back. I don't want to think about Worcester, about the windows that will be sealed shut until

April, the stripped trees. On the boat going back, we stand on the upper deck to look for dolphins, but the landscape looks like an industrial park on water, and we wonder if the waitress was joking. It's still sunny, though, and you show me a game where we throw pennies overboard and try to get them to land on the lip that extends around the base of the boat, the last stop before the moiling waters. We lay our arms as flat as we can against the body of the boat, and when that doesn't work, we try dropping the pennies way out over the railing, hoping that the wind will carry them back. And when that doesn't work, we try throwing the pennies as hard as we can, and we try dropping them gently. Each time, the pennies hit a frame, a post, a window, and ricochet into the water, never to be spent again. We are down to our last penny and we each hold one edge, even though this is hard because, you say, my fingers are too fat — you are pleased by your joke — and this penny lands on the edge but on its side, and for one shining moment it stays. Then it rolls off into the water to meet its brethren at the bottom of the Gulf, and the waters swallow it up in some shade of blue that we don't yet have a word for, and I get such a piercing happiness, I can't breathe.

I know that this will be one of the happiest moments of my life. I know that, even though I do not know that when we get to the shore, we will learn that the Atlanta outbreak has leapfrogged five states in less than a week and we are in a state of emergency, and in the chaos we will only get as far as Houston.

I want so terribly to hold on to the spot in the sea where our last penny fell. I keep my eyes fixed on it, but the motor has turned the water into a swirling target. And then I blink, and I lose it.

But we lean against the railings and you clasp your hands behind my back, like a bridge, and forever I promise to remember your face against that beautiful sky and the sea tossing us up and down and the merry creaking of the boat and how you say, Polly, I can't unlove you.

They arrived at night. Polly would've missed her stop if not for her cabin mate, who told her to get off.

"This isn't Buffalo yet," Polly said.

"They announced Buffalo."

"It's a mistake. This isn't Buffalo. I would recognize it."

"Last call for Buffalo, last stop before Canada," the loudspeaker said.

The passengers were herded into a Plexiglas tunnel no higher or wider than the biggest man. A megaphone shouted, "Single file! Single file!" The lights were prison bright. At the front of the line was a row of card tables, and at each table was a man in a hazmat suit and an empty chair.

"Approach and sit! Approach and sit!" the megaphone said.

The man in the hazmat suit said, "Open!"

Polly stared without understanding.

"Your mouth, your mouth! Let's go!"

367

Before she could properly part her teeth, he gripped her by the chin with his rubber-gloved fingers. With a single hand he jammed two abnormally long cotton buds into her mouth, stabbing the inside of each cheek. He rammed one up her nose so hard her eyes watered. He withdrew with his bounty and used a dropper to apply a clear liquid to the head of each cotton bud. The liquid turned violet as soon as it hit the cotton. He took a box that looked like an electric pencil sharpener with three holes and stuck a cotton bud in each hole. He drummed his fingers on the box, waiting. The membranes in her nose were still stinging from the cotton bud, and though she tried to stop it, she could feel that inexorable force gathering until out it came: a sneeze.

All eyes snapped towards her. The man across the table looked at her as if they were in the pause between the click of a land mine and the boom. The box on the table emitted a cheery ding. A green light flashed. The man exhaled.

"Free to go," he said.

Her cabin mate was a silent, short, square old lady, who spent hours lying in her bunk, staring dolefully at the rivets in the ceiling, but as soon as they got off the barge, she changed entirely. She whistled in the customs line, immune to the threatening looks of the passport officials. Polly distanced herself from the old lady, joining a different lineup, the longest one, already anxious about what the official might think of her red conditional passport. A young man examined Polly's papers for a long time, massaging the center of his forehead and sighing. He glanced at her, then at his computer, then at her again. For one mad moment she thought he had records of everything that had happened to her: the reroutement, the customs police, the Elvis yearbook, Frank's searches, the abrupt and suspicious end of her bond. Then, in sleepy tones, he said, "Welcome to the United States," and that was it.

She got as far as the double doors outside the port building, and she was lost. She found herself in the middle of a crowd. What day was it? She had never seen downtown Buffalo this busy, not even on a Saturday night. Perhaps a concert or a game had just let out? People walked in pairs, or in groups, or with dogs, shouting and laughing and throwing sticks in the canal. The ground sloped up from where she stood, the city bathed in reassuring orange lamplight, and not one building doused in weeds. But nothing was the same. It couldn't have been a concert or a game, because where the old arena had been, there were tall brick buildings instead, a wall of concrete, like a book held too near to read the words. She saw a street sign and didn't recognize the name. Of course. They had moved the harbor. That was what had happened.

A group of trishaw drivers clustered around the port building, looking to pick up fares.

"You looking for a ride, miss?" one of them called.

"Where am I?"

"Where do you want to be?" he replied. The rest laughed.

She felt a tap on her arm. Polly looked down. It was her cabin mate.

"Where are you going?" the old lady asked.

"Where are we?" Polly said.

"Erie Canal."

"But they moved the harbor."

"They didn't."

"But everything looks different. The street names are wrong."

"My ride isn't coming to get me until tomorrow morning and I know a clean hotel around the corner. Share a room for the night?"

Her cabin mate still shuffled, but she was

surprisingly speedy, and Polly, carrying the woman's old leather suitcase, with its tiny, useless handle, struggled to keep up. Now and then the crowd swung between them and her nerves spiked, then the back of her cabin mate's head would emerge into view again, her hair flat from the bed. She skated forward at the same even pace, never turning to check for Polly and her suitcase. Polly had imagined she'd go straight to Frank's as soon as she arrived, but it was too late to call on him now. She knew that made no sense, but it was just easier to follow the old lady down the orange streets. Had this always been the color of the light?

Her cabin mate opened a door out of nowhere and brought Polly into a narrow, high-ceilinged lobby. The whole edifice looked to be half the regular width, like one building had been split into two. A letter-board directory with white press-in letters listed dentists and notaries.

"The hotel is on seven," her cabin mate said.

Polly made for the stairs.

"Where are you going?" the old lady asked.

"Stairwell?" Polly pointed to a marked door.

"You can take the stairs if you want, but

I'm going to take the elevator."

"Of course. An elevator." She heard her own voice, astonished and stupid, but her cabin mate took no notice, frowning at the lit-up call button.

On the seventh floor the old lady banged her fist on a dented green metal door. Something electric buzzed and the door opened. The receptionist did not stand up behind her high counter, so they conducted their business with her eyebrows. Because her cabin mate was too short to see over, Polly handled the exchange.

"How much is it?"

"Ten dollars per, twenty dollars total."

"Twenty dollars? That's it?"

Her cabin mate jabbed a sharp elbow in Polly's side. "You want her to charge more?"

"Tax-free if you pay in cash," said the eyebrows.

"I only have this." Polly withdrew a twenty from the $213 they'd given her when they closed her bond.

"Wrong currency," her cabin mate hissed.

But the receptionist said swiftly, "I'll accept American dollars." An elfin hand snatched the bill off the desk.

Her cabin mate pulled down the register and filled it out on a bended knee.

"What's your last name?"

"Nader."

"Lebanese?" She smiled up. "I knew it. I can always spot my own."

As soon as they were in their room, the old lady undressed. On her hands and knees, in baggy men's briefs, she raked through her suitcase until she found a cloth bag, and she dumped its contents into the sink in the corner, a shower of dirty socks and underpants. She filled the sink with water and soap, and she dug a travel radio out of her suitcase and unplugged the lamp on her nightstand so she could plug the radio in. In the new dimness, music unlike Polly had ever heard piped out of the mini speaker: a man sang like a woman, in high falsetto, and an electric piano noodled a riff, both chipper and melancholic. Her cabin mate unlatched the casement window, a little glass door that opened inwards. Polly sat in a daze and watched her bustle.

"Feel that?" the old lady said.

"What?"

"That. Have you forgotten? It's called a breeze." She laughed. "I hate Texas." She sat down and lit a cigarette.

"Why did everyone say it's expensive up here?" Polly asked.

"Who's everyone? These are expensive" — she eyed her cigarette — "that's for sure.

First time back?"

Polly nodded. "Since 1981."

The old lady raised her eyebrows and blew an appreciative smoke ring out into the night.

"A liberated Journeyman. I'm a courier," the woman said. "I work for a big law firm. Mostly, I tool around this region. But if they have really important documents for clients down there, I have to take the barge, five days each way, to get the documents south."

"People up here have business with people down there?"

She nodded vigorously. "A lot of employment now. TimeRaiser has become very popular for staffing up here."

"You must go up and down all the time."

"No. Thank God. Only once or twice a year."

They listened to the music while a haze of smoke layered the ceiling.

Then Polly asked, "But what about the rest of the time? There's only business once or twice a year?"

"There are other couriers. And they put the low-priority stuff in the mail."

"The mail?"

"Yeah, the mail."

Norberto, sitting on the edge of the bed, ringed by everything his lover left behind, insisting there was no postal service.

"You look spooked," the woman said. "Five days in a sardine can will do that to you. Go wash your face, you'll feel better."

And yet later, inexplicably, whenever Polly thought back to that first night, it was a happy memory. The old lady, so content smoking cigarettes and listening to that sad, sweet music and the sounds of the street in a cloud of blue while the breeze ruffled the underpants drying on the table. And everything yet to be decided, all the options still intact.

When Polly woke up, her cabin mate was gone. She'd left ten dollars on the table and a note describing where the trustworthy money changers could be found. The whooshing of the town filled the room: the sound of a bus's air brakes and a truck accelerating, honking, mists of speech. From up high, the echoing noises sounded hyperreal, as if all of Buffalo was inside her head, riding around her eardrum in big-top circles.

At reception there were some stale, hard cookies and a pot of gloppy tea on a side table. No one was behind the counter. Polly took a cookie and put another in her pocket, in case she didn't see food for a while.

Outside, it was raining. She held her cabin mate's map close to her chest so the ink wouldn't smear. She would change her money, she would buy an umbrella, and she would go to Frank's.

Again the streets were crowded with pedestrians, everyone running to get out of the rain, and an even more extraordinary sight: the road thick with cyclists in every color of slicker. They flocked like cars, filling the street from curb to curb. She could not figure how to get across the street until she saw that the cyclists stopped at the traffic lights. The hand-drawn map took Polly to a vast indoor market at the corner of Swan and Pearl, which still had their names. The market was sliced up into a million tiny stalls, selling bread and live chickens and bolts of cotton, the whole place shoulder to shoulder with women doing their weekly shopping. The money changer was stationed in a cage in a mirrored stall. He took her bills and put them in a machine that spun them around and counted, and then he handed her the exact amount she'd given him, but in a different currency, with a slip.

"That's the exchange?"

"Rate is one-to-one. It says on the slip."

"Then what's the point of changing money?"

He frowned.

"Do you know where I can buy some clothes?" she asked.

Deeper into the market, there were secondhand clothing sellers, their floors so heaped with rugs that customers kept tripping and the racks kept jamming on furrows of pile. There were bins with clothes for fifty cents, seventy-five cents, a dollar. Misty would have lost her mind. Anklelength dresses made of slinky material, with high collars and elasticized cuffs, and Polly found herself thinking of Marta. Feeling sick, she tripped over to the men's side, and found only Springsteen T-shirts. The denim rack had so many pairs of jeans, you could hardly move them, and she didn't know what style was current. A doe-eyed girl with a ribbon tied around her head, who probably hadn't been born when Polly was last home, came to help. As she heaped slacks and button-ups and scarves in Polly's arms, Polly's eyes filled with inexplicable, horrible tears.

The fitting room was a series of curtains defining a space just big enough for feet. In the safety of this little room, Polly tried to soothe herself. But she was coming unfastened.

It must have been that all the terror and

377

grief she'd bypassed had decided it was safe to emerge now. But this was the day she'd waited for for so long, and it was being ruined. This was a foolish way to think. It was only a day. The lifetime they'd have together after this day was more important.

Somewhere a great epiphany broke forth: there's only ever going to be one of every day; there will be other days, but they won't be this day. This was the true source of the tears. Yet she could manage not to see this truth, lying in the corner of her eye, for just a while longer.

In the end, because they were at the top of the pile, she chose a short-sleeved blue shirt with dots, a black shoulder bag, white canvas shoes, and a pair of brown pants.

"I like," said the salesgirl. "That style gives you a cutie booty. Take this scarf, on the house! A welcome present." Everyone seemed to know that Polly wasn't from around here.

She bought some lipstick and some blusher in a shade she'd used once and she stumbled out of the market, out the wrong end, and she didn't see any of the things she'd seen on the way in. Instead, behind a cyclone fence, there were tents. Tents and tents. Some actual tents, many partly collapsed, others made of blue tarps and sticks posted in the ground. The rain had stopped and the July heat made fog rise off the damp streets and the canopies. Everyone living there looked old, though some of them were probably still young. They sat at the mouths of their tents, bare feet sticking out into the walkways, some people trying to hang blankets, wet from the storm, to dry along the fence.

She should go back to the hotel; she could pay them to let her use a bathroom, where she could shower and change. But she had lost her cabin mate's map. It was probably buried somewhere under a pile of slingback heels.

She stopped at every corner and looked up the street, and each time it was the same thing: an infinite row of towering buildings, tapering to an unseeable point, the friendly, spattered Buffalo landscape she had known, the squat, gappy skyline shredded into tall, gaunt strips. It was as if they had picked up the roads and shuffled them like a deck of cards. Once or twice she thought she found a building that she recognized by the crown molding or the configuration of windows, but when she looked beside these familiar figures for corroboration, where there had been a teeny parking lot or a stand of trees,

there were skyscrapers, like matching senti-
nels.

On and on she walked, following the
crowds, believing that, once she got away
from the canal, once they were out of Al-
lentown, once she got past downtown, once
she got to Elmwood, she would turn the
corner and see something she knew. The
stretch of anticipation, between corner and
corner, became dire. At first she only hur-
ried, at the pace of the fastest walkers in the
crowd, ready for the moment when the city
would return to itself. But the more blocks
she crossed, the more the line where the
unknown turned into known receded, and
she ran as if there were still time to catch it.

She stopped only when she had to, when
the soles of her feet were burning and sweat
was dripping from her chin. She had
reached a small park. She came to her
senses. She had to find Frank first. A kiosk
next to the park was selling used paper-
backs, heaped in color-coded pillars and
fanned like exotic feathers to belie their age.

"Do you sell current maps?" she asked.

She spread out her map on a bench. The
map was hand-printed and duplicated with
some kind of imprecise, smudgy technique,
but as far as she could tell, it was accurate.
It even had an index. She looked under *G*.

Using her finger to measure the inches, she found that she was about a mile and a half from Grape Street. She had never heard of Grape Street. She could not picture the neighborhood, which was just as well.

A nearby sandwich board advertised a swimming pool and public baths. It cost two dollars to go swimming and five dollars for the deluxe package, which included a swim, shower use, towel rental, and soap.

She scrubbed the soap bar in her hair. It made her smell like chalk. She put on her new clothes and untangled her hair with her fingers as best she could. She put on the lipstick and the blusher, her hand shaky. The makeup felt like wax.

It was as if she were wearing some sort of absurd camouflage. She wiped off the makeup, washing her face three times, and even then a pinky shadow stayed. She wanted to get her coveralls out of the garbage, but other women were filing in, and she couldn't go through the trash in front of them. She had forgotten to get the cookie too, before she ditched her old clothes.

She sat in the bleachers by the pool and looked at the map again, memorizing the turns, so that she wouldn't have to take it out and consult it later on, like a tourist in her own home. She put her head back and leaned weakly against the steps. It was humid, the air tanged with the smell of chlorine. She watched strong women do the butterfly, up and down and back again. The pace clock read nearly five o'clock. She wished she didn't have to go alone. She wished Frank were with her on this journey to find him. What was in the corner of her eye almost slipped to the center, but she got going on her way before that could happen.

It was rush hour. Trolleybuses ran on electrified poles, looking like puppets. They idled behind the masses of cyclists, their motors revving aggressively whenever a gap opened. Trishaws went by, with as many as three passengers tucked within. On a highway flyover, she saw dump trucks and cube vans, but hardly any cars. Her new shoes were made of nothing, and she could feel every crack in the sidewalk. She was sure she was lost again, then she reached an archway over Carlton Street and Michigan that said, *The Fruit Belt.*

Past the archway, it got very quiet, as if a cloth had been dropped over the city squawking behind her. Big, ropey maple trees lined the street and old, grand houses were set back behind winding driveways and laboriously constructed gardens. Sometimes there were smaller houses, thoughtfully appointed quaint cottages that must cost just as much. There was no one on the sidewalk or in a yard. She passed Lemon Street. There were only two more streets until she reached Grape.

She was overcome with stupor. She had the idea that it would be lovely to lie down on the pavement and go to sleep just for a few minutes. She was as tired as if she had traveled here on foot from 1981. Maybe she should come back when she was feeling better. She had the money for at least a few nights' lodging. She could manage on her own for a while.

It was a big white house on the corner, with four-pane windows and rosebushes. There was no cover out front, no hedges or benches. Anyone looking out the window would see her in plain view.

She rang the doorbell. She imagined it ringing and ringing and no one coming, but almost right away the door opened. It was a teenage girl with a sleek ponytail and pressed clothes.

"I'm sorry," Polly said. "I have the wrong address."

When she was almost away, back at the curb, she saw a fancy stand-alone mailbox with carved birds. It had *Casa Marino* printed across it in scrolling script.

Polly rang the bell again. The same girl opened the door; this time her face clouded with irritation.

"So sorry. I'm looking for Frank?"

"Frank's not here," the girl said in a weird, almost mocking monotone. "He's out of town and we don't know when he'll be back."

"Oh. Are you . . . his housekeeper?"

"No!" the girl shouted, offended.

Not his wife, Polly thought, bile rising in her throat. You can't be his wife.

"I'm his daughter," the girl snapped, and slammed the door.

She found herself at a bar on Main, in a single-seater booth in the window, with no recollection of having walked there. The server came over to take her order. Polly unthinkingly asked for water.

"That's all?" the server said, sighing.

Polly thought for a second. "A beer?" she said, racking her brain for the name of a beer.

"How about a Bud? Would you like a Bud and a glass of water?" the server said, with weary helpfulness.

Dusk was falling and crowds were going home for the night. The sun was pouring its last breath in through the window and directly into her eyes, but she didn't turn away.

She felt the bite of the bubbles on her tongue and remembered that she had never really liked beer. Within five minutes the alcohol had intensified her stupor to an agonizing degree. If she could just sleep, if she could just put her head down and close her eyes and sleep, everything would be fine. But the server kept glancing at her suspiciously and she did not want to do anything that would get her kicked out, because she didn't have anywhere else to go.

Polly was aware that something was wrong with her, but she was not able to put her finger on what it was or what to do about it. She imagined this was what it was like to be in a car crash, where you can't quite figure out if it's your leg or your arm that's pinned, but the shock of it keeps you serene. Shock — that was what this was. Yet knowing that did nothing to lift the fog.

Later, the bar filled behind her. It sounded like a party of old friends. She thought of her own friends, Cookie, even Norberto. Cookie had risked her neck to help her. Norberto had sold his dream to get her here. And for what? If her own suffering was inaccessible, theirs was not. They had given so much to send her to this very moment because they wanted to believe that love endured, and she had failed them.

She put one hand over her whole face. She felt her breath whistling between her fingers, getting faster and crazier, and she gulped down the remaining beer to make the stupor return. The cacophony of the crowd built to a sudden peak. A man in a dark suit had come in and the bar staff were greeting him. He accepted a kiss on the cheek from Polly's server before he took a stool, tapping a pack of cigarettes on the rail, patting his pockets for a light.

She knew that back. It was changed, more bulging at the shoulders, a different curve to the spine. But she would recognize it anywhere. The back of his hand. The line of his jaw.

She waited for him to turn around. She sat absolutely still. She could wait forever.

The server leaned over and whispered something in his ear. She cocked her head in Polly's direction. And he turned around, and he saw her.

How many times had she thought she'd seen those eyes?

And then he turned away.

There was a frantic beating in her throat, and she realized that she had stopped breathing. She tried to take a breath but couldn't. Her face was burning as if she had been slapped.

But then he stood. He took a step. He was walking towards her, the love of her life, and he was saying her name.

She saw his arm coming towards her and his chest pulling level with hers as he bent, about to embrace her, and her shoulder cried out for his palm. And then their breastbones met and her arms made a halo around his ribs and his chin docked against her ear. At last they were back in that beloved space, the circle of each other's arms. And all the days and all the trouble were blanked out by the pealing of her heart.

Then he stepped away.

"Sorry," he said.

She laughed, giddy. "What are you sorry for?" She stepped towards him, to reclose the space.

"I don't know." He laughed too, but it was a courteous, impersonal sound. "That was forward of me." He stepped away again, until the table was between them. "Please, sit." His words were alarmingly formal.

His hair was longer, blacker, slicked straight back, like a banker's. His features were more strained, as if they had outgrown his skin. She concentrated on how his face was still his face. Under his suit jacket, he was wearing a crisp, white dress shirt, with the neck unbuttoned at the collar. When he sat down, he positioned himself far from the table, and he had to reach to grab her glass of water. He took a drink, a fat, hasty swallow, and then his eyes widened.

"That was your water, wasn't it? God, I'm sorry!" He smacked his hand to his forehead. He waved the server over and ordered more drinks and another glass of water, explaining that he had accidentally drunk hers, could you believe it?

"It's okay," she said, and then, puzzled by his fuss — imagining that maybe, in his post-flu life, he'd become a germophobe — she said, "I only had a sip."

"So embarrassing," he said. He apologized again. "I don't know what I was thinking. What an idiot."

"It's me!" she cried. "You can drink my water!"

He made a face like the inside edges of his eyebrows were trying to touch each other.

At the clinic, in August in 1981, when she finally arrived at his bedside after reams of bloodwork and red tape, they had touched hands through the isolation tent and his

388

eyebrows had reached to catch each other as he tried to smile. A face like a dissonant note, the look of someone who has just made an indelible mistake.

Or had he made that face? Was it probable that she'd remembered such a traumatic moment so clearly? Her memory could just be filling in gaps, transposing his look from some other, minor time onto the clinic. Maybe it was a face he made when he used the last of the milk, or spilled water on her book.

There was no way of ever knowing for sure.

Then, in a wink, like a hologram, his face changed. It took on an opaquely cheerful, blank expression.

"Well!" he said. "How've you been?"

It was the strangest question she'd ever heard.

She rubbed her fingers across her temple and heard their rustle through her skull. When they had been in each other's arms, it was as if the world had gone into a softer focus. But now she was back to the dreadful sharpness of reality.

"You have a daughter," she said, because it was the only thing to say.

His hand had been lying open on the table. He took it away, buried it somewhere below.

"Yes. Felicia."

"How old is she?"

"Fourteen."

Only ten years younger than Polly.

"You aren't surprised I know you have a daughter?" She had nothing left in her, nothing to act as a buffer or a filter, and the words were flopping out of her mouth any old way, as soon as they came into her head.

"Okay. How do you know I have a daughter?" He cleared his throat and stuck his chin out to scratch his neck.

He looked like someone else wearing Frank's skin. But she knew this movement well. She could read his gestures as clearly as if they were players on a baseball team. He was pretending.

"I went to your house. She said you were out of town." Could he read her too?

"Did she?" Again he stuck out his chin.

Then she saw what had happened, as clear as if his skull were made of glass. He had been at the house. He must have told his daughter to say he was away. But why would he do that?

Her knees were trembling and she couldn't make them stop.

The server placed two drinks in front of them: something clear and fizzy in a rocks glass for him and another Bud for her.

"Cheers!" the server said.

He picked up both drinks and clinked them together and put hers in front of her, unsmiling.

She wanted to touch him. She wanted him to come and sit next to her and put his arm around her so badly she was in actual pain. Her stomach was cramping and her knees just wouldn't stop.

"Do you mind if I smoke?"

She saw that his hands were shaking.

They sat in appalling silence, the ice in Frank's glass melting to a film as he smoked a cigarette, and then another.

"Why did your daughter say you were out of town?"

"I don't know. Being a teenager?" He blew smoke out of the corner of his mouth, and then he gazed after the trail.

Why are you acting like this? she wanted to shout. But that would be to behave with intimacy, tantamount to saying this was the person she'd loved.

"Where are you staying? Are you staying with Donna? Is she the one who told you where I live?"

"Donna?"

"Yes." He laughed. "You've forgotten your aunt?"

His smile plunged as she put her head in her hands and, at long last, began to weep.

"I thought she must be dead."

"No. She lives around the corner." He touched her elbow gently.

He led her up the street. The rain had started again, a drizzle misting their faces with wet. His gait was different. It was looser, sleeker.

"You're married," she said, those flopping words coming again.

He shook his head. "Separated. In the midst of divorce."

"You're rich."

"I'm in real estate. I opened some bars too."

"Do you own that one? The one we just left?"

He nodded. "It was just timing. Louisa, my ex, her parents got us across the border. They have money. A lot of people were moving to Buffalo then. We had power, because of the dams, when lots of other places didn't. Her family was good at taking advantage of that opportunity. I started off working for them, and then I got my own company. It was sort of a fluke. Could have happened to anyone." Of all the things to apologize for, he was apologizing for being rich. "What do you think of Buffalo?" he asked.

"I don't recognize any of it." The desire to cry came again, but she managed not to.

"What was America like?"

She would get this question over and over, for the rest of her days, the chummy, innocent asker never understanding that it was an impossible question.

"It was okay."

He paused, and she thought he was about to throw off this awful disguise and become himself again. Then he said, "Did you know that we're a closed system?" He explained, in great detail, how the United States had to supply all of its own goods and services, either because of strict trade regulations to prevent the spread of disease, or because import and export partners of the past had not yet reached the level of solvency necessary to resume trade partnerships — an unstoppable, vomited monologue.

They arrived at an apartment building set off on its own, fenced in wrought iron, milky lights illuminating the cornices from below.

Polly eyed the opulent facade. "Is Donna in real estate too?"

"I bought her this apartment."

"Why did you do that?"

"Because. I owed it to you to take care of her."

Polly tried to open the gate but it was locked.

"You need the access code. Wait, Polly — wait. When did you get here?"

"Last night."

"I mean, when did you get here, to *now*?"

"Last September."

"I tried to find you. But they didn't know when you were going to arrive until you actually arrived."

"I know." The cramps were now so acute that it was difficult to stand up straight. "Frank. Do you remember . . . things?"

"What things?"

She wanted to ask something that would uncover him, like testing for a replicant.

"You put a photo of us in my bra. Do you remember that?"

He blew out his cheeks. Another tell. Nerves. Discomfort.

"I can't recall. Why did I do that?"

Where was the man who rescued the rocking chair, who darned her socks, who loved his mother, who saved bottle caps, things she had mocked, to force the minutes to stay? She would study his eyes and hands and the inside of his wrist, but she was no longer allowed to stare.

"Can you tell me how to get in?" She shook the gate. "Please tell me the code."

"It's your birthday."

The foyer was ablaze with dynasty lamps and crammed with sofas and beefy rugs. A suited security guard waved when he saw Frank climb the stoop.

"Now what do we do?" Frank said when they reached the top.

There was a shriek from behind the glass. Donna was in the foyer, her fist at her temple, crying out. The security guard averted his eyes and they ran to each other and put their arms around each other and held on for dear life. Polly was gulping and trying not to suffocate and Donna's flowered sweater was in her mouth. Then Donna took Polly's face in both her hands and said, "How long have I waited for this day?"

Frank had left them at the elevators. "Maybe I'll come by on Sunday?" he'd said, but Sunday came and went, and he never showed.

Polly didn't notice Donna's limp right away. Her aunt pulled up her pant leg and tapped her ankle with her cane. It made a hard, hollow sound. She removed her sock to show Polly her artificial foot. "Looks like a picture of a photograph," Donna said. "Managed to avoid getting the flu, did not manage to avoid getting sepsis." She blew raspberries at concern. "I've still got the other one!"

Donna had taken up sewing. From cut-up scraps of abandoned dresses and T-shirts, she made blouses and trousers and track-suits, in splendiferous colors with gold piping and sequins. She sold them on consignment at the markets. Her sewing machine buzzed and whizzed while Polly lay on the rug in the sewing room, which doubled as her bedroom, listening to her cabin mate's radio station. It took a few days, but eventually Donna got comfortable enough around Polly to go without her prosthetic.

"You look exactly the same," Donna kept saying. "I knew you would, but still, I can't believe it. You're like a vampire. You finally look young enough to be my niece." She had somehow managed to find a Polaroid camera with film inside, and she used up this entire precious resource on photos of Polly. She stuck these photos on the fridge, propped them on the buffet, tucked them inside of books. "I always wished I had more photos of you," she said.

Donna's apartment was on the nineteenth floor. Her favorite thing was her balcony, and she spent ages with her watering cans and flowerpots. Birds came and sat on the branches and ate from the sugar water feeders that hung the length of the colossal terrace.

Donna didn't ask what happened in America. Every moment they spent together, Polly was grateful for this reprieve and devastated by her apathy. The push and pull kept Polly in the middle, sedate. But Polly too did not ask Donna the details of her injury. So they understood each other's wounds, without knowing them.

One day Polly woke at dawn, sweaty and cold. The phone was ringing. She reached for the receiver and braced herself for the voice, ill with dread. Then she saw there was no phone and that she was somewhere else altogether.

Polly went into the living room.

"Sorry," Donna called from the kitchen, "that was just Al, my neighbor. We're both early risers."

At dawn you could see everything from the balcony, the entire sky banded with rose, lavender, and gold, the whole beginning of the day. After that, Polly got up at dawn always to watch the sunrise with Donna and Derek, Donna's tubby little terrier. Polly didn't ask what happened to Chicken and Noodles.

"I didn't think that birds that size could get up so high," Polly said.

"Tenacity," Donna said. Then, after a pause: "Frank wanted to buy me the penthouse, but that seemed unnecessary. Blood money." Donna sniffed. "I couldn't forgive him at first, for what he did. Marrying some rich bitch, not four years after you were gone, when he'd promised to wait twelve, after you gave your life for his."

"We don't have to talk about Frank."

"But twelve years is a long time, right? And eighteen? That's a very long time."

Polly said nothing.

"I was trying to suggest another way to think about it."

"Do you think anyone has photos of the way things used to look?" Polly asked.

"That's a funny question. Why do you ask?"

Polly yearned to hear that, even if her home had been converted from its full sidewalk-and-smokestack body into the flatness of the second dimension, it still had corporeal form. If there were photographs of how things used to be, then she still lived in a world with a Buffalo.

"Al would know. He lives at the library."

Polly only left the apartment to take Derek for walks. They went for hours-long journeys, Polly carrying Derek when he started to wheeze, but never beyond the boundaries of where Polly had already been. She stayed away from the old places: her mother's bungalow, where she was born; Frank's apartment near Hertel Avenue; and all of Riverside, where she had lived with Donna until that December day when Frank decided they should drive south. Until she saw them those places were preserved, as they once were.

Once or twice she walked Derek all the way down to the canal. They watched the boats come in, until it got dark and Derek whined for his dinner. She was looking for her cabin mate. Polly had this outlandish, unshakable notion that she alone recognized who Polly was.

Every day was laced with hatred for Frank.

Al was from Greece. He had a big belly and a weakness for puns, and after dinner one day, he withdrew a lumpy envelope from his satchel and put it on the dining room table.

"These photos were donated by the son of a local photographer. We haven't sorted them yet, but I'm told they're all dated around '75. I understand you, my dear. The first time I returned to my town, it was like going back to a childhood home where all the rooms had jumped up in the middle of the night and traded places."

Polly wished to say how completely she knew what he meant, but words failed her. She was even more distressed moments later when the photos weren't the salve she had expected.

It was true they were photographs taken by a local photographer, but they were family photos. Someone had been visiting from somewhere far away, an aunt or cousin, and they'd taken pictures in front of all the necessary landmarks. There they were at Anchor Bar. The aunt had hair to her waist. There they were in front of City Hall. Polly tipped the photo as if it were a window, and at the right angle it would reveal something of Frank's bar. Here they were in Delaware Park.

"No?" Donna said. "Not what you're looking for?"

"It's not . . ." Polly tried. "I don't know. What was right there?" She pointed to where the frame cut out the rest of the park.

"This is not a systematic record. We just get slices. They organize the photos by date in our collection, not specific locations, so if it's specific locations you want, that's more involved. But we have photo plates going back to 1901! We'll find you something."

How brittle an existence Buffalo led, living only inside these strips of feeble paper. Faced with this, her brain emptied. She studied the photo of Delaware Park. This was their beginning, but she had no feeling at all, as if necrosis was setting in along the seams of her memory.

In late September, Polly started making wider and wider circuits with Derek, pushing the edge of what she could bear, and one day she made it to the high school at the rim of the Fruit Belt, minutes from Frank's house, just as school was letting out. She watched the teenagers, a stream of ponytails and shouting, until just a trickle was left, then no one. She returned at the same time the next day, and the next and the next, each time waiting by a different gate, until she found Felicia.

Polly missed her at first. Felicia was under her eyeline, at the lip of the soccer field, knees up, her back to the fence, the pearly fabric of her purple bomber bulging through the chain link. Polly stationed herself on a stone bench a breath away, near waiting parents drinking real coffee in glass jars. She pretended to fiddle with Derek's collar.

Felicia was powerful; others came to her. The only time she raised herself was to greet an equally magnetic girl. They kissed each other on the cheek, like the French. Felicia was all legs. She glided, walked like a celebrity. She must have learned to walk like that from her mother. Her mother who is not me. Polly felt unwell; her eyes wouldn't focus. It was like looking through a broken camera. She wanted to leave, but she was screwed to the bench.

A boy, not in their league in his one-color outfit and unremarkable hair, came to talk.

"You girls going to the game this week-end?"

"Uh-huh," her friend said. Felicia was doodling in a notebook and didn't look up.

"Okay. Where do you think is the best place to sit?"

"Near the front, I guess?" The friend's voice lifted into mirth, not nicely.

"Okay."

But he was brave, this boy, standing over them, exposed like a house in a desert.

"Okay, bye," he said.

When he'd gone, Felicia leaned in close to her friend and said, *"You girls,"* in a teacher-type voice. They giggled — loud, showy laughter. The boy's shoulders curled over as he retreated.

Another, a soccer ball bobbing between his hands, came over. He slithered down the fence to sit beside them.

"What was that?"

"Huh?" The friend made Bambi eyes. Felicia kept doodling but smiled. Polly was mesmerized by her, as if by fire or water.

"Don't talk to that clown."

"I talk to who I want to." Defiant words, neutered by a singsong tone.

"Psshht, whatever. His family are Journeymen. You should stay away from him."

"Why?"

"They're old-school. They're afraid of microwaves. They want to make abortion illegal."

"They're afraid of microwaves? You're so weird."

"Really. They're backwards. They don't believe in equal rights. For women."

"Why?"

"My sister had a Journeyman neighbor. She was always waiting at the peephole, judging my sister for having guys over. Unlike me, I'd never judge a lady for liking the bone."

"Gross." This was Felicia's first contribution. But shouldn't she say, *A Journeyman saved my father?*

"And it's on the news. The government is considering —"

"The government," the friend interrupted, in a self-serious voice.

"Whatever. The government is considering changing driver's licenses so they don't list year of birth, just age."

"So?"

"That does not sound like something true." Felicia again. Confident, matter-of-fact intonation. But shouldn't she use that voice to say, *Without that Journeyman, I wouldn't be alive?*

"Mr. Cherry told us all about it. They

want to differentiate between —"

"Differentiate —"

"Between age and birth date, but that could breed statutory rape, voter fraud —"

"Voter fraud! You are such a nerd." Felicia's friend leaned over, fingers fanned, to defile his hair. He danced his head out of reach, smiling.

"It's a gateway to pedophilia!"

Laughter. Rage rent a hole inside Polly.

"How old is that Journeyman clown?"

"He was six when he arrived," Felicia said.

"How do you know that?" asked the friend.

"He's a pedophile!" The boy erupted. "It doesn't matter how old he was when he arrived. He's still at least twelve years older than us. He's twenty-seven. Dirty old man."

"I gotta go."

"No! Fefe!"

Felicia bounced off in a cloud of passionate farewells. Here, Polly could have stopped.

But this girl had grabbed the gift of her life so greedily. Her pea brain could not fathom the debt owed to the woman following her with a dog under her arm. This thieving girl had snatched the body and the life meant for Polly's baby.

It did not take long to catch up with Felicia. She'd stopped in the middle of the sidewalk to riffle through her knapsack, blocking foot traffic. She groaned, lost the halo of confidence bestowed by her friends. She was a child, still too inexperienced to know to muffle her emotions in public. Vulnerable.

Her head snapped up. She'd found what she wanted: a portable cassette player. A bus arrived at High and Main. As Felicia ran, her headphone wires billowed in the wind and her knapsack careened from side to side, the zipper not secure, some kind of wrapper flying out.

Polly gathered up Derek and climbed on the bus.

Felicia sat three rows back from the driver. Polly took the empty seat behind her, Derek organizing himself in her lap. Low-roofed residences condensed into office towers. Felicia pressed play and sang along under her breath. She moved the air with her little mouth, her shoulders dancing in time with her sighs. What was she listening to?

Polly wanted to see her. She wanted to squeeze her smug little jawbone between her fingers, fix her in place, so she could stare at her. What in her was her father's? But Felicia's hair made a screen. Half of you should have been mine. Felicia's hair cascaded over the back of the seat. Brown curls. Polly lifted her fingers, wiggling them in the wash of Felicia's hair.

A cyclist raced across the road and the driver hit the brakes. Everyone jerked forward and Polly's thumb twisted in the waves.

"Ow!" the girl shouted. She turned to see what had hurt her pretty head.

Polly stared forward with a voided face.

Felicia gasped. "Cute dog!" she said. She reached over the seat rail and then paused, her hand in the air, her shoulders bunched up to her ears. "Is it okay if I pet him?"

Polly hoped she was smiling, but she couldn't feel her lips.

Felicia plunged her fingers under Derek's collar and Derek obliged, smacking his stubby tail against the seat.

"He's a good boy!" Felicia proclaimed.

"What are you listening to?" Polly asked.

"Oh, crap! My stop!"

She grabbed the bell cord, nearly swinging from it. The bus screeched to a stop, its contents complaining once again.

"Bye-bye, doggie!" Felicia shouted, and bounded off.

Polly and Derek scrabbled to their feet and followed. They stepped into the glare of the late-afternoon sun, so bright it erased the faces crowded around the bus stop. Polly heard her name. It was easy to mishear among the click and hustle of the street. She heard it again. A sick feeling cracked over her.

An old woman had a hand on Felicia's shoulder. She was wearing a visor and the kind of shirt that's meant to be creased.

"Dear Lord, it's you."

She was bent over and age had leached the color from her hair, but it was Mrs. Marino.

Polly held Derek like a baby, using him to protect her soft, armorless chest, gripping him so hard her fingers must have been digging into his meat, but with the mysterious kindness of animals, he did not protest.

It was rush hour, the streets flush with commuters. A woman walked her briefcase into Mrs. Marino, but she didn't seem to register the pain.

"Felicia, this is, uh . . ." Mrs. Marino stopped. She laughed, a creaky sound. Felicia looked from her grandmother to Polly, her hair swishing and her face peeved and worried.

Polly was bound to these people. But not by blood, not by marriage. Something common, but not normal, not enough to have a legal name.

"You look just the way you did when you were a girl." Mrs. Marino stepped close. She smelled of dough and roses. Polly meant to turn away. Mrs. Marino put her arms around Polly.

She was still the same. The kind of person who was unembarrassable, who would hug whether or not you hugged back.

"Thank you," Mrs. Marino said. "Thank you." Felicia kept staring, alarmed and angry at her grandmother for crying.

Here was the payment that, seconds ago, Polly had demanded. But it was wrong, seeing his mother like this: a pencil stroke the artist forgot to hide, the remains of some failed experimentation, never meant to be seen on the painting's surface. And in his mother's face was Frank's, the little nose, the sweet eyes.

Polly turned away, her chest stuffed with tears. All she had done, every day since she returned to Buffalo and found Frank lost, was to try to forget all that love. She had gone through every pocket she owned looking for ticket stubs and pencils and bits of hair. But it lived on, in the atmosphere. Frank existed.

"Are you all right? Do you need money?" Mrs. Marino called.

Polly stepped to the left and let the human tide wash her away.

They all lived so close. Every night, they all slept on the same axis. Early mornings, Polly marched up and down Donna's street with Derek. Each time she got to North Street, she almost took that left to Felicia's school. But along with everything else, she'd lost that bionic ability to drown out doubt. Always by first school bell she returned to Donna's.

Donna took her swimming every day. "You can't just lie on the floor." Polly sat on the bottom of the pool and imagined the world above was the way she remembered it. But she could never sit long enough before the air in her blood floated her to the top.

One day in November, management replaced the fall-blooming flowers flanking the front door with heavy, wide-bottomed concrete planters, each holding a delicate, diminutive evergreen bush pruned in the shape of a double spiral. There were no cuttings, no shears tucked under the foot of a bush. The evidence that a person had done the work was erased. You could pretend the bushes just grew that way. Cookie and the women of 4A1 and so many others were still trapped under the border, where Polly had left them behind.

When she entered the apartment, Donna came in from the balcony.

"The security guard called. Why the hell did you steal that?"

A spiral bush was in Polly's hand. Her arms were sticky with sap and her hands were scraped where the plant had tried to resist her violence.

"I don't know."

"What's the matter with you?"

Polly didn't answer. Donna came over and took the plant out of Polly's hand and laid it carefully on the dining room table. One side of the spiral was crushed. Polly had wanted to destroy it, but once she severed half its roots and wrenched it from the basin, she had felt no satisfaction. She felt only anguish.

"Maybe we can replant it," Polly said.

"Let's wash these hands."

Donna led her into the bathroom and gave her rubbing alcohol and a warm towel, and while she watched to make sure Polly got all the dirt out from under her fingernails, she said, "Do you want to tell me about what happened to you?"

"I just went for a walk."

"I don't mean this morning. I mean since you arrived. What happened in America?"

"You never asked before."

"I was waiting for you to bring it up."

"There's not much to say. It was only a few months."

"Will you tell me what happened?"

"It's hard to explain. It's difficult to understand."

"I'll try."

"How did you lose your foot?" Polly asked.

Donna breathed like the atmosphere had thickened. "All right," she said. She sat down on the toilet lid with her cane between her knees.

"I was trying to get to Texas. Took me so long that they'd erected a border before I could get south of Ohio. Pathetic. Anyways, I was still in the US, but very close to America. They were putting everyone within a certain distance of the border in quarantine camps. Do you know how long it takes for symptoms of the flu to show?"

"Twenty-one days."

"Right. But they wanted to keep us for six months. Extra precautions. But after two weeks of quarantine I was going nuts. So I tried to jump the fence. Barbed wire." She shrugged.

"Why were you trying to get to Texas?"

"Why do you think?" Donna's old sharpness remained.

Polly felt a new kind of pain; she had not thought there were new kinds of pain to know.

"I was trying to get to Houston. I was going to join you in the future."

Something broke free in Polly, like ice calving from a glacier. She took her aunt's hand. Donna was making a fist, so Polly wrapped Donna's knuckles with her own fingers. Polly talked very slowly, and at the end of each sentence her voice rose uncontrollably, like she was reading from a passage written in a language she hardly knew.

"You know how I told you I'd arrive in Houston in 1993? They rerouted me. To 1998, in September. I thought that as soon as I arrived, Frank would be waiting for me. But he wasn't. We had a plan, but it didn't work. I tried to keep my head down and just get through, but I had some bad luck with my boss. Then I had to work in a factory. I had to move to a worse place, sort of a shed, with lots of other women. But everybody was nice, so it wasn't so bad. Then a guy I knew, from the first place I lived, asked me to move in with him, to help him with some housing scam, for money. Then I had to leave his place too, because we had a disagreement. And then my bond was over and I came back up here. And that's it, here I am."

Polly waited for Donna to say, *Okay then,* and pat her on the shoulder, like she would.

Instead Donna said, "You must have been very scared."

"It wasn't for too long."

"It was almost a year. That's a lot of days to be completely on your own like that."

"Others had it a lot worse than me."

"I'm sorry that happened to you."

"It was all right."

Donna started to cry. Polly had no memory of ever seeing her cry before.

"We didn't know where you were. I kept waiting and waiting. I relied on Frank for news. I should have just come to get you. But I was scared. I'm so sorry."

She was shuddering with sorrow and Polly put her arms around her.

"It's okay, Auntie. I'm okay."

For in that moment she did feel okay. A light filled her, beginning in her belly, then shooting up her windpipe and swelling into her mouth.

They made tea and put some cookies on a plate and sat on the balcony.

"Are you afraid of heights?" Donna asked. "You never used to be afraid of heights."

"What makes you think I am?"

"You always sit with your back to the edge."

"No I don't."

"Yes you do. We got a million-dollar view and you never look."

"I don't really like the view."

"You don't like the view?!"

"I don't like to look at the city."

"What's wrong with the city?"

"It's changed so much. Buffalo is gone."

"It's not gone. It's right there."

"It's gone and I can never go back."

A sob blasted its way out of Polly. Donna rushed to her and pulled Polly's head to her chest, as she might have done when Polly was a little girl.

"It's not gone," Donna said. "Look. It's right there."

It was the beginning of a millennium. It was a new year, the year 2000, and Donna started murmuring about Polly getting a job.

"I got some contacts at the market. Maybe we could get you a stall. People could bring old things they find and you could fix them up."

No response.

Donna tried inserting a disclaimer, "The apartment's paid for, and I make enough money off my suits to feed us both. I just think it would be good for you to get out of the house."

Donna made other suggestions. "If you don't want to do furniture, there are so many other things. You could be a baker. Didn't you like cooking? Or computers, you could learn computers. They're the way of the new millennium, Al says. We're in the twenty-first century now, we have to upgrade ourselves."

Polly just rolled over on her side and tickled Derek's belly methodically.

"We should get your papers sorted out," Donna said, one sunrise. "We should ask Frank. He must have connections that can fast-track your application and get you permanent residence."

Polly gathered the dog hair embedded in the rattan runner.

Al came over for dinner. Over a dessert of sour-cherry preserves, Al asked Polly if she had any background in literature.

"Not really, why?"

"Peggy, at one of our city libraries — I'm on the board, you know — she's leaving us. She's having a baby. So now we need someone to man the circulation desk."

Donna was quiet — a rare occurrence.

"Or I suppose I should say, we need someone to woman the front desk. Ha! I mean, we don't pay much. Or I mean, we don't pay. It's a volunteer position. But it could be more one day."

"Polly's still finding her feet," Donna said.

"That sounds nice, actually, Al. Thank you for asking me."

"It's the Riverside Library. It's been somewhat . . . neglected."

"That's where we're from. Me and Donna, that's where we used to live."

"You never told me that," Al said to Donna.

"It was a lifetime ago," Donna said. "Or it was, for me."

In the end, the library saves Polly's life. Half of the books hadn't even been catalogued, and no one had even selected a standard system of classification. Some sections are alphabetical, others are Dewey Decimal. It is pandemonium. Many of the books are so bedraggled that there's no way they can go out on loan without being mended. There is no Mylar, so Polly uses double sheets of old newspaper and prints the name of the book on the spine and the cover in thick, black crayon. There is work for days. And, by some miracle, Riverside Park is still there. It is only a matter of time before they build something on it, but until then, when the thin winter sun allows it, Polly eats her lunch there with her mittens on, and watches the Niagara River flow.

These days, her senses have been recalibrated. She can pick out golds and reds and pinks in Derek's coat, when before she thought of him as only brown. She sees all of the lines on Donna's hands, one hundred rivers, a mark of all the years she weathered while Polly slept. She can hear little birds walking in the snow behind her lunch spot by the river, a sound as loud as blinking, these birds who stay through the winter, while everyone else goes. She can smell the icy nip of the million waters the Niagara carries past her feet, waters that maybe once lapped up to Norberto's boat. All these meager things are so wonderful and yet sad. It will never be the twentieth century again. It will never be 1999 again. This must be how people feel right before they die: absurdly sentimental. But, as silly as it is, she can't help it. On the first warm day in March, a house on the edge of the park leaves its windows open and the curtains toss in the wind.

Four months into the new century, on an April evening, a grumbling crowd gathers at the bus stop.

"Friggin' construction," someone says, pointing to a posted sign. "They're detouring us around the whole neighborhood. This will add ten minutes to my commute."

Polly looks at the map to see where the detour will go, and she sees a route she has traced with her feet one thousand times, to Donna's house.

Street by street, she has given up her old city. She has opened the lid to let this air turn everything to dust. Except her old home, only a short walk from the library, she has spared. It is the last place she cannot bear to know is gone. But now the hour is upon her.

She usually lets the moms with kids and the elderly get on the bus first, but this time she shoves to the head of the crowd and rushes the first empty window seat. The roads still cling to their old shape. If she squints, she can see the old city underneath.

The bus makes a turn and a turn and another, and the crowd complains about the dizzying ride, and Polly is nervous, as if she's going on a first date. How can the house still be there? What if it passes before she sees it?

As the bus makes its final turn, she gets this ridiculous idea in her head. When they go by her house, she might see herself. Like in an old time travel movie where the time-lines cross and there's two selves. The original self hums in the kitchen, making a pie, while the new self crouches under the sill, waiting for the moment to send a signal of the bad things to come.

She could go back and tell her old self not to go to 1998. They could all stay together.

But what will happen to this self? She'll have no place in this world. She will have to be killed off.

And then the house is passing her. The

oak tree in the front has grown monstrous. The yard is littered with plastic toys and bicycle parts.

But still, there. There's the pink siding. There's the white paint stain on the footpath. There's the bedroom window looking down to the street.

The places of a life gain a type of magic. Going back will have a cosmic effect. The two yous cannot occupy the same day and territory; there will be a rip in the space-time continuum.

But of course, nothing happens. The bus takes another unpleasant turn, and they're back on a main street. There's only the people, still complaining, and the smell of old bread, and the fact that it's a Thursday.

Polly sits with a dry mouth and her hands wedged between her thighs, trying to feel all right and failing.

There's a boy, sitting with his feet propped on his porch railing, bouncing a misshapen basketball between his legs, watching the traffic go by. There's a girl, wearing a white hat and climbing the stairs to a house, then turning around to check a piece of paper in her hand.

Polly thinks, But this is life. This is living, and there's still so much more to come.

DECEMBER 1999

It was the end of a millennium, New Year's Eve 1999, and Donna wanted to have a party. She bought a cassette player and they borrowed chairs from the neighbors. Al made "champagne" — apple juice with vodka and fizzy water. Polly selected the most restrained outfit from the ones Donna had picked out for her: a blouse in ever-gradating shades of pink. During the party, Polly stayed in the kitchen and washed glasses, and every time the front door opened, she thought her heart would stop, but Frank didn't come. More than anything, she was enraged with herself for wanting him to come. After all this time, it would not leave her. And then the clock was going and everybody was kissing and it was too late: it was already the new century.

After the last guest had left and Al had fallen asleep sitting up, his chin halfway to his crumb-covered belly, Polly took Derek out for his pee. The night sky was a cold purple, and Polly had that feeling that something was about to happen, though she'd long mastered how to repress that kind of thing. But there he was, sitting on a bench by the gate in a velvet tuxedo, with an unopened bottle of whiskey in his hand.

"I thought about coming up," Frank said. "Then I didn't."

It had been snowing, and the wet had melted his hair gel to reveal that he still had his curls after all.

She was working very hard to keep breathing at a normal, even pace.

"Will you come with me?" he said, and that same hope she was dismayed she still possessed was all over his new face.

"Somewhere like where we used to go," she said.

She gave Derek to the security guard and Frank took her around the corner, down Elmwood, to where a grand hotel stood, where once there'd been grocers and liquor stores.

"The Ritz," he said. "Just launched."

Her heart sank.

"You don't want to go in? I don't know where else is still open."

"No. Okay."

The bartender knew Frank's name. They

sat down at a low, round table in a dark corner, almost lost in the folds of plush blue curtains that swooped down from the great heights of the ceiling. Polly had to sit on the edge of her deep armchair to reach the table. She kept her coat on.

"Two screwdrivers," said the bartender, delivering drinks. "Hold the cherry."

The screwdriver was such a bright color, it glowed. The ice formed glossy, orange ridges, and moisture beaded on the outside like tears.

"I ordered for you. Or if you don't drink them anymore, I can get something else."

"You remember."

"Of course."

"I haven't had one of these since 1980."

"Good night!" This was a new saying for him. "Maybe you should have both."

It was too pretty to drink. So many nights she had lain in the container, picturing a glass that looked exactly like this, conjuring up its curves and angles until it floated in the darkness before her eyes, there to hold if she only put out her hand.

"Costs the same whether or not you drink it," he said as a puddle gathered at the base of the glass.

She took a sip. She gasped a little as it lapped over her tongue, and for a second she was transported. For the rest of her life, as long as she lived, she would never again taste anything so wonderfully, painfully sweet.

His eyes were wet. He was angled towards her, but the armchairs were heavy and high armed, almost like sitting in a bucket, and any movement towards each other would have to be deliberate, conspicuous, difficult to conceal. She kept her hands in her lap.

"I'm so sorry I never came to see you since you've been back."

"Why didn't you come?"

"I was ashamed. I walked to Donna's every week. The gate was as far as I ever got."

"You were at your house. That day in July when I came to the door."

His movements went slow. He blinked. He moved his mouth. He nodded.

"I panicked. Like a child. I thought about that moment for eighteen years. But when it came, I still had no clue what to do. Immediately I realized what I'd done, so I went after you. I followed you to my bar. But when I got there, again I had no plan. I'm stupid."

There was nothing gratifying in this. Polly only felt hollowed out.

"I want to know what happened to you

down there, but I have no right to ask," he said.

"Why do you want to know?"

"It was all I wanted to know for many years."

She nodded. He had spoken in the past tense.

"Why don't you tell me what happened to you?" she said.

"Oh. All right. They sent me to the hospital. I think I hoped I'd die."

"Why?"

"I thought I would never see you again."

"But I told you I would find you."

"I didn't believe that we would make it."

"That's clear."

He squeezed his eyes shut, making asterisks out of his eye sockets. Then he opened them. "Maybe I shouldn't keep going."

"Keep going."

"After six months I was in the clear. But I had nowhere to go."

"Did you ever consider keeping your promise to meet me?"

"Of course I did. I stayed in Houston. I started volunteering at the hospital. I'd been there a year when I met Louisa."

"Louisa?"

He nodded.

"Your wife?"

He nodded.

"So you met her after just a year?"

"Closer to two years."

"You're right. You shouldn't keep going."

But she couldn't have said how many years would have been enough to make it feel all right. She drained her glass, no longer tasting the drink.

"I don't know what to say," he said. "Anything that you say, you'd be right."

"There's nothing to say. You know when I left, they didn't tell me they weren't going to send me to 1993. I thought I was arriving in 1993. They only told me in the airport, when I arrived, that it was 1998. And even still, I thought you'd come anyway. I went every Saturday to the place where you said you'd meet me. I risked so much because I thought you would come. Every day, for weeks and weeks, I waited for you." She hated herself like this, so pathetic and loose-lipped.

"I tried to go," he said.

"What?"

"I tried to get to Galveston to meet you, in 1993. But the border had only just opened. There was no way to go except by private boat. I made a search for you instead. All they could tell me was that you hadn't arrived yet. I kept checking."

427

"In '95 and in '97."

"How did you know?"

"Why didn't you check every year?"

He rubbed the side of his nose.

"Why didn't you check last year?"

"Louisa," he said. "We started divorce proceedings two years ago. It's a mess. If she noticed the money missing, I could lose custody."

Polly had fabricated a mythology to withstand what was, in the end, so brutally banal. She didn't want to talk anymore.

"Why did you come tonight?" she said.

"I couldn't go on not seeing you. I've been desperate to see you."

It was suddenly sweltering hot. She struggled to undo her coat buttons.

"That doesn't make sense. Before, you were too ashamed to see me. Now you're desperate to see me?"

"Both."

She couldn't get her arm out of her sleeve.

"Let me help you," he said. He held the sleeve while she pulled, but her bracelet was caught on the lining. So he took her hand and slipped the bangle off, over her wrist. Then he let go. It was an unthinking action, a reflex, as if they were still lovers.

They stared at each other, both understanding what he had done, a sensory memory reactivated. She could still feel the kiss of his hand on her own, the joint, the pad, those particular bones.

"You're sweating," he said, and then he took a napkin and dabbed her forehead, his face close enough to block out the light.

Her nose was full of saw-toothed tears.

He said, "You look exactly the same, you know. Like a mirage."

His face was red, his neck was red, even the tips of his ears were red.

"I'm not a mirage," she said.

He encircled her shoulders with his arms. He placed his cheek against her neck. She leaned into him, their collarbones meeting like the sides of a steeple. She could hear the breath whistling in his throat.

"Can we go somewhere else?" she said into his ear.

She led Frank down to the canal, to the only hotel she knew in town. He hailed a tri-shaw and they went clattering down the street. As they passed City Hall she thought she saw the bar flying by where first she'd seen his face. Their faces glowed in the red dynamo light from the back of the bike and the fringed edge of the canopy was shaking like crazy, and he asked if they could hold hands, just one last time, and she said, "Why does it have to be the last time?"

Down by the water, the New Year's traffic was too thick, so they got out a few blocks up and walked the rest of the way with their arms around each other, holding each other up, and you would have thought this contact would be monumental, but instead it was as natural as switching on a lamp.

But his shape was not where she had left it. His shoulder blade had shifted and his waist pinched in more sharply. She clutched the coat fabric bunched at his side.

The eyebrows at the front desk were ragged and exhausted from a night of screaming revelers and Frank's demands that they get the best room.

"We're not going to get crabs here, are we?" he whispered to her.

The room was all wrong. It had a private bathroom and an adjoining living room with a sofa, and plastic fruit on the coffee table and a minifridge. But Polly was sure that if they lay down and closed their eyes, they could pretend they were in that salty room at the Flagship Hotel, everything mauve.

He sat down on the bedspread of pastel diamonds and patted the place next to him.

"You're quiet," he said.

"Sorry," she said. "You know me."

"I do," he said.

She sat down, afraid that he would touch

her and afraid that he would not.

"Can you take off this tuxedo?" she said. She wanted to make him look like himself.

But when he stripped, it was even worse. He was wearing tight bicycle shorts. He had gleaming muscles everywhere, and when she commented on their newness, he didn't understand. He smiled happily and said, "Thanks. I box now."

"Are you going to undress?" he asked her. "You don't have to."

"Okay, but turn off the lights first."

She thought the dark would blur his unknown edges and his familiar self would come to the surface. But it was almost six in the morning, and the dawn was drawing its fingers across the sky, and there was not enough dark. She could only bring herself to take off her pants and her cardigan. She got under the covers and they lay still, side by side, and something was coming in like a wave and her chest was in the swells. It was something she had tried to hide from herself for so very long, something horrifyingly, cruelly simple: it was not going to be like it was.

"What do we do now?" he said.

"I don't know."

"You're shaking."

He reached for her with his stranger's

431

hands, and she couldn't help it. She flinched.

He scrambled out of the bed like he'd been burned.

"Where are you going? What's wrong?" She followed him but he kept trying to get away. He bumped into the fridge.

"You recoiled, you winced," he cried.

She tried to deny it, but it was hard to talk. He backed himself into the bathroom.

"Don't close the door," she wept. "Please, don't close the door on me." Finally she said, "I thought it was going to be like it was. I didn't know it would be like this."

"I don't deserve anything from you, but if you don't love me anymore, I can't stand to hear you say it."

"I'll love you for the rest of my life. Forever."

"But you don't want me to touch you."

She searched ardently for an answer.

"I wish I was still young, but I'm not," he said.

"You're still you."

"Oh." The air seeped out of him. He collapsed on the bathroom floor in a bedsheet, between the toilet and the sink.

"What did I say? What did I do?"

He dragged a towel from the counter and unfolded it at her feet. "Can you sit down?"

When she did, he said, "I met Louisa in the hospital. She was a medical student."

She put up her palm for him to stop. "I don't want to know, don't tell me."

But Frank kept talking. "At first, it was because I wanted somebody, just a body. And I told her that it couldn't ever be a love thing between her and me, because I was waiting for you. But she got pregnant, and we were in a war zone, and we had to leave. And when Felicia was born, it started to seem impossible that I could be the same person, the same guy who was with you and the guy who had this lovely baby. The memories of you and me, they must be someone else's memories. A story someone told me. Nobody could have felt that way about you, and lost you, and carried on. I split in two. Do you understand what I mean?"

"No."

"I could pretend to be him. But haven't I already done enough wrong?"

"No. No. No."

"Then kiss me." He reached out his hands. She took them and rolled onto her knees and brought her face up to his and closed her eyes. The bathroom lights were the brightest lights on the planet. Someone upstairs was taking a shower and the pipes began to talk.

Polly inhaled. Smoke, mint, men's soap. She took the deepest breath in the world. But it was true. That scent, Frank's smell, the rain and the sweetness, was gone.

She opened her eyes.

"See," he said. "You see."

He hugged her, wrapping her in the sheet.

They went down to the street together. There was garbage everywhere: chestnut shells, shattered plates, Napoleon hats made out of newsprint.

He asked if he could walk her home.

"What do you remember?" she said.

A group of teenagers were galloping up and down the sidewalk, screaming, "It's the apocalypse, motherfuckers!"

"Everything," Frank said. "I remember you laughing, I remember the dress you were wearing that first day in the park. The diner by your house with the tabletop jukeboxes, the way you put your arm through mine whenever we walked. The car ferry in Texas, throwing pennies from the deck."

She thought all those days had been lost, like beams of light at the end of their reach, scattering into darkness. But he had kept them safe after all.

He put her in a trishaw. He kissed her cold

cheeks and they said, "Good-bye, good-bye." But this time as she was driven away, she could look back. And they waved and they waved and they waved and they waved and they waved, until they were each completely out of sight.

ACKNOWLEDGMENTS

My agents, Karolina Sutton, Lucy Morris (queen of titles!), and Alexandra Machinist, pulled me out of the slush pile and into the light, and have worked indefatigably on my behalf ever since. To my editors, Cassie Browne at Quercus Books, Helen Smith and Lara Hinchberger at Viking Canada, and Tara Parsons at Touchstone Books: thank you for summiting the mountain with me; for pushing me up, and up, until we reached the peak.

Mat Johnson was this story's first friend. His tough-guy exterior belies superheroic generosity and kindness, but nothing hides (or hides from) his insight. I will always be grateful. Thank you to the University of Houston Creative Writing Program, especially Robert Boswell and my classmates, whose seriousness, openness, and commitment to the grit and glamourlessness of hard work showed me what it takes to be a writer, and made me proud to be one. Thank you to Inprint Houston, without whose fellowships and prizes I never would have met these people who changed my life. Thank you to the VONA Fam, who kept finding me when I got lost.

I am immensely lucky to live in a country that invests so meaningfully in its artists. Thank you to the Canada Council for the Arts, the Toronto Arts Council, and the Ontario Arts Council for your support, long before I showed any sign of being a safe bet.

Thank you to Margo Keirstead at Maple Leaf Furnishings, Sarah van Maaren at the City of Toronto Archives, and Monique Peterson, for patiently and passionately explaining to me the ins and outs of your professions.

My front line of early readers, sounding boards, ideas guys, and child-minders: Ryan Yao, Elisha Lim, Julia Gruson-Wood, and Kristin Wheatcroft (who each endured a thousand years of questioning), Brené Brown, May El-Abdallah, Tony Neale, Sharon English, Michelle Mariano, Alison Northcott, Anthony Van Pham, Angela Lee, Aja Gabel, Jameelah Lang, Rebecca Vogan, Max Arambulo, Meghan McClenaghan, Winnie Ng, Maureen O'Hara-Lim, and Vincent Lim. Your feedback, corrections, and help were invaluable, but thank you even more for your enthusiasm, interest, and company during the years of gestation.

Stephen King says, "Writing is a lonely job. Having someone who believes in you makes a lot of difference. They don't have to make speeches. Just believing is usually enough." To my family — my mother, my father, my sister, my husband, and my daughter — thank you for being my some-ones who believe.

ABOUT THE AUTHOR

Thea Lim's writing has appeared in publications including *The Southampton Review, The Guardian, Salon, The Millions,* and others. She has an MFA from the University of Houston and has received multiple awards and fellowships for her work, including artists' grants from the Canada Council for the Arts and the Ontario Arts Council. She grew up in Singapore and now lives in Toronto, where she is a professor of creative writing. *An Ocean of Minutes* is her first novel.

The employees of Thorndike Press hope you have enjoyed this Large Print book. All our Thorndike, Wheeler, and Kennebec Large Print titles are designed for easy reading, and all our books are made to last. Other Thorndike Press Large Print books are available at your library, through selected bookstores, or directly from us.

For information about titles, please call:
  (800) 223-1244

or visit our website at:
  gale.com/thorndike

To share your comments, please write:
  Publisher
  Thorndike Press
  10 Water St., Suite 310
  Waterville, ME 04901